Out of Such Darkness

Out of Such Darkness

ROBERT RONSSON

Patrician Press • Manningtree

Robert Ronsson lives in the Severn Valley with his wife Valerie. They have three children and two grandchildren. Robert retired early from his career in financial services to start writing full-time. His first novel *No Mean Affair* was published in 2012. Robert is on the organising team of his hometown's blossoming literary festival and he and Valerie help run the community cinema.

Published by Patrician Press 2015

For more information: www.patricianpress.com

First published as a paperback edition by Patrician Press
2015
E-book edition published by Patrician Press 2015

British Library Cataloguing in Publication Data. A
catalogue record for this book is available from the British
Library.

ISBN 978-0-9930106-2-0

Printed and bound in Peterborough by Printondemand-
worldwide

www.patricianpress.com

To Norah Geraldine Ireland and Cooper James Robert Byrne

Oh Fatherland, Fatherland,

Show us the sign

Your children have waited to see.

The morning will come

When the world is mine.

Tomorrow belongs to me.

(John Kander and Fred Ebb *Cabaret* 1966)

Chapter 1

On a late summer's morning Jay Halprin drives his VW Golf Cabriolet westward along Route 22. The roof is down; the wind tugs at his greying hair; the sun flashes meaningless Morse in the rear-view mirror as the car speeds under the overhanging boughs. He will arrive at Burford Station in good time to catch his customary 07.14 train to Grand Central and he intends to be in his office shortly before 08.30. He will sweep into his allotted space in the station car park accompanied by the crunch of protesting gravel. His carton of take-out coffee awaits him in the drug-store.

Rachel Halprin, Jay's wife, is at home tidying away the breakfast things as she contemplates an empty day. Her greatest challenge will be to find places in their rented house for the superfluous furnishings from England. She curses that the town's swimming pool closed on Labor Day. Her afternoon visits had given her structure and routine. The sun will be warm enough later to sunbathe and swim – why did they close the pool? Her neighbours would tell her that you can't trust the summer to stick around. It has packed its suitcase already. Fall is creeping up on Burford Lakes bringing lower temperatures and wet winds.

Jay and Rachel's son Ben, having mastered the Pledge of Allegiance, is now familiar with everything he needs for a smooth passage through his seventh day at Jefferson High School. He stands on the street corner alongside neighbours Tyler and Peach Cochrane waiting for the school bus. His toes hang over the front of the kerb like a penguin on a cliff. He's pondering whether or not to take part in the upcoming soccer trials.

The upheaval of the family's re-planting in American soil is behind them. Tender root-tips are emerging, feeling their way through this fertile loam.

Jay, the agent of the family's move, waits in the Burford Station drugstore line silently rehearsing his order – double-shot-American-black. He glances at the shelf of magazines. His camera-pan stops at the red masthead of the *Burford Buzz*.

This is wrong. The editor, Melissa Rosenberg, told him that the magazine would be out on the second *Thursday* in the month. He checks the cover and finds the date. He's right; the drug-store owner has put it on the stand two days before time. If Jay wants to read the interview 'fresh off the press' he should buy it today.

The dollars in his hand are only enough for his coffee so he feels in his pocket for more folded bills. Nothing. He curses under his breath remembering how, the evening before at the grocery checkout, he had handed over the bulk of his cash. He had intended to use the ATM when he arrived at Grand Central.

He pinches his lower lip between his forefinger and thumb and looks over the sharp-suited shoulder of the commuter in front of him. How long is the line? Jay's train is due any second. If he crosses the square to the bank he'll have to wait for the next one. But he needs to read the interview – to see what Melissa made of him.

A woman turns away from the counter with her coffee and a copy of the *New York Times*. The queue steps forward one pace. It's two months since Jay moved to Burford Lakes but he's yet to develop a newspaper habit. His daily routine is to buy only the coffee and to catch up with business reading while the train soothes its way past the copses and reservoirs of the northern suburbs of Manhattan. If Jay ignores the premature

Buzz and catches his usual train, he will arrive at Grand Central in good time.

An alternative scenario comes to him. He's in the station car park lounging in the cream leather seat of his car. The roof is down and his jacket is draped over the passenger seat. The take-out carton of coffee is in his right hand and, in his left, the *Burford Buzz* is open at the page where he had explained to his new neighbour why he and the family had come to New York; why they had chosen Burford Lakes as their home. The sun, still low in the sky, caresses his hair.

So it is that, as the 07.14 to Grand Central glides into the station, Jay strides away along one of the diagonal paths crossing Burford Station square. He passes under the statue of Chief Kisco in full ceremonial dress, pointing the way to the Bank of America.

Burford Buzz - 13th September 2001

Melissa Rosenberg meets her new English neighbor and warms to the idea of a British invasion!

It's been 125 years since Lord Percy led his Redcoat stragglers into the settlement of Burford Lakes and ordered it to be pillaged and burned to the ground. We guard our memories jealously so, despite being allies in the world wars of 1917 and '41, we stay cool when the cry goes up that 'the British are coming!'

These thoughts flashed through my mind as I stood on the steps of a tidy colonial house on The Ponds Estate waiting for Leslie 'Jay' Halprin to answer the door. Would this man, who had brought his family to our shores, be a true successor to Percy – taking the food from our mouths, destroying our livelihoods?

Based on my meeting with him, I have to say that nothing could be further from the truth – unless you're a Brand Recovery Consultant, that is. And Jay told me that in New York they're as rare as nuggets in a Croton River prospector's gold-pan.

Jay's delightful wife Rachel made tea in a teapot the English way and graciously departed to meet some of her new friends at the town pool. She's wasted no time gathering round her a circle of Burford Lakes townswomen who share her taste for sunshine and exercise – but not too much of either!

But back to Jay: why is he here?

'I was one of Europe's top brand-recovery experts and Glenn Straub and Francois DuCheyne wanted me for their team.' According to Jay, 'Straub, DuCheyne is *the* world leader in brand management. My specialty [he says *speciality!*] is helping companies rebuild their brand after negative publicity.'

'How long have you been here?' I asked, casting a critical eye over the oddly-assorted sticks of patio furniture that gave the living room a transient look.

He beamed a broad smile. (All those bad things we hear about British dentistry certainly don't apply to Jay!) 'The neighbors here have been very kind. Rachel was – we all were – going stir-crazy cooped up in a hotel. We decided to move in here with just a television and a sofa-bed. The people around us were soon knocking at our door offering to lend us the things we need until our furniture arrives. Everybody has been so friendly. They're even holding a welcome party for us.'

I wondered how long the Halprins intended to stay in our fair boro.

'Who knows? Our first impressions are that we couldn't have found a more welcoming locality than Burford Lakes. We have everything we need here. I can't see why we shouldn't make the move permanent.'

All work and no play would (possibly!) make Jay a dull boy so I asked him what he does in his spare time.

'On the first Sunday we were here I heard the familiar shouts of men playing football [he means *soccer!*] somewhere behind the house. So I went to the end of the garden [*backyard!*] and
discovered a pick-up game in the park. I only had to show an interest for a few minutes before they invited me to join in. I now play every Sunday.'

So there we have it. Here is one Brit whose diplomatic skills are definitely an improvement on Lord Percy. But it's not all plain sailing – Jay offered a story to illustrate that there is some grit in the oyster and asked, 'You sure you want to hear?'

I found the combination of Jay's dark eyes, his winning smile and that quaint English accent irresistible – it was as if Hugh Grant himself was asking for my permission to keep talking. No way was I saying nay!

'Well, one of our first big purchases was a car – a Subaru 4x4. At the dealer's, I asked to see "under the bonnet". The salesman gave me a very puzzled look in response.'

As all the good folks of Burford Lakes would! Jay's joke made sense when he explained that, on his side of the pond, what we call the 'hood', they call the 'bonnet'!

We laughed together as the sun went down behind the trees lining the backyard. Rachel returned from the pool and my work was done. As I closed my notebook, the lady of the house poured me a glass of European Chardonnay (small at my request!) and long-time Burford Lakes residents and next-door neighbors Bob and Katy dropped by. Here is one Brit family that looks as if it's going to fit right in. Once they get to grips with our 'foreign' language, that is!

Jay is half an hour behind his original schedule as he steps down from the train and joins the crowd hurrying up the ramp to the Grand Central concourse. He consults his watch. On a sunny day he prefers to walk the mile or so along Park Avenue to the subway at Union Square. The trains going south are more frequent there. He jostles through the commuters who scuttle like cockroaches across the marble floor.

Outside, on Park Avenue, he crosses to the western side, the sunny side. The city's workers are making the most of the weather in shirtsleeves with jackets hooked by fingers over shoulders or folded into commuter backpacks.

The boulevards of New York fire up Jay's system and it runs hotter than a pan of French fries. Jay has read *The Bonfire of the Vanities* by Tom Wolfe but the moral was lost on him. He loves this city – this cauldron boiling in the heat of capitalist enterprise. These commercial cliff-sides that tower over him, this special Manhattan muscle-bustle, the blue sky of September, the grid-locked yellow cabs that honk like geese: all these things come together to convince him that his decision was correct to take the job with Straub, DuCheyne.

Buoyed by NY fever and the *Burford Buzz* puffery, his chest is pumped and his stride is long. He swings his shoulders in a poor-imitation pimp-roll and hums the song by Sting – *Alien in New York* – while he imagines his arrival at the office. He'll throw his briefcase onto the couch by the coffee table, move to the narrow floor-to-ceiling-window and scan the view across to Brooklyn. He knows he'll never lose his fascination with the insect-scurries of the ferries criss-crossing the reflective surface of the East River. Nancy will enter the office. They'll discuss the morning's post and e-mails. Although he's worked at Straub, DuCheyne for only a month he's secured one new client already. Nancy – statuesque Nancy – will flash her perfect teeth and congratulate him on his progress with a possible new client in Texas. He's making his mark. Not bad for a working-class lad from England.

A spark in the sky makes him look up as he passes Stuyvesant Square. It's a flash of light reflected off the wing of an aircraft as it banks low towards the twin towers of the World Trade Center. How low Jay doesn't register until his mind clears and, for a millisecond, he goes back twenty years and is in his Student Union bar watching in slow-motion as a stray dart embeds itself in the soft panel of a loudspeaker. Then, back in the present, the plane plunges into one of the towers.

Time freezes. He's mistaken, surely. His eyes have betrayed him – there are billows of flame from the tower's near side but there is no noise. Has this horror happened with no sound – distanced from reality – a video with the mute button on?

Jay's heart jolts. There is a scream of engines and it's as if the scene is being re-enacted with sound. The *whoooumpf* comes as the point of the aircraft pierces the building and the wings slice through its core. Then the roar, as a fireball bursts through the northern facade. Debris showers down, trailing fire and smoke.

Jay points up and looks around. The other southbound pedestrians who saw it are slack-jawed and gaping. People who had been coming towards him turn back. Their heads twist round and upwards, like tree-tops lashed by a storm-wind. An unrecognisable force jerks the New Yorkers around him into movement. They stagger towards the stricken tower.

Jay's mind is tumbling with images he doesn't understand. It's crashing with stimuli that he's not equipped to process. The majority of people around him are responding to an urge to get closer but his instinct is for flight. He turns against the streams of flocking New Yorkers and hurries back to Grand Central.

Within fewer than fifteen minutes, Jay is on a Brewster-bound train. The other passengers are brown-skinned, Spanish-speakers. For them this is the normal commute, leaving the city when the suits move in. They whisper mostly, chins sunk into their chests. The ones who had seen what Jay witnessed have passed on the news. Huddled in the carriage, they reflect his shame. They also are outsiders. They also are running away.

Iced water floods into Jay's veins. Sweat damps his forehead and, under his shirt, cold dribbles of moisture track down his sides. He closes his eyes and slumps further down in his seat; he needs to feel the movement, the progress away from disaster. He shivers and, like a screening on the inside of his eyelids, he watches once more the missile plunge in and the plume of fire spew out. It was the nearer North Tower; he doesn't doubt it.

He tries to count floors from the top but only has an impression – about one-fifth of the way down. There are 110 floors. So it must have happened around the 85th floor. The offices of Straub, DuCheyne are on the 95th.

His mind is in turmoil. Had one of his colleagues – Nancy perhaps – glanced out of the window and seen it coming? How fast do they fly? He had read somewhere that planes gobble up hundreds of metres per second. If she *had* seen it, Nancy wouldn't have had time to scream.

He takes out his mobile phone and hits the office number. It's busy.

The percussion of the wheels of the train as they cross points outside Fordham echo the rhythm of Jay's startled heart. *Bm-ta-ta, bm-ta-ta, bm-ta-ta-ta-bm-ta.* His eyes are closed and, as he will remember it for the rest of his life, the clatter is not loud enough to mask the sound of light footsteps stepping in time to the train's beat. Somebody, somebody who evidently doesn't know, is skipping in the aisle. The sound stops level with him and Jay is aware that the light weight of a small person is now perched alongside him on the seat. When Jay opens his eyes nobody is there.

It's not surprising that his brain is playing tricks. He isn't being incinerated only because he didn't catch his accustomed train. He owes this to the mistimed appearance of a gossip sheet that's tucked inside the briefcase nestling against his leg. The *Buzz's* pages are folded back at the interview and the photograph of the Halprin family chafes against the bag's Italian leather divider. A separate article, a space-filler that earned scarcely a glance from Jay, completes the two page spread. It records the recent marriage of a man and a woman, both in their mid-eighties, in a White Plains retirement home. The bridegroom is described as a long-time Burford Lakes resident and 'a survivor of a Holocaust death-camp'.

Chapter 2

MY CABARET YEARS – IN THE FOOTSTEPS OF ISHERWOOD

A memoir by Cameron Mortimer.

Quentin Crisp's American odyssey as 'The Naked Civil Servant' took off in the mid-1970s when his iconic television film was broadcast here. Am I being bitchy when I question whether its success prompted Christopher Isherwood to rush out his book 'Christopher and his Kind' in 1977? However it happened, I am content to admit that I would not be committing to paper this frank account of my life in Berlin were it not for these two 'stately homos of England' flouncing ahead of me in their open-toed sandals.

Like a deep-sea diver who surfaces in stages, I'm going to find it deleterious to my well-being if I go from this year, 1985, the full distance to 1932 in one step. So my story starts on 26 April 1950 and I hope it won't confuse you too much if we go backwards from there.

In the early afternoon, as was my custom, I set my rocking chair in front of the window and read by the light of the sun. I had a little over an hour before it travelled too far west and the angle into the window was too acute. I had viewed the house on a summer's afternoon and hadn't realised that it was only the absence of buildings in Jay Park that afforded the sun a glimpse of what was to be my living-room. For the rest of the day my narrow brownstone lived in the shade of the taller buildings on the south side of East 77th Street.

I was forty-five years old and already feeling the twinges of the arthritis that would cripple my knees in later years. A signed and

dedicated first edition of collected poems by W H
Auden lay open on my lap. It was all I needed to
spend my time in contemplative reminiscence. I
recalled a fleeting liaison with dear Wystan when
we worked together on a play that was never taken
up.

He declared at the time that the work and
the sex would have been more satisfying had I
been Christopher Isherwood. We both recognised
this as the catty prelude to schism and I forgave
him. We kissed and vowed to stay platonic
friends.

We didn't, of course. We both still lived in
Manhattan but Wystan's circle rotated at a higher
altitude than mine. In any event I would shortly
move out of the city to a northern suburb and saw
no reason for petty jealousy. Not to be vulgar,
but my Dexter Parnes VC mysteries were far more
remunerative than Wystan's poems would ever be.

The rat-tat-tat on the front door came as I
was succumbing cat-like to the warmth and I
jerked straight, causing my chair to rock
ferociously. I put out a hand to the sill and
this gave me a pretext to lean forward and look
down to the street. The man who had knocked on
the door had evidently stepped back and was
standing alongside a woman. She was hatless and
not somebody I knew. The man looked mysterious
with his face obscured by his hat which was set
at a just-so angle - a jauntiness I recognised.
The woman was carrying a baby. They presented a
shabby group and I could sense desperation in
their demeanour. Despite the attraction of the
man, I wondered if they were beggars and resolved
not to go down.

The man stepped out of view again and I
leaned forward to regain sight of him. The rat-
tat-tat sounded through the house. There was
something in the way he moved. It confirmed in my
mind that he was one of our tribe, but, this
being the case, what was he doing in the company
of a woman and a baby? Intrigued, I hoisted

21

myself out of the chair and made my way downstairs to the vestibule.

A mirror set into the hallstand gave me the
opportunity to check my appearance. I smoothed
down the front of my white shirt and re-tucked it
into my 'slouching' brown cords. A gold chain
peeked out at my open collar. That, and my white-
gold pinkie ring, were the only signs of
ostentation I allowed myself. I unbolted the door
at top and bottom and opened it on the chain.

The man stepped into view and took off his
hat. "Cameron?" he said.

"Wolf?" I closed the door, slid back the
chain and swung the door wide. "Wolf!" Tears
filled my eyes, obscuring the face that had
changed so much but at the same time held the
essence of the boy I had loved unreservedly in
Berlin. "Wolf! I never thought I'd see you
again!"

To mitigate the crassness of this remark I
can only say that it is at times of highest
emotion we resort to the commonest cliché.

Now we'll go back to the morning of 2nd July 1934
when I was also awoken by banging on my door.

"Herr Mortimer! Herr Mortimer!" It was Frau
Guttchen's voice, shrill and urgent.

I scrabbled around on the bedside table for
my watch. The luminous hands told me it was not
yet six o'clock. I groaned. Whenever my head
hurt, I regretted not spending a few more marks
on better quality red wine. "What is it?"

"Herr Mortimer!" There was more banging.

I had to raise my voice for the noise to
stop. "Yes! Frau Guttchen, I can hear you." After
two years in Berlin, my German was nigh on
perfect and idiomatic. "I'm coming."

Wrapping a sheet around my bare torso, I
twisted myself up and out of bed. I paused by the
door leading to the communal hallway and cocked
my head. The knock was civilised this time. "What
is it? This had better be good. What time do you
call this?"

"Herr Mortimer, you have a visitor. It is your young friend Mr Koehler. He seems to be very distressed. I have made him wait downstairs because of the hour. Herr Mortimer?"

"Yes, I'm listening." I tried to imagine why Wolf should be in Berlin. He was meant to be in Munich with his Hitlerjugend troop. "Did he say what he wanted?"

"He is in trouble, he says, and desperately needs to see you."

I turned the key in the lock and opened the door. Frau Guttchen's matronly figure was trussed into a tartan dressing gown with a faux sheepskin collar. What remained of her crimson hair was twisted into wraps of tissue paper arranged to reveal criss-crossing lanes of shiny scalp. I stifled a giggle and composed my face. "Would you be so kind as to send him up? Then, perhaps, you can go back to bed. I am so sorry you have been disturbed."

Frau Guttchen scurried away.

My befogged mind tried to unravel what was happening. Wolf was in trouble but what would its nature be? It had become increasingly difficult to be a foreigner living in Berlin and how might the authorities react if Wolf's problem implicated me? Whatever the danger, Wolf was my friend and I decided I would have to take the consequences.

I reached this conclusion as Wolf's booted feet sounded on the stairs. He appeared round the corner, his face flushed. His uniform shirt was dishevelled and its tails untucked. The mud on his shorts made it look as if he had endured a ghastly juvenile accident. His feet were bare inside his boots. "You have to help me, Cammie," he cried.

I stepped back and he brushed past me. The stale smell of him assaulted my senses and I had to force myself to cover the yard or so between us, arms outstretched.

"There, there, Wolf. Come to Cammie."

He threw himself into my arms like a wounded four-year-old. "It was horrible!" he cried, his eyes pumping tears and a bubble of snot beneath his nose.

I looked over his shoulder towards the bed. I hoped he wasn't going to ask to sleep, not in this state. "What's happened, lover? Why aren't you in Munich? Your weekend?"

He jerked down his arms and stepped back. "I feel as if I have walked the whole way. I couldn't risk using the train. They'll be looking for me."

"Who?"

"The Schutzstaffel - the men from the SS. They burst into our dormitory and started shooting. They were killing everybody - anybody."

"Hitlerjugend?"

He looked down at his boots and, as if he noticed his disarray for the first time, tucked in his shirt. "It wasn't a Hitler Youth weekend. I fibbed. It was with the Sturmabteilung - the Brownshirts."

My heart ached at the way he looked so miserable, so lost. I had nothing but compassion for my poor boy. "Come here, Wolf. You must have a bath. I'll make some coffee. You must tell me all about it but first let's clean you up."

Chapter 3

The train is pulling out of Woodlawn when they make the announcement. 'There has been an accident in the city. A passenger plane has crash-landed near the World Trade Center and there are a number of fatalities. The authorities are stopping all transport into and out of the city. This service is diverted to New Canaan and passengers are to make their own arrangements from there. This service is now non-stop to New Canaan.'

The passengers buzz like wasps in a sugar-trap. Some are translating the message for others. Jay will have to wait at New Canaan and Rachel will pick him up. He tries her number. Engaged. He wonders how many New Yorkers' lives have been disrupted and how many millions of people are trying to make a telephone call at the same time.

He pictures the Trade Center floor plans. If his office is below where the plane hit his colleagues will be safe. He imagines them labouring down the flights of stairs. How long does it take – 95 floors? Yes, they'll be traumatised but they'll survive.

What if Straub, DuCheyne's office is above where the plane burst in? (He remembers how the announcement had called it a 'crash-landing'. Why did they describe it this way?) There must be an evacuation procedure. They'll climb to the roof. There will be helicopters – an airlift.

Unwelcome thoughts press in on him. What would abrupt and immediate obliteration feel like? It's as if he's picking at a scab in his brain. I would have been there if I hadn't been so vain, he thinks. Vanity of vanities, all is vanity. Where did that come from? He feels a presence behind him – a spectre of his imagining. If he could turn round quickly enough he would see who it is.

Still the questions come as if this 'other' is interrogating him. They snap at him like unruly hounds. Would *you* have died bravely in the maelstrom of flame? What will *you* make of your second-chance life? He tries to quell the negativity rising within him. A song reverberates inside his head: *Who let the dogs out? Who? Who?* He shivers and murmurs to himself that somebody has walked on his grave.

Rachel! He straightens in his seat. She knows. She'll be watching news bulletins. What is she thinking? Does she know which floor was hit? Is she assuming he was below the impact and safe? Above it and waiting for rescue? In it – and dead?

He presses the 'home' button on his mobile phone and puts it to his ear. Engaged. He looks round the carriage. Many of the other passengers are doing the same thing. Pressing buttons, putting mobile phones to their ears. Shaking them. Inspecting the screens. The networks must be overwhelmed. He will have to sit tight and wait for New Canaan. Jay starts chewing the skin around the thumbnail on his right hand. He shifts on the seat and the damp patch on his back cools in the air-conditioning, a sensation that is soon overwhelmed by the heat from his adrenalin-pumped heart.

When the train approaches the terminus he moves to stand by the door. There is a sweat-perfumed scrum waiting as the carriage glides alongside the platform but Jay is aware of an unspoken understanding by the brown-skinned people: they will defer to his Anglo-Saxon height. As soon as the doors are open he runs towards the exit where he spies a bank of payphones. There's already a line formed at each one. The train, the swarming crowd, the misery of the lines, a newsreel image from the Holocaust springs unbidden into Jay's mind and he shakes his head to send it spinning away. 'Where did that come from?' he asks himself as he sizes up the lines.

Having decided on the shortest queue, Jay delights in elbowing others aside so he can join it. He shifts his weight from foot to foot and jiggles coins in his hand. He strains to overhear the woman making her call. Can he tell from her tone whether she's reaching the end of her conversation? He counts the bodies in front. Four. He turns round. There are already three people behind.

The other lines are at least seven or eight deep. He will have to wait his turn. The tension of frustrated communication clings to him like a Boston fog. The woman uses a clawed finger to click off the connection and leaves the handset dangling. Jay watches it spin on the twisted chord like a ghetto corpse strung from a wire and he has to shake his head again to detach himself from the image. The woman pushes her way through, pressing close by, weeping. Jay turns to the front and curses as the next man fumbles his coins, drops one and scratches around on the floor before finally fingering it into the slot.

By the time he reaches the booth, Jay has observed the previous callers and memorised the process for getting a connection. With the sweaty instrument snapped to his ear, he listens for the ringing tone. He notices dregs of spittle in the mouthpiece.

'Hello?' The voice on the other end is unknown to him and cautious.

He thinks that in his panic he has he pressed the buttons in the wrong order. 'Who's that?'

'This is the Halprin house. Who *is* this?' The woman who's answering sounds scared.

'Where's Rachel? Who's *that*?' He looks up at a woman in a fuchsia-pink jacket who stands behind. She's listening and tutting at his lack of progress.

'This is, Katy from next door. Is this … Jay?'

27

'Katy. Where's Rachel? It's Jay.' There's a scream at the other end. 'Jay? Mr Halprin?'

'Yes.'

'Rachel! Rachel! Here, quickly! It's him. It's your husband.' He hears a scraping noise. Rachel says something indistinct in the background, then Jay hears Katy more clearly: 'Thank God! Quickly, Rachel. It's him.'

Rachel's voice is a monotone. Is it the shock of his resurrection? 'Where are you? Your mobile's dead. Why haven't you called?'

'I've been on a train, Rache. I saw it. I saw it fly in.' He's choking the words out. The woman in pink looks away. 'I saw it and ran.' This is only part of the burden weighing him down – his survival adds so much more.

'We thought you were dead. I've been waiting for somebody to tell me. Katy's come to sit with me.' She's weeping and the sound of it makes Jay's throat constrict.

'I would have been.' Something within him dredges up the notion that perhaps he was always going to miss the train. He dismisses it and says, 'Can you come and get me? I'm at New Canaan station.'

Rachel sniffs. He pictures her taking a grip of herself. 'Why New Canaan?'

'I'll explain when you're here.'

'Okay, I'm on my way.'

'Thanks, Rache.' He replaces the handset on its rest and the woman in pink steps forward. He looks at her eye to eye. It's no matter to either of them that there are tears tracking down his cheeks.

He spies a Starbucks across the road. The backs of jackets and blouses are pressed flat against the windows and people are crowding round the door. The rest of the town is deserted. When he reaches the doorway, he sees that someone has rigged up a television. Nobody is serving or drinking coffee. A gaggle of women in T-shirts and jeans detach themselves from the interior and come out shaking their heads, their chins in their chests. They have smudges of mascara under their red-rimmed eyes.

The group round the door eases and Jay is inside. The onion-bitterness of body odour makes it smell like a cheap hamburger joint. All eyes are fixed on the screen.

'How bad is it?' Jay asks nobody in particular. 'I've just got off the train.'

The man in front of him, who's wearing UPS brown overalls, answers from the side of his mouth, cocking his head so that he doesn't miss anything. 'Poor souls have been jumping.'

He tries to interpret what this means. Where from? Why? 'I've missed it. I only know about the accident – the plane, the tower.'

The man turns to him. 'Two of 'em. Two planes. Look. They've got both towers – that's both towers burning. Motherfuckers!'

Nobody in the room reacts to the profanity. Plumes of white smoke are curling up from both buildings. He shakes his head. 'They'll get them off with helicopters, right?'

'It's too hot. They got no chance – those poor fuckers on the roof. If they were above it they're–'

Toast! Jay jerks his head back in reaction to the word that sprung out from his brain. He thanks God he didn't say it aloud. But he can't stop his mind throwing this stuff at him.

They're toast, Jay. And you're down here instead of up there with them.

Jay feels the people around him tense. There's an explosion in the South Tower. It shudders and a cloud of smoke and dust erupts from the top floors. The twist of debris spirals into the sky but it's not the building growing. Seconds pass as they try to resolve the image. Then it becomes clear; the

29

building is disappearing. It sinks and settles on its haunches like a stricken zebra resigned to a lion's final throat-ripping snarl. A collective groan sounds its death-cry.

'What the fu–' UPS-man says.

The commentator screams that the building is collapsing and the view cuts away to street level where people are running, running, looking over their shoulders as a monster clad in a billowing cloak of white chases them down the street.

'I don't understand,' Jay says. 'What's happening?'

The voice – this new unwanted voice – speaks. *It's death. Death is loose on the streets of Manhattan.*

A woman answers this time. 'They say there are twenty planes in the sky unaccounted for. They're bombing us with our own planes.'

'Who?'

She sounds tired. 'They don't know. Terrorists? They hit the Pentagon with another one. But the World Trade Center – well you just saw it.'

The TV cuts away to a camera on Staten Island. There is an absence, the imagined outline of a space filled with sky. 'Did they get out?' someone whispers.

'Who knows?' It's somebody else. 'You have to pray ...'

A ticker tape at the bottom of the screen mentions a man called Usama Bin Laden. His terrorist organisation has been boasting of making an attack like this. Jay looks at the North Tower, still standing. He tries to count floors from the top but there is so much smoke and the angle switches too often. Is his office above or below?

They continue to watch as the pictures switch between views of the tower in Manhattan and the hole in the ground alongside the Pentagon. Jay turns to the window from time to time to see whether Rachel has arrived.

By the time he sees the gold 4x4 draw up, Jay has assimilated what has happened but he still doesn't know how bad it has been for Straub, DuCheyne. He leaves the coffee shop and crosses the road. There's a delay while Rachel unbuckles her belt and grapples with the door before she jumps down from the driver's side and runs round. She throws herself at him, sobbing. 'I thought you were dead.' Her voice is distorted and if she had said anything else he wouldn't have understood.

He holds her close. Her fists beat against his back. He pulls away and uses his thumbs to wipe the tears from her cheeks. She looks up at him, her eyes brimming and her top lip crumples. 'Oh, Jay. It's your floor. They flew into your floor. None of them can have lived through that. We have to go home – to England. Can we go home?'

Rachel's driving along Route 22. Jay's sitting in the passenger seat. The silence invites the presence in Jay's mind to intensify his torment. *Choose a scene*, it suggests. *Which one makes you shudder most?*

The camera is following a woman as she falls. Her hands are tight to her sides to stop her skirt from billowing. She's concerned for her modesty even as she plunges to her death. Jay looks closer at her right hand. She holds it awkwardly and he can make out a pair of shoes with high heels.

Did she think she was going to need them when she reached the ground?

Jay tries to remember the formula for computing the speed of a falling object. The phrase '32 feet per second per second' surfaces from the swamp of his grammar school education. What does it mean? The building has a hundred floors. So, 15 feet per floor, that is 1500 feet. How long does it take to fall 1500 feet? At 32 feet per second, rounded down, it's 50 seconds. Nearly a minute? It can't be right. The rate of fall: per second per second. It means there's acceleration but it doesn't answer the question, how long?

31

He plays back the woman's jump in his mind and counts to ten before the camera pans away as the ground looms up to meet her. Ten seconds.

Enough for her to anticipate the instant she hits the ground and becomes no more than a mess of butcher's slops on the sidewalk. When did she lose consciousness? What did it feel like in the moment of impact when Nancy's thighbones speared into her brain?

Jay shudders. What's got into him? Is he torturing himself because he should have been there? Is this how his life is going to be?

He groans and presses his hands to his face. Rachel reaches across and squeezes his knee.

Route 22 takes them past chic estates with high walls and robust electric gates. Trees lean out from either side and join arms overhead. The effect is of the 4x4 shooting along a tunnel like a hover car in *Blade Runner*. Jay wants it to stop. He doesn't know how to act when they get to the house. The neighbours are going to congratulate him on his good fortune but how can he smile when all his work colleagues have disintegrated into dust particles that drift across the East River?

There's a lurch in his chest. 'Ben! What about Ben? Does he know?'

Rachel is upright in the driver's seat with her knuckles white on the steering wheel. Her lips are pressed thin. There's a blue-veined tic in her pale temple. Her voice checks as if she is trying to swallow down bad words. 'He knows you're safe. Katy went to collect him and Tyler. He's home now. The school has closed.'

'What about others ... neighbours?'

'It's too early – who knows?'

Jay takes a deep breath and his body tenses. 'You said it hit our floor – SDC. Have you heard anything from anybody?'

There are spasms in Rachel's neck. She puts a knuckle to her mouth as if she's holding back sickness. 'You've only been there – how long is it?'

'Six weeks.'

'Six weeks.' Her voice is cold and flat. 'They don't know you. Nobody will think to call us. They have their own problems. Were any not in today?'

He shakes his head. 'I'd forgotten when I missed the train. It was a senior team meeting today. Everybody was due in early – by 8.30. Perhaps someone else was late like me.'

She turns to him. 'Why did you miss the train? You left in good time.'

His eyes look out of the windscreen but he sees only the morning's horrors. 'I saw it go in. I knew it was our floor, Rachel. I ran. I ran away.' He presses his fingers into his eye sockets to force the tears away and the accusations rain inside his head. *You survived. You left them to their fate. They were your colleagues but you didn't lift a finger.*

The car swings into Ponds Lane. Jay registers Ben sitting with the screen door wedged open by his body. He's bent over as if examining the ants' nest that Jay knows is there in the crack between the steps. Of all the things to say that scroll through Jay's mind, the one he elects to use as he approaches is, 'Don't leave the screen door open like that, Ben. The house will be full of flies.'

Chapter 4

Wolf was shivering as I undressed him in the bathroom. Naked, his ribcage showed blue through his vellum-like skin. His shrimp-like penis cowered in the seaweed twist of his pubic hair. His buttocks were hollowed out and pale. The steam from the bath rose around us and I sensed Wolf's fear passing from him to me like an infection.

I sat on the edge of the bath dribbling hot water on to his chest from a sponge with my right hand as I massaged his neck with my left. Despite myself, I could feel the stirrings of my arousal and I was disappointed to see that he was unmoved by my ministrations. "What happened?" I said. "You're safe now. You can tell me."

He closed his eyes; the fair lashes fluttered. "I'm sorry, Cammie. I lied to you. You are not my only friend."

It was a dagger in my heart but it was something I knew had to be true. Beautiful boys like Wolf were in demand and I often wondered why he had chosen to spend his time with me. I was generous, of course, and I knew he held a genuine affection for me - but I was only one of ... how many?

"Ssh, Wolfie. Don't worry about that now. You can tell me anything. Where have you been?"

"I've been staying with an SA troop at a barracks in Munich. I will be too old for the Hitler Youth soon and I, and some other boys, had been singled out for officer training with them. I always wanted to join the SA."

I didn't let him know how much this disappointed me. The SA rabble were the worst of Hitler's thugs. They beat people nearly to death for no more than not giving way on the sidewalk. The sight of their brown uniforms made Jews

34

scurry in any direction to avoid being in their
path. "So it was a recruitment weekend?"

"An induction. We were introduced to the SA
tradition."

It was difficult to imagine an organisation
of quasi-criminals having "a tradition" when it
had only been in existence for a decade but I
declined to demur.

He closed his eyes. "The Hitler Youth boys
were all chosen because we are ... the way we
are. They paired us up with experienced men – men
who are also like us. We were all in the
dormitory together."

I had heard rumours that Ernst Roehm, who
founded and led the SA, had adopted the Sacred
Band of Thebes as the model for his bodyguard.
"You were to become lovers?"

He covered his face with his hands. "Yes.
For the good of the unit. We would have
incredible fighting spirit – willing to sacrifice
ourselves for each other."

I shuddered. "Tell me what happened."

His tears started and I held his shaking
shoulders as he leaned forward, head bowed,
sobbing. "We were settling down after ... you
know ... it was an orgy ... I am so ashamed."

"Try to tell me, calmly," I said, stroking
his back.

"Suddenly, the doors at the far end of the
barrack-room burst open and the Blackshirts ran
in. They lined up against the wall and started
shooting. My man, Max, was hit in the first
seconds. I used him as a shield. I could feel
more bullets hit him. I slid back onto the floor.
I was one of many scrabbling around. My clothes
were there next to me so I grabbed them and
crawled under the beds to the end of the room
where the showers were. I escaped through a
window. I ran away naked. Others stopped to get
dressed. I don't think they made it."

His forehead was touching the water. I
spooned some suds onto his blond hair and began
to rub the soap into his scalp. "Go on."

"I hid in some trees and put my uniform on. I knew better than to go to the railway station. I got my bearings and walked to the road. I waved down a truck and the driver took me to Leipzig. I hid there for most of the day and then persuaded another truck driver to bring me to the outskirts of Berlin. Then I walked here. I knew you would look after me. You will, won't you, Cammie?"

"Can't you go home to your parents?"

"The SS will have my papers. They know I was in Munich. They will go to my house looking for me. You are my only hope."

I knew then my time in Berlin was over. I would leave and, somehow, I would smuggle Wolf out with me.

In his book Isherwood admits that "To Christopher, Berlin meant boys." This implies that he was an open and obvious bugger in those days but none of us was 'out' in the same way as we are now. If you were like Crisp - which I never was – you flaunted your campness in London and risked ridicule, arrest or outright hostility and violence. For the rest of us it had to be enough to move in the same shadowy circles and haunt the same dubious nightspots. I could never live truly as myself.

I went to live in Berlin because of money. I had written the first Dexter Parnes mystery, *The Silver Eagle Device*, when I was still at Oxford. After I came down I had a job in a dreary insurance office in Cheapside, London. For three years, while I tried to impress a publisher, I filled in forms, calculated premiums and copied line after line of policy details into ledgers. It truly was a Bob Cratchit life. My only adventures involved furtive gropings with men in the public gardens behind the back entrance (yes, really) of the commuter station in my home town of Surbiton in Surrey.

Sidgwick and Jackson took *Eagle* when I was 23 and published it the following year. It earned out its advance inside twelve months by which time I had finished the sequel, *The Seven-Second Timepiece*. It too sold well. Sidgwicks contracted me for two more Dexter Parnes adventures.

With this behind me I worked out that, if I could find somewhere inexpensive to live, I could leave the insurance business and write full-time. That's where Berlin came in. With the outline for the third book in my suitcase I caught the boat-train to Paris and thence to Berlin.

Anybody who, like me, went to a minor public school during and after the First World War will admit that adolescent fumbling - mostly involving mutual masturbation - was rampant. In fact, it was quite the norm. Most boys knew that they were going to 'grow out of it' when they had the opportunity to interact with girls.

But, even at school, I knew I was different. Boys weren't second best. I enjoyed giving pleasure and this made me a popular onanistic companion. If I could find a boy to love, it would be a relationship of the heart as well as body. Despite my promiscuity I failed to find the right boy at school.

At Oxford I had my physical urges satisfied by the occasional fling, once or twice even with young women, but without a true love appearing. So, in terms of a fulfilling relationship, I was still a virgin as the train steamed into Bahnhof Zoo.

Besides my valise, which was large enough to have smuggled in a small boy for my gratification, I carried my passport and the name of a hotel near the station. This had been arranged by my agent, Peter Everley. "I know you'd prefer to be in the Nollendorfplatz area, Mortimer, but you'd never get any work done. Carmerstrasse is opposite the University of the Arts. The academic air will be good for you. Stay away from the Nolli," he had said.

My heart was thumping as I hauled my bag along Hardenbergstrasse. In London I would have accosted a likely-looking layabout and asked him to carry it for me for a few pennies but I had no

way of knowing whether this was the done thing in
Berlin. Goodness knows there were enough men
loitering on street corners with their jackets
hanging off their wasted frames and with sleeves
or trouser legs pinned up because they had thin
air where the limb should have been.

I was unsure how to buy a ticket for the
tram that ran along the centre of the bustling
street. Motor cars beeped as they passed the
occasional horse-hauled cart piled high with
barrels, crates or bound sacks each stencilled
with words I didn't understand. There were
unintelligible posters on columns that seemed to
have been constructed purely for their display.
The air was tainted with the exotic tang of
foreign cigarettes.

The nearside traffic came towards me as I
walked along the left-hand pavement and this
added to my sense of disorientation. I worried
about how I might cross the first road I
encountered. The city was strange to me. But I
was the stranger, the outcast. Perhaps I had made
a mistake ...

Chapter 5

The Halprin's next-door neighbour Katy Cochrane had left Ben in the house alone. 'You don't want me around when your father gets home,' she had said.

As soon as they turn on the TV, Jay notices that the North Tower has gone. His legs give way and he collapses onto the sofa where he slumps watching the screen between his fingers. He can't imagine ever being anything other than cowed, stunned, uncomprehending ever again. If only he could sleep and never wake up.

He has to 'pull himself together' for Ben and Rachel, who sit alongside him like relatives at a death-bed, and robot-like he turns to one of his business techniques – an 'action pathway'. First, he'll find out what has happened at Straub, DuCheyne. If, as seems likely, all his colleagues have perished he'll talk to the widows of the men who brought him to New York. He can't imagine how these conversations will go. After that, he'll know where he stands workwise.

While the images flash and the commentators prattle he tries to think of something normal – routine. He recalls the evening of Ben's first day at school nearly a week ago when he had made sure he was home in time for dinner. The garlic-rich smell of a pasta sauce had met him as he opened the screen door.

'Jay, how was it?' Rachel tried to lift her tone but the fragility in her voice was obvious.

'You know that company *Heroes of the Alamo* – the one I went to see in San Antonio?'

Rachel shook her head. 'Companies here and their strange names …'

'Well, they're coming round.' He shucked off his jacket and hung it over a chair-back. 'That'll be two clients inside a month. Glenn and Francois are already talking end-of-year bonuses.'

'That's good. Ben has news as well. He's happy with how it went.'

Jay loosened his tie. 'Where is he? Up or down?'

Rachel signalled 'up' with her forefinger.

Jay went to the bottom of the stairs. 'Ben, I'm home. Want to come down and tell me about your day?'

Rachel was at the table pouring sauce over the tagliatelle by the time Ben's fast feet percussioned down the stairs and he fell into the room.

'This is good, Rachel. Delicious.' Jay said it before the food had passed his lips. He rubbed his hands together. 'So what's your news, Ben? Everything okay, first day?'

Rachel looked across the table. 'Go on. Tell your dad your news.'

Ben looked down at his plate. 'They had an audition for chorus–'

'Chorus?' Jay said.

'It's what they call the school choir. Anyway, I sang a bit and they got all excited.' He blushed. 'I've been a bit self-conscious about my voice – haven't sung anything since it started to break and it was all over the place. Well, they loved it. Said I'm a natural counter-tenor, whatever that means.'

'And ...' Rachel tapped a fingernail on the table-top.

'And they want me to audition for the school show at Christmas.'

'Really? What is it?' Jay asked.

'*Cabaret*,' Ben answered.

A frame from the film loomed up in Jay's mind. The cabaret's Master of Ceremonies, in white-face makeup and painted-on eyebrows was leering into the camera. Jay tapped a foot as the music crawled into his ear. 'Doo doo de, Ca-ba-reyey,' He swayed his upper body in time with his singing and clicked his fingers. 'Doo doo de, Ca-ba-reyey.'

'Da-ad!' Ben put his fingers in his ears.

'Sorry, Ben. It's great. Go for it.' He looked up and saw Rachel frowning and making round, dark eyes. 'You won't hear any more singing from me – promise.'

Now, there's something more significant about the image that came to him that day – the chalk-complexioned, ruby-lipped Master of Ceremonies. An idea as elusive as an eel on a boat-deck is squirming in and out of the foreground of his mind. He focuses on it, trying to pin it down but it slips away.

He switches to yesterday when Ben came home agitated with news of the audition.

'They've given me a part!'

'Who? What?' Jay said, looking up from the dinner plate. Rachel gave her husband a scowl.

Ben put on his talking-to-a-moron voice. '*Cabaret*? The audition on Friday?'

Jay noted how his son now punctuated the majority of his statements with question marks.

'Dad?'

'Jay!' Rachel put down her knife and fork. 'Ben wants to tell you something.' Her articulation was precise and she emphasised her warning with a nod of her head.

'Sorry, Ben. I was miles away there for a moment. The show – *Cabaret*. Go on.'

'They want me to sing a solo.'

'Wow!' Jay was impressed but at the same time was concerned. He couldn't imagine his shy son carrying it off. 'Which part?'

'Not one of the main characters. They showed us the movie in lunch-break? So we'd know the setting – the rise of Nazis in Germany and all that?'

Jay nodded. 'I've seen it hundreds of times. It's a great film. Liza Minnelli as Sally Bowles – what a great performance. What a tremendous character. I read the Isherwood book that started it all – *Goodbye to Berlin* – years ago. Have you read it, Rache?'

Rachel gave him her turn-to-stone look and nodded towards Ben. 'Tell your dad about *your* part, Ben.'

'Well, mine is the bit where the American writer and his German friend go to the park? And the boy sings. It's a sort of traditional German song? Only it turns out the boy's a Nazi and it's actually a Nazi song. And the crowd all sing along? Well, that's me. I'm going to sing the song, *Tomorrow Belongs to Me*. I have to do it twice?'

As Jay recalled the scene from the film, chills prickled his neck. He pictured the rosy-cheeked boy with the fascinating voice and looked at his son. Ben sat opposite, straight-backed and blond. His brown eyes gleamed with the obligation to carry one of the key moments in the show.

Jay saw a Ben he hadn't recognised before. Yes, he thought, he can surprise me. He can be that boy, this son of mine.

One side of Jay's brain focuses on the rolling news coverage. The other recalls the voice that has taken up residence inside his head. Its intonation has always sounded foreign and Jay now decides it has a German accent. The presence from the train – dancing along the aisle, perching on the seat beside him – assumes a white face, centre-parted hair and it leers into a non-existent camera. His was the insistent voice that urged Jay to replay the horrors of the victims over and over in his mind. It was the Cabaret's Master of Ceremonies who let the dogs out.

Now it's the MC who leans in so close that Jay can feel his breath on his ear as he whispers: *Ben is your salvation. It will be a distraction – therapy even – to help him. Show an interest. Activity is the best antidote to depression.*

The television news presenter is saying that 20,000 people worked in the two buildings of the World Trade Center and up to half of them could be dead. The casualties on the ground at the Pentagon, where the third plane crashed, are fewer but all the passengers and crew died. It emerges that there was a fourth hi-jacked aircraft and it plummeted into a field in Pennsylvania. Again, all on board were lost.

New film footage comes in and the Halprin family watches over and over again, from this perspective and from that, as the planes strike, as the towers collapse, as the people run. The pictures of the men and women jumping etch themselves onto Jay's retina. The MC's voice encourages him to superimpose the faces and mannerisms of his colleagues on the jumpers.

If they were in the office they would simply have vaporised. Come on Jay, which was the worst fate: vanish in an instant, jump or burn? Which would you have chosen?

Workers in the floors above where the planes struck were able to phone home and talk to their loved ones knowing they would never get out. Passengers on the fourth plane, United Airlines 93, used the on-board telephones after it had been hi-jacked and had described their plans to recapture the aircraft.

Each development reinforces Jay's sense of survival and cements the MC's invasive voice in position. Rachel and Ben stop watching and creep around as Jay sits mesmerised by the screen – a voyeur at an auto-wreck.

Rachel calls both sets of parents in England. 'No, he's really not up to talking. He's in shock, I think. We'll talk again tomorrow. He'll feel better then.'

43

As the sun sets, Jay goes to the window to pull the curtains. His face is swollen, his eyes raw. His caustic tears sting as he watches the houses opposite shine out their flickering TV-blue lights. Nobody in America is going to sleep worry-free tonight.

It's 3.23am on 9/12 and the MC prods his finger into Jay's side. In the fug of waking Jay watches him blow a kiss, smile and hunch his shoulders with delight. When Jay shakes his head, the image falls from his memory as mercury slips from a tray – leaving only a smear. He checks the illuminated numbers on the bedside clock.

A vision of the collapsing North Tower creeps into his head. The top floors concertina down as if a vacuum below is drawing the building in on itself. The MC's voice: *The fragments of your colleagues' bodies that still remain after the explosion were pulverised into powder. All mixed together they're a Cup-a-Soup version of the company that was there. 1) Open the sachet and pour into a medium mug or cup; 2) Make sure there is enough water in the kettle and switch on to boil the water; 3) When the water has boiled, pour into the cup or mug and stir with a spoon; 4) Leave to cool a little and drink. Go on, Jay, drink my tasty soup. Could it be thicker? Could it have more body? Are you the missing ingredient?*

There's solace for Jay in knowing these are the MC's words, not his own. In the immediate aftermath, on the train or in the car with Rachel, when each morbid obsession or ghoulish thought entered his head, he wondered whether he might be going mad. But now he can assign these grisly introspections to a second person, surely this means he hasn't lost his mind.

The MC interrupts these fragments of half-asleep thoughts with another, more collected idea: *the complete personnel roll of Straub, DuCheyne, is understood to be dead.*

As one of the workers on the 95th floor, he'll be listed among the missing. Only his family and the Cochranes next

44

door know that he's alive. He resolves to tell 'the authorities' in the morning. This only prompts more confusion about whom 'the authorities' might be. He drags a pillow over his head.

He hopes, prays even, that his colleagues have souls. Something of them has to be left for their families to cleave to. In this country where 'which church do you go to?' is a more common question than the British 'what do you do?' the families will have the compensation of knowing their loved-ones' souls are safe. They will have already consulted their priests, their rabbis, maybe even their imams.

Rachel has nobody to visit her. The family has no spirituality. There's no religious element to their Jewishness. Out of nowhere, Jay sees the image of a clothes hanger. He thinks about the story.

Hymie Shapiro, a great-uncle on his mother's side, ran a tailoring business in London. Jay had never met Great-Uncle Hymie. He didn't even know of his existence. But, when Hymie died some twenty years ago, he decreed in his will that every traceable relative should receive a clothes hanger from his shop. So one day, without notice, Jay received a parcel from Gold and Oppenheimer Solicitors and in it was a letter and Jay's clothes hanger. The letter only explained the fact of the bequest; it gave no clue as to Great-Uncle Hymie's motive.

The clock now shows 4.13, two hours before Jay would normally rise and make a cup of tea. But the thought of the clothes hanger has taken root and the tendrils fill his head. Rachel's unbroken snoring reassures him as he slides off the mattress and creeps to the wardrobe. He opens the door and silently thanks the landlord for installing an interior light. He looks across to check Rachel's still form.

Taking the weight from each clothes hanger before sliding it, he moves his suits one by one. He's looking for a white plastic plaque and there it is under his well-loved but seldom-worn Harris Tweed jacket. He takes the jacket down

45

and, with all the exaggerated stealth of a cartoon burglar, he leaves the room and tip-toes across the landing to the bathroom. He closes the door, flicks on the light switch and squats on the toilet. The MC sits opposite him on the tiled floor with his back against the door, watching.

Jay removes the jacket from the clothes hanger, absent-mindedly checks its distinctive trademark label and leans forward to drape it over the side of the bath. Now he's holding the clothes hanger by its metal hook and he caresses its shoulder as if it's an artefact plundered from a museum. He imagines Great-Uncle Hymie himself describing it.

'Look at the hook in your left hand, Jacob. See the gauge of that steel wire? It's over-engineering, but such quality. This hook is never going to straighten out. No matter if it's carrying an extra-outsize, double-lined astrakhan coat with mink collar. And the bobble on the end, Jacob. That's it. Pass your thumb across it. Even a mistress's tender skin would not take a scratch from such smooth.'

Jay runs his palm down the flank of the arm. 'Slick as a rabbi's blessing, Jacob. Only a dense-grain wood could take such sanding. No suit lining, not even my finest silk, could pick a snag from such a finish. Notice how I have designed an angle to the arms. This way the jacket drapes just perfect. A customer could only be impressed with a jacket on such a clothes hanger.'

Tears cascade from Jay's chin onto his shorts as he hugs the hanger to his chest. The chamber echoes with his low moan. Great-Uncle Hymie's voice is now fading, 'Thank you for keeping my clothes hanger, Jacob. A blessing upon you for this.'

The faux-ivory plate pinned across the join where the two angled arms come together captures Jay's attention. There's an old-style telephone number, **Wat**erloo 5561, and then the word 'Hymie' in slanted, black script across the centre. To the right of this in red are the words, 'The Tailor' and an address, like the telephone number in smaller, black font, '48 Lower Marsh, London, S.E. 1'. Jay traces the indented characters with his fingertip.

Great-Uncle Hymie's clothes hanger will never again be the silly joke of a dying old man. Jay places it reverently on the windowsill. He will find a proper place for it in the morning.

He returns to bed, moving gently. The MC is tiptoeing theatrically behind him with a white-gloved forefinger pressed against his pursed lips. Jay is awake for another thirty-four minutes while the MC nips at the open sore – *if you had been in the office on time there would be nothing left to show you had existed.* But eventually he desists. He's not cruel. He's not an inconsiderate spectre. He knows Jay has to have enough sleep for there to be something to work with in the morning. As Jay's eyes close and he loses consciousness the MC loosens his arm from around his waist and turns to face the other way.

Chapter 6

Peter Everley had assured me it was a short walk to the hotel and, true to his account, the hotel came into view the instant I turned into Carmerstrasse. I climbed a few steps and entered through the open outer door into a porch. A glass panel in the inner door allowed me to view the reception desk by the staircase. I took a deep breath, opened the door and went inside. "I have a booking. My name is Mortimer." I spoke carefully, enunciating each consonant.

"Herr Mortimer, of course. Welcome in the Carmer Hotel. It is an honour for us to have such a famous guest."

Peter had evidently paved the way with a little exaggeration but I was happy to find that this man spoke good English. "I don't know about that ..."

The man pressed a bell and the "ting" echoed around the enclosed space. "You will need help in the stairs with your bag, yes? We have not the elevator. Now if we can deal with the registration?"

I soon settled in as a resident of the west end of Berlin. Most of the sights of the city were to be found towards the east near the boulevard called Unter Den Linden. But Peter was right, I did not need distraction. My room on the third floor was perfectly adequate for me to work in and it had a tall French window that I could open inwards. For the next few days I sat at my desk and worked on the book. I took breakfast in the nook below the stairs with a cast of other guests renewing itself daily. They were always men dressed in suits and carrying heavy bags of samples.

It became my habit, around mid-morning, to take a walk down Carmerstrasse to Savignyplatz where there was a coffee shop on the corner. It was gay with a dark-green awning which hung over the tables arranged outside. As long as I was there before midday, the sun illuminated the tables and I would customarily enjoy a coffee with a cinnamon pastry while writing notes for Dexter Parnes. The white-aproned waiter spoke very good English and after he realised that I would become a regular customer, he asked my name. From then on he would call across in English as I arrived, "Your normal order, Herr Mortimer?" I would wave my notebook in response and this became our ritual.

On one such occasion there was a tall, wild-haired man of about my age sitting at my preferred table and I had to take the one next to it. I may have looked at the man distastefully but he seemed oblivious because he started up the conversation straight away. "You're English."

"Yes," I said, taking out my notebook and pen and placing them carefully in front of me.

"Cigarette?" He held out an open tin. The white tubes had tan-coloured ends.

"Are these the new ones? With cork tips?"

He lifted his chin as if his neck needed a stretch and spoke with lazy assurance. "Yes. Regatta brand by Greiling. The cork tip makes for a smoother smoke. Go on."

"I will." He flicked his lighter and I discovered that I had to suck quite hard to get a draw.

"Takes a bit of getting used to – but worth the effort."

I blew out the smoke and touched my tongue against the roof of my mouth. "Takes away a lot of the taste. Is the goodness still there?"

"Supposed to be. If you look at the cork afterwards you'll see it's trapped some dark brown matter. Looks bad. Better not to have it inside you, they say."

"Who?"

"Greiling - the advertisements."

"Well ..." I didn't need to say any more because he nodded and snorted blue smoke as he suppressed a laugh. For the first time since I arrived I felt my guard - the resistance to company that one feels in a foreign country - drop. I offered my hand. "Cameron Mortimer."

"Leonard Plomer. Call me Leo. Everybody does."

"Cameron."

The waiter appeared by Leo's shoulder and started to shuffle behind him.

"Look here, Cam," Leo said. "Sit with me and take in the sun." He signalled and patted the table. The waiter deposited my order alongside him. "Noch einen Kaffee, bitte," Leo said.

I shifted across so I was alongside him with my coffee and pastry in front of me. We both faced out into the square and I could hear the klaxons and beeps of traffic from beyond the trees. "You speak German."

He waved a hand, "Enough to get by."

"How long have you been here?"

He rubbed his stubbled chin as if trying to recall a difficult theorem. "About a year. You?"

"Less than a month. I need to organise German lessons. You don't know anybody, do you?"

Again it seemed as if I had asked him to disclose a terrible secret. There was a long pause during which his coffee arrived. "Danke."

"Bitteschoen." The waiter bustled away.

"There must be somebody in my digs but I can't think. They all come and go."

"What do you do?"

He held out his hands. "Guess." His fingers were long with large pads on the end and I would have said he was a musician but for the spatters of all the shades of blue and red that coloured his palms. He turned his hands over. I could also make out other fine spots of yellows and browns.

"Painter?"

"In one. You?"

"I write."

I expected him to ask about my writing. Most
people did. Instead, he sipped his coffee and,
with my ego lightly bruised, I took the
opportunity to take a mouthful of the spiced
pastry which was usually the taste highlight of
my day.

"Where are you staying?" Leo asked.

My mouth was still churning the sweet ball
round and I had to swallow quickly. "Carmer
Hotel. Just along the road. My agent in London
booked it for me."

"Hotel? You must be doing well."

I stubbed out the cigarette and took a gulp
of coffee. It boosted the blandness of the smoke.
"I hadn't thought about it. I assumed an
apartment would be more expensive."

"Apartment?" He snorted. "That's not the way
it's done. Look-" he waved a hand regally as if
showing me the extent of his demesne, "-look at
all these grand houses. Most are owned by people
who once had pots of money. But they were done
for in the inflation. What with that and the
crash they've had to find ways of earning money
you wouldn't believe. You'd get a room for much
less than you're paying at the hotel. But you
have to be careful. You'll need a bit of space
and privacy if you're working."

"How do I go about it?"

"You're already doing it, Cam. You talk to
someone who knows. When you've finished your
coffee we'll take a stroll and I'll introduce you
to Frau Guttchen."

Within ten minutes he had walked me up
Carmerstrasse, past my hotel, to the point where
it joined Hardenbergstrasse. There was a circular
lawned area where four streets intersected.

"You are now standing in Steinplatz." Leo
pointed to a green-painted kiosk on one of the
corners. "Ernst runs it. He's a veteran of the
war and deserves our custom. You can't see it
through the little window but he's lost his legs.
You must buy your cigarettes from him."

I said I would.

51

"If you don't like Regatta, try Enver Bay. They have a strong Turkish taste and Fritz will give you a good price if you buy them a hundred at a time. Now, let's meet Frau Guttchen."

We crossed Uhlandstrasse and found ourselves in front of a muddy-green building with gothic-arched windows. Leo led me through an entrance into an open courtyard. I guessed that when the block was new - as few as ten years before - this had been laid to grass but now it was fenced off and divided into vegetable plots. They looked like the kitchen garden at home but the soil was sandy dust and it seemed able to support only a limited variety of plants.

We turned left and climbed a staircase to the first floor. "Frau Guttchen owns two apartments here. She is a widow. I think, when her husband was alive, they may have owned the whole block but I don't like to ask. She rents me the loft space in the top apartment. It's bloody cold in the winter and can get stiflingly hot in the summer but the light is good. I can get on the roof when the city heats up. It's all mine up there."

"Does she have a room spare?"

He pulled at a bell knob. "Not on this floor but the one below me. It's at the front. View over the square. It has a gas ring, I think. You share the bathroom, of course." There was a sound inside. "Here she comes."

Chapter 7

The alarm goes off and the heat builds as Jay's systems fire into life. His blood pump wheezes into an acceleration cycle, spinning its wheels like a steam engine on an icy track. His brain reboots and he comes to life. Why? Why has he woken so early? It's not as if he's going anywhere. He turns to Rachel who's invisible except for a spread of hair across the cream pillow. 'Is Ben going in today?'

'Uh?'

'Ben, is he going in?'

She groans and mumbles something about the time.

'Wednesday. We have to treat it like a normal Wednesday. I have calls to make. Ben is going to school, isn't he?'

Rachel sits up and Jay's blood fizzes because the nipple of her left breast is pushed out above the twisted neckline of her top. The sight of it stirs him and the MC asks whether after twenty-whatever years such a reaction is sweet or pitiable.

Don't make a grab for her.

Jay leans across to nuzzle into her neck and his right hand touches her breast; his thumb flicks across the nipple. She brushes his hand away. 'I have to pee. I have to get a pot of tea on the go for Ben, make sure he has a good breakfast and see him off. We both have a lot on our minds. Do tell me you're not thinking …'

Jay places his offending hand flat on the duvet. 'I was … I was just being affectionate.'

She leans into him. 'You can be affectionate later.'

His thoughts turn to the realisation that the MC has crept into his life again and he considers the implications. Does it mean he's mad? He shakes his head. The MC is a defence mechanism dreamed up to help him deal with the unthinkable. As long as he keeps him in his place, he can't see any harm.

Breakfast is a cheerless procedure. They're following the script like actors in a first read-through.

Jay on the musical: 'Have rehearsals started yet?'

Ben, toast halfway to his lips: 'They were meant to start today. I'm not sure it will happen now.'

Rachel, sipping her tea: 'They'll want to keep things normal.'

Ben: Yeah, but what if one of the cast has lost somebody?

Jay: Have they?

Ben: Don't know. Who knows what's happened to anybody?

Rachel: They'd be missing, I suppose.

Ben: Well, the kid wouldn't come in until they knew.

Jay: Shall I turn on the TV – find out the latest?

Both: No!

Rachel: We had enough yesterday.

Ben: I'd better go.

Jay: I hope rehearsals start. It'll give you something to think about.

His wife and son glance at him.

'What?' He considers what he said.

It's not Ben who needs something to fill his mind.

'You know what I mean,' Jay says.

All three of them cock their heads as if responding to a noise off-stage; it's the blare of the school-bus engine.

'Gottarush!' Ben says.

'Have a nice day.' Jay steps forward and hugs his son. There's tension in the embrace. He pulls away.

'You too, Dad.'

Jay and Rachel follow Ben out and arrive at the corner as the bus draws up. Ben is acting as if his whole life has been spent in line waiting for the school bus.

Rachel nods to the children from next door. 'Good morning, Tyler, Peach.'

They nod back. Their faces are pale with deep, dark eye-sockets.

Jay shakes his head. How does she remember their names?

The bus doors fold back and the kids clamber up into a leaden atmosphere. The doors whisper shut. The bus moves away past Jay and Rachel's house on the left. Three-hundred-or-so metres further on at the far end of the lane, where it turns right, another group of kids stands by the entrance to the town park.

'Look! Josh and Leah Edler are there.' Rachel stands on tip-toe, her back arched, and she waves. Jay takes her hand. They watch the bus slow and stop. Its rear lights blaze and a red disc swings out to warn cars not to overtake. Jay wonders at how different life is in America.

When they go back to the house a silence fills the large space in the small kitchen vacated by their son. Avoiding eye contact, they tidy the used crockery and utensils into the dishwasher. Jay looks at his watch. Coming up to eight o'clock. Nearly 24 hours on. No point calling anybody until at least 08.30. His case is nothing like an emergency.

'I'm going down to the den,' he says.

Ben has left the computer switched on. Jay, prompted by what he remembers as his own decision to support Ben, uses the webpage *Yahoo!* to locate a site that provides information on the movie *Cabaret*. The page has scenes from the film embedded in it including the one where the boy sings *Tomorrow Belongs to Me*. Jay has time to make a cup of tea while his machine loads with the necessary software. Finally, the computer unfreezes and the extract is ready to play.

The quality of the boy's voice is the first thing to make an impression; it is youthful, just-broken. Jay hasn't thought about it before but the young actor doesn't seem to be singing in a recognisable register. Perhaps this is what Ben meant when he said that he had been told that he was a natural counter-tenor. Jay's mood shifts as the song morphs from something bucolic and wistful. It creeps up on him but it starts when the *volk* around the singer join in and the song swells into a menacing anthem. By the end, when the singer gives the Nazi salute, the garden is bursting with nationalistic fervour. Michael York turns to his aristocratic companion – a German: 'So you still think you can control them?'

One person in the scene stays unmoved. An old gentleman in a blue, peaked cap, nursing his beer in his left hand. He's seen it before. He shifts his cap to one side and scratches his head at their folly.

Jay's also shaking his head. There are Americans who will be looking for a nationalistic response. Their country is at its lowest since Pearl Harbor. Who can they turn to if it's to be raised up again? Can their President, who distinguished himself on the day by his absence, step up to the plate, as they say? Is he capable of taking war to the Muslim extremists? Or is it the terrorists themselves who offer the parallel with that scene?

While Jay waits for the film's opening to load, he tries to determine a profound way of linking what he's watched to the horrors of the day before, but he's unable to grasp it. When the computer's ready, Jay clicks on 'play' and immediately recognises the *bm-ta-ta, bm-ta-ta, bm-ta-ta-ta-bm-ta* introduction. It's the rhythm of the train wheels as they crossed the points when the presence moved in alongside him. Joel Grey's face appears in close-up to sing the first word *Willkommen* and consolidates it – these thoughts and images that spring from nowhere, they are not Jay's. They come from *him* – the MC.

He hears Rachel's feet on the rush-matted stairs and clicks 'pause'. She's carrying a plastic basket of washing. She shrugs. 'Life must go on.'

He watches her disappear behind the open door to the laundry area and hears the lid of the top-loader swing back.

'What were you listening to?' she calls.

'Ben's song from *Cabaret* – the film version.'

'What do you think?'

'I'd forgotten how scary it was.'

'Mmm.'

'Has he told you about how it works in the musical?' He hears the washer rumble into life.

Rachel emerges wiping her hands on a towel. 'Only that he has to sing it twice. First time he's off stage. The MC guy, you know, the Joel Grey part in the film …' Jay experiences a jolt of guilt as she names his white-faced, carmine-lipped secret '… he plays it on a gramophone. Only a few minutes later, Ben has to do it properly on stage. There's a party and one of the guests asks him to sing it to embarrass some Jews who are there.'

Great-Uncle Hymie's clothes hanger! 'People like us,' he says.

Rachel turns the corners of her mouth down. 'If you put it like that …'

'Have you wondered about it, Rachel, our Jewishness?'

'What makes you ask? Is it yesterday?'

'It's this country. Everybody has a religion. It was the first question that guy Edler asked me at their party. "Which synagogue do you go to?" What would *you* say to that? ' He recalls the evening they had prepared for the Edler 'soiree'.

'It feels like we're "coming out".' Rachel was standing with her black dress gaping at the back.

'We will be a bit "on show".' Jay was halfway through a decision whether or not to wear a tie but automatically he reached forward to pull the dress's zipper to the top. Rachel made to step away but he put a hand on her shoulder. 'Just a second, love. There's a claspy thing.' As he fiddled the hook into the loop of cotton he studied the nape of his wife's neck.

He had loved her thick hair from the first time he saw her and even now, after nearly thirty years, he was excited by the way she flicked it behind her tiny ear, stabbed through with a black pearl stud. Finally the hook was in. He nuzzled his lips into her collar bone. It always made her shiver and scrunch up her shoulders. 'Okay. You're done.' He patted her bottom to help her on her way to the dressing table. He hoped they would return to the house neither too drunk nor too tired. He groaned. It was work next day. 'Any idea why we're doing this on a Thursday? Why not the weekend?'

Rachel was putting a lipstick to her mouth and sounded like a ventriloquist with a swollen-tongue but Jay still understood: 'No idea.'

When they had arrived at the Edler house Beth Edler and Melissa Rosenberg snatched Rachel's comfortable presence away. Ben rushed up the stairs to join Josh Edler who had beckoned him from an open doorway and Jay was suddenly alone – facing the backs of people as they pecked at each other's party blah. He felt like a mariner set adrift in a rowboat.

'Jay, you seem to be far away, there. What, no drink? What's your poison? Follow me, I'll show you what we have.' Howard Edler led the way to the kitchen and a worktop with enough booze to tank a party in a bordello. He waved at the selection of drinks like a conjurer's assistant demonstrating something that would shortly disappear.

'White wine?' Jay said.

'No problem. But it's not as cold as it should be.' At the same time as he pointed this out, and before Jay could protest, he poured a slug of wine into the glass and followed it with a sloppy handful of melting ice cubes. He wiped his hand on a paper towel and handed over the slush.

Jay offered it up like a priest's chalice. 'Cheers!'

Raising his beer glass, Howard responded, 'L'chaim!'

Jay took a sip and grimaced. After some seconds, in which time he looked into his wine glass, he said, 'How long have you lived in Burford Lakes?' Then, realising that he was talking to the party host, 'It's Howard, right?'

'That's right, Jay. Howard Edler. Oh, Beth and I have been here … what? A couple of years before Josh was born … fifteen years?'

Jay tried another swallow of wine-flavoured water and it sloshed across his tongue without troubling his taste buds. 'Fifteen! Have you seen a lot of changes in that time?' He looked up into Howard's face. The man loomed over him. He had an enormous head. His features filled it, so they too were magnified. His greying moustache hung from his upper lip like Spanish moss. His hooter – it's the only word for a nose such as his – was a bulbous Tube map of broken veins.

Howard rocked his head from side to side as he weighed up his response. 'Let's see: the Kisco Skies apartment building, the mall and the High School they're all newish but they're more Burford Station. This old part, Burford Lakes, hasn't changed; couple of new smarter eating places. Oh! And the little movie house, which had been derelict, that re-opened.'

'Sort of gentrification of the old part, then.'

'Hmmm.' Silence.

Jay looked down into his glass hoping the next topic would float by on the slivers of ice. He wanted to flee to the main room but Howard's bulk was between him and the door. It was a relief when Howard reached forward and took him by the elbow. 'I'd wanted to ask you,' he lowered his voice and steered Jay towards the door to the backyard, 'which temple are you going to join?'

'Temple?' Jay remembered the research he had done before coming to America. He had read that men in the suburbs had their strange lodges of Mooses and Buffalos and other animals it was their habit to kill. Did one of these meet in a temple? Was Howard trying to recruit him into a Freemason-like sect before anybody else could tie him in?

'Temple. Synagogue. Have you and Rachel decided where you're going to worship?'

Synagogue? What was he saying? 'No. I mean: not, no, we haven't decided; more no, we haven't thought about it.'

Howard nodded. He was frowning. 'It's too early, right?'

Jay shook his head. 'No!' His voice sounded squeakier than he'd hoped. 'No. It's … we're … we're not … religious.' He felt like a child-molester who had just confessed. In his mind, the room next door had become shocked into silence but the continuing hubbub reassured him this wasn't so. He leant into Howard. 'We're not Jewish – I mean we're not practising.'

It was Howard's turn to be puzzled. He placed his paw on Jay's arm. 'I'm so sorry, Jay. I misspoke. I shouldn't have assumed. It's just … your name's Halprin, right? I looked it up; it's Ashkenazi in origin – possibly rabbinical. You're Jacob and Rachel. You can see where I made the mistake, right?'

Jay relaxed. *He* was on the front foot. 'No problem.' He gripped Howard's upper arm. 'We are Jew-*ish*. It's just we're not practising. We don't do religion.'

Howard stroked his moustache down as if he could pull it over his top lip and this would take back what he had said. 'It was when Josh told me your son's name – Ben Halprin – another good Jewish name. You can understand how I could have got it wrong.'

'It's an easy mistake, Howard.'

They chuckled like conspirators.

'Anyway, Jay, I'm with the Reform Temple myself. That's the easy-going branch. So if you ever feel in need – well, you know where to come.'

'It's very kind of you, Howard, thank you.' He slugged back the tasteless dregs in his glass. 'Now, if it's okay, I'd like to try some more of your excellent wine.'

After the party, Rachel and Jay strolled back along Ponds Lane. Ben trailed behind. Jay had drunk more than he'd meant to and already the next morning's headache was germinating behind his eyes. He groaned and a thought bubbled up from the magma flowing thickly in his head. 'I know why it was a Thursday night "do".'

'Why?'

'It's because they're Jews – Jewish – whatever you're meant to say. The Edlers. Tomorrow's Friday. The Sabbath – is that the right word? It starts Friday night, doesn't it? And Saturday's the holy day so you can't have it then. So, ipso facto, it has to be Thursday.'

'Is it *all day* Saturday? Can't they have a party on a Saturday night?'

They turned up the path to the front door. 'Don't think so. It's all day isn't it? Anyway, Howard – old man Edler – thought we were Jewish too. Asked me which Temple we're going to.'

Rachel opened the screen-door and fiddled the key into the lock. 'We *are* Jewish aren't we?'

He suddenly had the urgent need to pee. 'Well, yes, but, like I told him, we don't do religion. We're not practising.'

Rachel giggled. 'No we're very good at it.' She followed this with a loud extended belch. The front door opened and they tumbled inside.

'Jay! ' Rachel interrupts his reverie. He's forgotten the conversation. He drags himself back to the present and recalls that he had asked her about their Jewishness.

'I'm happy as I am. I don't see the need for it.' She sits next to him. They're on the sofa that, folded-out, had been their bed at the time of the party. She reaches up and strokes his head. 'I can understand if you need something – religion whatever – after yesterday.'

Jay laughs. 'I'm not going to let myself turn into a basket case.'

Are you sure about that?

Chapter 8

Leo Plomer became my Berlin fixer. Within 48
hours I had moved into Frau Guttchen's upper
property at Uhlandstrasse 187 - a building I had
dubbed 'das gruene Haus' - 'The Green House'. As
Leo suspected, my room - evidently once the
living room of the apartment - was large enough
for a double bed, a sitting area with a sofa and
an easy-chair, and a work space in front of the
window which overlooked Steinplatz.

The windows were strange affairs - stretched
vertically and arched, framed in dun ceramic
tiles. The space within was busy with green-
painted wood frames set with glass and strange
harem-style outward-hinged wooden blinds that had
no glass behind them. Leo mentioned that I should
notice that the architecture was clearly
influenced by Rennie-Mackintosh. Frankly, at that
time I neither knew nor cared what he was talking
about. I had very adequate accommodation and it
was a lot cheaper than the hotel.

Frau Guttchen even provided a breakfast of
sorts with a slice of bread smeared with what she
called butter. This was served with cheese and a
slice of ham or sausage. It was a fixed meal for
a negligible price and sitting down to breakfast
was a good way of socialising with the other
tenants and practising my German. There were four
of them with, sadly, not a Sally Bowles character
among them. They were all male because Frau
Guttchen didn't take women. According to Leo this
was because the sort of single woman who needed
this sort of room would be earning her living on
her back. So the other four tenants were men. All
respectable looking with administration jobs in
one or other of the educational institutions
strung out along Hardenbergstrasse.

After breakfast, I worked through the day, except for my stroll down to the square for coffee. From my desk, in moments of inactivity over the next month or so, I was able to watch the trees in Steinplatz bloom and then burgeon with leaf. In the evenings Leo and I would stroll along the railway arches, dodging the beggars, and take in a low-cost meal with beer or cheap wine at one of many cafes that catered for the less well-heeled Berliners.

It took Leo a surprisingly long time to mention girls until one night, over a plate of ham, cabbage and potato, he said, "Do you have a girlfriend in Blighty, Cam?" The building shook as a train thundered overhead. The candles gutted in unison, creating a theatrical effect of the building being tossed at sea.

"Nobody special." Luckily I was able to focus on the forkful of mashed potato in front of my mouth.

"Me too. But you must need to ... relax in the company of a woman some time."

"Not especially." I dared not look at him. "You?"

He seemed to be oblivious to my discomfort. "God, yes. In fact, I'm thinking of taking a stroll along Potsdamerstrasse tonight after we've finished here."

"Where?"

"Potsdamer – the Bahnhof Bulowstrasse part. Where the ... ladies are to be found. The ones you'd want to spend time with, anyway."

"Right."

"Mind you. It's best not to hang around too late. The Brownshirts get a bit lively later on. Strutting up and down as if they own the place." He looked round to make sure we weren't being overheard. "Between you and me, if the National Socialists ever get into power, I'll have to bail out of Germany."

"Mmm." I nodded as if I knew what he was talking about. I did understand fragments of the political state of the nation but it was mostly too complicated and transient to bother with. You would invest time in finding out which of the minority parties was forming the government and in what proportions and when you had it all off pat another election would come along and change everything. There seemed to be no prospect of one party taking control – not in the foreseeable future.

"Are you totally blind? My name, Leonard Plomer - what does that tell you?"

This was just the situation where my eyes go starey and my mind goes blank. I shook my head.

"My mother's maiden name is Cohen," he whispered. "Get it now?"

"Right. Yes, I see. But the National Socialists aren't going to get in, are they?"

"Do you go around with your eyes shut? Why d'you think they have put out all these flags and march up and down all over the place? They're in the middle of a Presidential election, for God's sake."

I took a drink of beer. "I did actually."

"Did what?"

"Think the flags were all part of being in Berlin."

"Sometimes, Cam, you strike me as terribly naive. What date did you arrive?"

"March 21st."

"Well, a week before, the 13th, if I remember, they had an election which Hindenburg won easily but with just under 50%. So there's a run off with one candidate dropping out. Basically, it's Hindenburg against Hitler. The next round is April 10 - Sunday week."

I shook my head. "Sorry, I don't read the papers. I'm writing or teaching all day."

"Look, all the action - the non-violent action, that is - happens on a Sunday. I'll take you to a rally and you can see for yourself. OK?"

"Thank you."

He stood up and handed me some notes to pay his share of the bill. "Glad to be of service. As

for me, I'm heading into the arms of a young
lady. Sure you don't want to come?"
    I shook my head.

The following Sunday morning, after Frau
Guttchen's special breakfast (which was the
weekday one with the addition of a boiled egg)
Leo led the way out onto Steinplatz. We waved at
Ernst in the cigarette and newspaper kiosk - I
had by now developed a taste for Enver Beys with
the Turkish flavour - and being reminded of our
habit we both stopped to light up. The sun was
shining and we both sported brimmed felt hats set
just-so. I was wearing a light-grey worsted suit
with an open-necked white shirt. Leo, rather
ostentatiously, wore dark blue but unmatching
cotton jacket and trousers with a grey-striped,
collarless shirt. This attire made him look for
all the world like a train driver. We swung along
Hardenbergstrasse under the Zoo Station bridge
and on past the Kaiser Wilhelm Church.
    "Where are we going?" I said.
    "I'm taking you this way so as you remember
it but there is a short cut."
    "To where? Short cut to where?"
    "It's a lake on the edge of the Tiergarten
near here. Look." he waved in the direction of a
pagoda-roofed entrance with elephant statues
standing guard on both sides. "The Zoo."
    I nodded. My shorter legs were struggling to
keep up with Leo's stride.
    "We'll cross the canal in a minute."
    Immediately we were on the far bank we
turned left so that we were alongside the water.
Looking across the canal beyond the fencing, I
spotted an ostrich pecking at the ground while
three long-horned deer stood impassively beyond.
I could hear to our right the oompah-oompah of a
Bavarian-style band.
    "Hear that? It's the Biergarten." We were
approaching another bridge. Leo pointed at it.
"See that? It's known round here as Rosa's
Bridge."

"Rosa?"

Leo stopped, took a last drag of his cigarette and ground the stub into the gravel path with the sole of his canvas shoe. "You are dangerously ignorant of Berlin politics, Cam. Rosa Luxemburg. She and Karl Liebknecht declared Germany a communist republic in an attempted coup after the war. She was murdered and they say she was dumped into the canal from here."

The music was louder as we turned right under the bridge and now the scene in front of us was a riot of black, red and white. Long vertically strung flags hung from flagpoles all around and swastika bunting swaddled the trees. There was a cordon of Brownshirts in front of us.

"Say nothing unless you're spoken to," Leo said out of the corner of his mouth.

Chapter 9

It's mid-morning on the day after 9/11 and Jay judges it's time to tell the world that he's alive. There's a contact number scrolling across the bottom of the screen as soon as he turns on the TV. In the few moments that he watches, Jay establishes that Usama Bin Laden is behind the attacks and that all the airlines around the world are closed down. The skies are empty.

He calls the number. The woman who answers already sounds tired.

'I think I ought to report that I'm *not* missing.'

'Sorry?'

'This is the line for missing persons, right?'

'Yes, for people to report that somebody who may have been caught up in what happened has not come home.'

'Well, I should have been in the building and I *have* come home.'

'That's good for you, sir, but I don't think you need to tie up one of our lines telling me.'

'Even if everybody thinks I was in the North Tower when it was hit?'

'Do you work for Cantor FitzGerald by any chance, sir?' There's a change in the pitch of her voice and Jay pictures her moving the headset microphone closer to her mouth.

He marks her use of the present tense. 'No, why?'

'It's just that Cantor FitzGerald is the biggest employer of people who work above the ninetieth floor. We're anxious to trace anybody who worked there. Everybody is listed as missing. You being English …'

'Is Straub, DuCheyne one of the companies on your list?'

She asks him to spell it. 'It's not on our list.'

'We had offices in the North Tower – on the 95th floor.'

There is a heavy silence, a sigh, then: 'I'm so sorry, sir.'

Jay shrugs and stiffens as if he's receiving an unwelcome embrace and reaches for a chair. 'My name is Halprin, Jay Halprin.'

'I'm so sorry, Jay.'

He's surprised that she uses his first name. Before he can react, the woman explains that because of the special nature of his call she's going to pass him to her supervisor. When the man answers, Jay has to repeat his reason for calling.

'And your company, Straub, DuCheyne ...'

Jay presses an open palm to his forehead. Every muscle in his body is straining. His laboured breathing communicates his frustration.

'I'm sorry, Mr Halprin. I was reading from Joy's note.'

The man's voice fades as Jay processes this information. The name of the woman he spoke to is Joy. They have a line for bereaved people to call and one of the women operating it is called Joy. Did they not think it might be a good idea if she used another name, just for the duration?

The MC sniggers. *What about Joy's human rights? This is America in the 21st Century.*

Jay tunes into the telephone receiver again. '... on the ninety-fifth floor. Is that right? We don't have any North Tower survivors above ninety-one. How did you get out?'

'I was never in. I was late.'

Silence again. Jay hears what he thinks is the man choking back a sob. 'I'm going to have to be honest here, Jay. I don't know what to say.'

'That's all right. Don't say anything.'

The conversation proceeds with the man, Tony, asking for a full list of the other employees. Jay's mind flashes to his customary arrival in the office. He throws down his briefcase onto the meeting couch and turns, knowing that Nancy has followed him in.

The MC gatecrashes the scene, pursuing Nancy. He presses close against her back with his tongue lolling, imitating her walk with a piston strut of his thighs. He licks his fingers and pretends they sizzle when he touches them to her sheathed backside. He turns to Jay: *Nancy! She's put the wares on show for you since your first day. You're not immune; I know you've filed away all the 'indiscreet' flashes of lace-edged bra as she leant forward to point out a detail on your papers. You've marvelled at the way her hinterland stretches the seams of her pencil-skirt when she sashays out of the room. You poor sap. Didn't you know she was as prepared to have an after-work liaison as a puppy is prepared for a biscuit. She was showing you the green light and you didn't even see the traffic signals.*

It was something Jay innately knew to be true. He wipes away tears. It feels as if his Adam's apple is choking him.

'Mr Halprin? The other employees?'

Jay tells him what he knows: that there were seventeen of them including two full partners and they were all scheduled to be present in the office yesterday morning. The only way of escaping was to have been ill or late as he was. 'Can you let me know if you hear that anyone else has survived, Tony?'

'I have your number, Jay, and I'll make that call, with pleasure. Do you think there's a way we can get a list of employees?'

'I'll talk with the other partners' relatives today and see if there are any papers in their homes.'

'That would be good, Mr Halprin. We have you and your company logged. Thank you for calling.'

In the hiatus that follows, Jay senses the man swallowing the automatic final words he always hears as, '*Have an iced A*'. A long time will pass before anybody says them again.

Jay decides to take a walk to work out what's going on in his head. He has to make some sense of it before making the two calls he's dreading. Rachel asks if she can join him. He weighs up what's more important, clarifying how a fictional character has set up home in his brain or staying on the right side of Rachel.

Don't even think about me. We can get cosy any time. Go with Rachel.

They turn left in front of the house, following Ponds Lane away from Route 22. Ignoring the entry to the park, they walk on through the Ponds estate of mock-colonial houses with their porches and dormers. There's a gap on their right, through which they can see the lake with bulrushes on the margins. Small birds cling on with claws encircling the stems and their bodies whip as the rushes swirl. The breeze picks at the birds' feathers with a violinist's pizzicato touch.

Jay and Rachel turn into the park at its farthest entry from the house. The ozone freshness of clear-running water has the effect of de-fogging Jay's mind. The sun is high over a row of poplar trees and he looks across expecting to see a pillar of smoke or dust. But there's no sign of what they now call Ground Zero.

The MC's voice is scolding: *Don't go looking for torture. The dread will come to you at a time of its choosing.*

Rachel reaches for his hand and entwines her fingers in his. 'You know what you were saying about whether I think about us being Jewish? Well, if you need something like that ...'

'I know. You said.'

She snaps back immediately, her voice encouraging, upbeat. 'You know that place we've been to on a Sunday – the beach where we had to pay.'

'In Greenwich?'

'That's it, Greenwich Point Park. Well, at the pool one time, the girls told me how it's free to get in after Labor Day. Do

71

you remember we could see Manhattan from the beach there? The Empire State Building and ... well, we could see the Twin Towers.'

'Yes.'

'Perhaps ... I thought ... you and I could go there this afternoon. Maybe take a wreath and float it out on the water. You know, for the people at the firm.'

The MC is skipping and clapping his fingertips under his chin. *A wreath for the people at the firm! Wreaths are good. I like wreaths.*

Jay presses his forefingers against his temples as if he can bore through the hollows to relieve the pressure.

'I know it's a terrible Americanism, this thing they call "closure" but it could help. Quite honestly, doing anything, however futile ...'

There is no 'closure' for you, Jay, actually. You survived. Rachel believes that 'saying goodbye' will bring you to a conclusion? I don't hear the fat lady singing.

Involuntarily, Jay nods at the logic of the MC's words. But he's aware of Rachel's tone of voice and persuaded by her concern. He takes her hand. 'It's a good idea, Rache'. She moves his hand to her waist. They finish the walk joined at the hip.

'Hello? Is this Mrs DuCheyne?'

'I shall ask her if she wants to take the call. Whom shall I say is calling?'

'It's Jay Halprin. I'm her husband's English business partner.'

'I shall tell her.' Jay hears footsteps click-clacking on marble followed by two sets of heels sounding in unison accompanied by muffled conversation. Somebody lifts the receiver as the first voice is saying, 'It can't be him, then.'

'This is Francois DuCheyne's mother.' This new voice has an accent. Jay is trying to place it – possibly South African? She curtails her vowels as if she has cut them with shears and she hammers her consonants into place.

'I'm calling to offer my condolences, Mrs DuCheyne, to you of course but also to Mr DuCheyne's wife.'

'Thank you. She is here but I am sure you will understand that she is unable to take calls.'

'Of course.'

'And you are?'

'My name is Jay Halprin. I work with your son.' He emphasises the present tense.

'My daughter-in-law remembers you but ...'

'I wasn't in the building.'

Her voice emerges as a feeble, high-pitched whisper. 'What?'

'I missed my train. I was still Midtown when it happened.' He counts to twenty beats before the response comes.

The voice regains its edge. 'You have been very fortunate.'

The MC interrupts: *Fortunate is not the word I'd use.*

'Yes,' he says. 'I'm sorry, I have to ask this because I haven't heard from anybody. Is Mr DuCheyne missing?'

'We are assuming he is. We have been told that there are no survivors from the ninety-first floor and above. We are thinking that the worst has happened. But we are planning to go to Ground Zero and post a "missing person" notice.'

'Of course ...' Jay doesn't know how to proceed – how to change the subject to the business. He decides to be direct. 'I'm sorry, Mrs DuCheyne ... but, because of your son's ... absence, there are things to do with the firm I need to attend to – perhaps with your son's attorney?'

'We don't have to do that with any haste, though, do we?'

'Perhaps only for the peace of mind of the employees – and their families.'

'Let us leave it until next week, shall we? Call again then.'

'I'll do that. And I'm so sorry, Mrs DuCheyne.'

'For what? You have nothing to reproach yourself for.'

But Jay is thinking, as he replaces the phone, that he would feel more comfortable had she rebuked him.

The call to Glen Straub's house follows the same pattern except that he speaks to the presumed widow. Again, Jay is guarded and sticks to the present tense. Again, news of his survival seems to disconcert rather than be the cause for celebration. As he finishes, Rachel signals that she's ready for their trip to the beach.

They stop at the florists in the nearby mall. The shop has sold its stock of wreaths. The lilies are expensive but Rachel purchases six and they head for Greenwich.

The kiosk is at the end of a two-hundred-yard-long causeway that joins mainland Greenwich to its residents' beach park. The border-crossing barrier is raised and unmanned; anybody can enter now that the season has finished. Rachel drives the VW through and turns left into the car park that overlooks East Beach. The roof is down and they sit for while watching the steel-grey water lapping against the coarse sand. It looks as if the ocean is washing up to a construction site. There's no wind but the maritime smell is tainted with the tang of smoke from a distant fire. Or is this Jay's imagination?

'Come on!' Rachel opens the car-door and swings out her legs. Jay turns to the back seat and picks up the lilies. He sighs. He catches up and takes her hand as they reach the beach.

They turn right and head almost due south trudging along the strand between the timid waves and the high-water line. Their shoes make dry impressions as they head towards

74

the wooded knoll about half a mile away which marks the end of the beach. They walk in silence but there is no silence for Jay: *Both the women you spoke to are bereaved but they haven't admitted it yet. They can't accept that Francois and Glen, leading lights in global brand management, are nothing but dust, leaving only you. As if the world needs a brand-recovery expert any more than it needed Straub DuCheyne. As if your life, Jay, was worth any more than the thousands of Americans who perished. As if there is any justice that you are here when the fire-fighters and police officers of Manhattan have lost their lives.*

His head is down. The tears are starting. He slaps the flowers against his thigh.

'Don't do that!' Rachel says and she releases his hand so she can climb up to join the sandy path that takes them past the salt-water lake and on towards the western end of the park.

As they emerge from the trees and the vista opens up, they stop. On the south-west horizon a column of smoke rises above the end of the smudged strip of land that is Manhattan Island. They can see the seat of the smoke. Jay's chest constricts.

Which way was the wind blowing yesterday? The MC asks.

'Which way was the wind blowing yesterday?' Jay repeats.

'I don't know. Why?' Rachel answers.

Where did all that dust end up?

'If it was this way ...' He looks down and shakes his head. His face is contorted as he swallows his sobs. One part of him is thinking he should kneel and sift the sand through his fingers, the other that he shouldn't make an exhibition. His stiff upper lip wins and he stays upright. 'Look!' He points to where the beach ends and the land turns back on itself to form the tip of the promontory. A group is huddled there – possibly fifty strong. They stand at the extremity of the park, as near as they can get to the distant funeral pyre. 'I'm not going down there,' Jay says.

'We can go a *bit* closer,' Rachel says and she leads him along the path to a break on the left where there is a shallow beach. It's dotted with random sculptured cairns where amateur artists have piled single rocks one upon the other until each tower is a millimetre below its tipping point. 'Come on.' She holds out her hand. He follows her and stands at the water's edge.

She turns to face him. 'You have to be strong, Jay. I thought I'd lost you and you're back. So we have to make the most of it; this is our second chance.'

Is this her best stuff? Is this motherhood-and-apple-pie her method for bringing you back to the life she wants for you? What about Nancy? Remember her, Jay? Leaning over your desk? That body. Her vitality …

He starts to blub. Emotion drains his muscles of power as he swings round and casts the lilies on their way. They flop down only a few feet into the water and nestle in their wrapping, like Moses swaddled in his wicker cradle-craft. The paper becomes waterlogged and the flowers lose the will to stay afloat. The sight of them embracing their drowning so willingly sends Jay into a moment of darkness even deeper than anything before. He groans.

Rachel speaks sharply. 'You should have taken them out of the paper. What about the litter?'

Jay swivels his heels into the millions of particles under his feet and heads back to the car.

Chapter 10

As Leo and I approached them the Brownshirts
stepped to one side to let us through the first
ring of trees and now we were on the edge of a
lake. Red-hulled wooden rowboats lined the shore
to the left as we carried on into the clearing
with others arriving ahead and behind us. Here
the surrounding trees and posts were festooned
with swastikas which also adorned the raised
wooden platform set with long pine tables and
benches. There must have been thirty tables and
two-thirds were already full.

There were two stages. The band dressed in
Lederhosen played from one and on the other was a
choir of young boys and girls dressed a little
like boy scouts with open-neck, khaki shirts and
light-blue, cotton neckerchiefs. They were joking
amongst themselves and I was struck by their open
smiling faces and their chubby knees poking out
from their dark knickerbockers. For all Leo's
imputation that the National Socialists were a
sinister cult I have to say that all I could see
was young people having fun protected by a
necessary ring of strong men who were needed to
defend them against any of the Communist Red
Front Brigades who might try and disrupt this
idyllic German scene.

A waitress in the traditional dirndl dress
served us with large beers and we started
drinking while taking in the scene.

We were on our second beer when a man in the
brown SA uniform stood to speak. His collar tips
bore red patches and an ornate lanyard dangled
across his chest where others of lowlier rank
wore dark ties. I was amused by how the
extravagant flared thighs of his jodhpur-style
trousers brushed together as he strutted about
but he seemed to be a capable orator and he

whipped the men and women around us into an
enthusiastic applause when he jumped off the
stage and gave a signal to a compatriot.

Immediately the swastika flags behind the
choir moved aside to reveal a cinema-style
screen. It was shaded by the trees and a
projecting awning and we could see the pictures
clearly.

A buzz went round the audience as the
credits stopped and, following a drum-roll,
Hitler himself was on the screen. Immediately
some in the audience stood up and gave the salute
"Heil Hitler!" I felt Leo's hand on my arm.

We watched the extraordinary performance
that kept the spectators spell-bound. At the end
the greater part of the audience stood up and
again raised their hands in the Nazi salute. I
had been swept up and was on my feet clapping.
Leo must have thought that he ought not be the
only one left seated so he stood alongside me
putting his hands together in a perfunctory way.

The swastika curtain closed over and the SA
officer was on the stage again, this time only
long enough to introduce the choir. They had
remained standing after watching their Fuhrer and
gave a concert of what I assumed where
traditional folk songs.

He steps forward at the end of the third song. He
has the most incredible face, blue eyes scanning
the audience imperiously. They are like binocular
lenses peering out between the right-angles of
his brow- and cheek-bones. The latter are
cushioned by an elasticity that age will destroy.
My mind is calculating involuntarily: he is young
but not too young.

I can sense that Leo is no longer looking at
the stage. Out of the corner of my eye I see him
watching me intently.

What he may deduce from my fixation with the
action on stage doesn't concern me. Adonis stands
before me and he has the voice of a songbird - at
once trilling but also broken, manly. He is

wearing the uniform of the Hitler Youth - but the
style of his covering is irrelevant. I see only
the detail of his body which creates a statue of
the naked David. The youth's sleeves are rolled
to above the elbow and I sense rather than
discern the down of fair hair on his forearms. My
mind travels on and I feel my arousal starting as
I imagine the pattern of blondeness that
stretches down from his navel. Beneath the roll
of his shirt sleeve a bulge of his bicep peeps
out and my mind fills in the same quality of
muscle on his calves, his thighs, his buttocks.

I have to shift my weight on the seat and
pull at the material of my trousers to make
myself comfortable and I give a furtive glance
towards Leo. He smiles and languidly turns his
face back to the stage.

The youth has sung one song and is now on
the second. This is a folk tune which is familiar
to the audience. The men and women start swaying
and some sing along. Men swing their steins of
beer from side to side. The last verse comes to a
crescendo and the crowd is singing and now
standing and clapping in one eruption of emotion.
I am standing as well, applauding and smiling,
hoping that the boy will turn to me and our eyes
will meet. But he merely stands, shoots his right
arm forward, hand rigid, and his lips mould
themselves around the words "Heil Hitler" which
are drowned in the flood of passion from the
crowd.

I know my eyes are sparkling as I turn to
Leo, nodding encouragement to show more
enthusiasm than his methodical clapping. He leans
towards me and whispers in my ear, "See how easy
it is."

We took a stroll down Kurfurstendamm after the
concert and cut up to Savignyplatz where we
stopped for a coffee in the same place we had
met.

"You could have told me, you know," Leo
said.

"Told you what?

"That you like boys."

The way he said 'boys' troubled me and I thought about how much I should say. I made a point of blowing my cigarette smoke away as if it was more important than the trifling conversation. "I'm not sure I like you using the word 'boys'. But, yes, I'm attracted to my own sex. Ho-mo-sexual."

Leo laughed and put his coffee cup down on the saucer with a sharp tap. "Cam. You're such a stuffed shirt. I had my suspicions before today. But the way you came alive when that boy sang. It was like watching a dog round a bitch in heat."

I stubbed out my cigarette and ground the butt down hard into the tin ashtray. "There's no need to be quite so mocking and graphic in your language. But, yes, guilty as charged." I leaned across the table. "He was quite the most beautiful thing, though, wasn't he?"

Leo turned down the corners of his mouth. "I'm sure I couldn't say. But you don't have to worry about me. I'm not going to blab or anything. Each to his own, I say."

"That's exactly what I say too," I said and we both chuckled.

We paid the bill and started the final part of the walk to Steinplatz. As we passed between the high buildings in this the most modern part of Berlin, which reminded me of the terraces around Shepherd's Market in London, Leo linked my arm in his and I felt a surge of warmth towards him. He was not one of our sort; he had made this clear. But he wanted me to know that he was comfortable with my confession and nothing had changed. In the past, men have often kept themselves apart from me once they know about my other life as if my sexuality was an infectious disease.

"Have you heard of Nolllendorfplatz?" he said.

"Is it called the Nolli?"

"Yes."

"My agent mentioned it. He warned me against staying in that part of the city. He said I'd never get any work done."

"It certainly has more distractions for a 'queer' - is that okay?"

I waved it away. It's a word we preferred to keep to ourselves but I didn't want to make a fuss.

"There are clubs. Where the boys go. It's very open down there."

"I had heard."

He stopped and turned to me. "Look, do you want me to take you there? It would be fun. We'll make a night out of it and then ... well if you want to go back you'll know where it is and how it all works. What do you say?"

I had been conscious that the moment with the youth on the stage had awakened my libido and I would need release and soon. I could have hugged him for his offer but I didn't want to appear too eager. "That would be very agreeable," I said. "Thank you, Leo. You're very kind."

Chapter 11

'What's this coat-hanger doing in the bathroom?' Rachel is holding the Hymie coat-hanger as if it's contaminated. Her nose is wrinkled and the edges of her mouth are turned down. It's the mannerism she uses when Ben discards a towel on the landing. They are only half-way into the morning, yet Jay's head already feels like a bag of popcorn in a microwave.

'Sorry.' He snatches it from her and strokes its smooth shoulder. He recalls Great-Uncle Hymie's imagined voice: 'A blessing be upon you for this'. 'I was looking at it the other night.' Jay is still wearing his night-time T-shirt and shorts.

Rachel cocks her head to one side. She's wearing a loose cotton top and jeans. 'Do you have any plans for today?' she says.

He's rubbing his thumb across the end of the hook. It's like a tear-drop of molten metal, generous. No cost has been spared to ensure that Hymie's clothes – and his customers – come to no harm.

What has happened to Hymie's values? Jay wonders. He talks about 'Customer Care' when he's coaching the employees of a client company on rehabilitating its brand. But it's not Hymie's model. It's the ersatz concern of the call-centre agent who asks, 'How may I be of service to you today?' with the callous disinterest of a pike swallowing a moorhen chick. Jay decides he will not ignore Great-Uncle Hymie's nocturnal visitation.

'Did you hear me? What are you planning for today?' Rachel asks.

'Does Howard Edler work?'

'What? Yes … he runs his own company, I think.'

'Pity, I was going to talk to him about visiting his synagogue.'

'He may still be home. See if his car's there – a big SUV.' She steps towards him and wraps him in her arms.

His reaction, a swell of blood to his groin, is immediate and the leering face of the MC appears over his shoulder.

Really? Shouldn't you be better than that?

'We need to talk.' Her lips are against his ear. 'We need to think about how we're going to earn a living. The company's gone. Your visa for working here is probably invalid.' She hugs him tight. 'We should go home.'

This is going to be her solution, Jay. We're not ready for 'home', are we?

His words stumble over the hurdles of his sobs. 'I can't, Rachel. Not until we're sure about them. All of them. It's as if they are on top of me, weighing me down. I have to get out from under them.'

Excellent! I could not have put it better.

Jay is now washed and dressed. He has the inkling that the MC is behind his sense of purpose and this nips at the edge of his consciousness. He makes for Burford Lakes library. The sky is still clear blue but the temperature has dropped. Jay has put on a sweater under his zipped top. He's on foot, orienteering towards the Presbyterian Church's white-painted spire that stands alongside the village green. Traffic speeds past; the act of walking to the village marks Jay as different. All his neighbours would have jumped into their cars.

The library building used to be a private house originating from revolutionary times but it's been renovated so often that not one nail from 1775 survives. Although some internal walls have been removed it's still a labyrinth of cramped rooms. Jay takes his proof of residence letters from his inside pocket as he ducks through the door. There's a small group of Burford Lakes women clustered like stick insects round the desk but they fall back when they see him. He doesn't recognise them but senses that they know who he is.

The MC is at his shoulder pushing him forward. *As soon as you open your mouth they'll recognise you as the English survivor. They think you're the man who tricked fate. But you no more 'tricked fate' than I did when I fled Berlin thinking I could outrun the Gestapo. Destiny is in control here, not fate.*

Shuffling so as to avoid brushing against any of the women's large handbags or ring-laden hands, Jay looks up into the blue eyes of the woman behind the counter. She's probably his age and, like the majority of Burford Lakes women, everything is carefully in place from her hair-sprayed-but-loose locks through her perfect teeth, the duck-egg blue of her cashmere twin-set with its twin peaks, to the narrow belt round her gym-trim waist.

'I'd like to join the library.'

The librarian inclines her head and genuflects with her back straight to reach a form from under the counter. 'Do you live in Burford Lakes?' Her voice makes him wince. It has the quality of a diamond cutter on a windowpane.

'Yes, here.' He lays the two letters flat on the desk.

'No Driver's Licence?' Familiarity doesn't soften the corrosive property of her voice.

'No. I'm using my British one.'

'That's cool.' She flutters her eyelashes. 'I *love* your accent, by the way.'

'Thank you.'

'So if you'll just fill out this form.'

The other women drift away while Jay writes. He's aware that the librarian is watching the pen move across the page.

'That's good, Lesley,' she says, as if she's his teacher congratulating him for being able to make the words. 'My name's, Prentice, by the way. While I'm putting you into the computer and filling out your temporary card is there anything I can help you with today?'

Her formulaic use of 'server' words makes Jay's temperature rise. 'My name is Jay. People call me Jay, not Lesley.' He can feel a heat on his back from the stares of the women who have moved behind him. They're whispering.

They know it's you. Their words are dripping with ersatz concern.

Prentice looks down at the card. She frowns and looks up at him accusingly for making her misstep with his name.

Overcoming the urge to apologise, Jay says, 'Do you have Christopher Isherwood's novels?'

'I'm not familiar with them. Would that be fiction?'

Dummkopf! And she calls herself a librarian.

'Yes, fiction.'

'You'll find fiction on the second floor.'

'Thanks.' Jay visualises the library facade as seen from across the green. It has two storeys. Where is the *second* floor? But he's manufacturing irritation as a reaction to Prentice's mannerisms.

From the top of the stairs he crosses to the 'I' shelves and there are three books under Isherwood. *Mr Norris Changes Trains* is in paperback with a see-through plastic jacket. So is *Goodbye to Berlin*. There's a hardbound copy of *The Berlin Novels*. He takes it down and reads the blurb that describes how *Goodbye to Berlin* was the inspiration for the stage-play *I Am a Camera* and the ensuing musical, *Cabaret*. He decides to borrow only the novel that is his primary interest.

So you don't have enough time on your hands to read two books?

He changes his mind and takes the hardback downstairs. He appears to be alone with Prentice now but there are hidden rooms where other residents could be lurking.

'Have you chosen something?'

'Yes, Isherwood.' He holds up the book and waits for a response.

She takes it from him and passes it across a reader. She enters the numbers from his temporary card into the computer one by one, her long fingernails tip-tapping across the keyboard like a ballerina on points.

'I had expected to find you fresh out of these.'

'Fresh out'? Did you say 'fresh out'? What are you turning into?

She raises an eyebrow and pauses until the last number is entered. 'Oh?'

'Because of the High School Production?'

Her eyebrow is tireless. 'Is that *Cabaret*? The one in rehearsal? My Briony is in the chorus. I'm so worried about her costume. Have you seen the film? I do hope that the costumes are going to be a lot less …' she shakes her head and presses her wriggling lips together '… revealing.'

'I saw it back in England. A long time ago.'

You want see it again, though. You'll have the opportunity to admire once more my singing and dancing.

The librarian looks at Jay with her eyes wide. Her head wobbles from side to side and her chin is tucked down towards her neck. Jay decides that it's a look that wouldn't be out of place in a comedy routine featuring gossip over a backyard-fence in a Northern town. 'We have the video, you know. It has been popular since they decided to do the play. But it's just come back.'

See? I knew she would have it.

'You have?' Jay looks round and then back at Prentice. She's pointing.

Jay heads in that direction, pauses and looks back at her from the entrance to a second room. She's nodding and the back of her hand is making a 'shoo' motion. The room has shelves of videos sorted by title and *Cabaret* is under 'C', sure enough. He takes it back to the desk.

The MC is jabbering in Jay's ear. It's as if Jay's a newsreader and the producer is cajoling him through an earpiece. *This is so wonderfully exciting, Jay! In my mind already I'm stepping my moves from the opening number. Where's my cane? Why do I not have my cane?*

Prentice is still holding the book. 'It's called *The Berlin Novels*.'

'Yes.'

'And it's connected to the school production?'

He feels awkward. Why did he embark on this? Is he showing off? 'Isherwood wrote the book which gave them the idea for *Cabaret* – the character Sally Bowles. I thought other parents might be interested as well.'

'But this Isherwood – he's from England like you, Jay.'

Jay decides not to explain that the writer character in the book was English whereas he's American in the musical.

Prentice is still turning the book in her hand. Jay would like to see her caress the cover and so demonstrate her passion for books.

She'd show more interest if it were a packet of Dreft *flakes.*

'So *you* have someone at the School?' she asks.

'Yes, my son Ben. He has a part in the production.'

'And this is the book?' She turns it over. 'All about Berlin.'

'Yes, actually it's *Goodbye to Berlin* that Cabaret is based on … loosely. You have it upstairs as a separate novel.'

'We do? I'll take a look. Perhaps I should suggest it for my book group.'

That'll be a middle-aged sorority meeting running on Chardonnay that gossips about a book's characters as if they're neighbours.

'Yes.' He's holding out his hand for the book. His feet are already turning for the door.

'Are you taking the film?'

'Yes.'

'The book is free – we are a free library – but the video rental is two dollars and fifty cents.'

The sky has clouded over while Jay has been inside and he zips up his jacket. He decides he will stroll past the rest of the shops before returning home. SUVs swing out of and into the car-parking spaces cut into the ancient green. He watches the drivers, women mostly, climb down from the high driving seats and set off for the cookshop or the deli, the greengrocer or the patisserie. They are there to buy the fripperies that accompany the 'main shop' that will have been planned and executed on the appointed day at the temples to consumerism strung along Route 84 farther north in Connecticut.

The movie house is showing films with titles Jay doesn't recognise although he has heard of two of the principal actors, Jake Gyllenhaal and Jennifer Aniston.

You like Jennifer Aniston? You're so predictable!

He's not ashamed to admit it. She *is* cute in *Friends*. Great hair.

And what about Nancy? Didn't she have great hair also?

Jay ignores him.

Did you fantasise about Nancy? Not just a little bit? Those tits? That ass?

OK. Maybe a little bit.

And where are they now? Those tits. That ass. The rest of her. The rest of them. Your colleagues. The thousands of others.

The tears have started and he sets out for home.

'Is that you, Jay?' Rachel emerges from the opening into the kitchen. She's wiping her hands on a tea towel. 'Don't take off your shoes. Howard came home for lunch not long ago. You'll catch him if you want to pop down there.'

The film, Jay, I thought we were going to watch the film.

'Later.' Jay catches himself speaking the thought as he places the video on the side-table. He turns back down the steps. Howard's SUV is parked in front of their double garage. Jay's feet shush through the first fallen leaves that litter Ponds Lane. As he approaches the Edler house, he thinks about what he'll say. He wants to rehearse the opening line but struggles to find the right words. Before he can resolve this, he has swung back the screen door and pressed the doorbell. There's an ornamental plaque alongside the bell push and he wonders what it signifies. He recalls that his childhood home had one.

Howard opens the front door and stands two steps above. He peers at Jay over the top of his reading glasses and this positions his bison-like head as if he's about to charge. 'It's Jay! Why, come in.' He flaps his arms as if he's shooing a flock of poultry across the threshold.

Howard touches a finger to the Mezuzah and puts the same finger to his lips. He removes his glasses and composes his face – grave and concerned. He has the manner of an undertaker persuading a client to choose his catalogue's most expensive casket. 'How are you, Jay? I don't suppose you've gotten used to it yet?'

Being alive, he means. Alive when every other poor bastard in the company is so much dust.

'That's why I'm here, Howard. I don't know what I feel.' His eyes film over with tears. He swallows down the lump in his throat.

'Come in. Sit down.'

'Do you have time? Don't you have to get back to work?'

Howard shakes his head and makes a tutting noise while pursing his lips into a grotesque kissing shape.

'I can come back later,' Jay says.

'No. Sit. Drink?'

As he lowers himself into one of the leather armchairs, Jay rolls his tongue across the back of his teeth. 'I'd be happy with water, please.'

'Gas or no gas?'

'Still is fine.'

'Wait there.'

The walls of the room are magnolia interrupted by framed prints set at regular intervals. The furniture is dark and European in appearance. Jay examines one of the pictures. It's a mediaeval street scene where the upper storeys of the buildings lean over at shoulder level like aunts and uncles embracing while children scuttle around their feet.

'Prague!'

Jays spins round guiltily.

'The series is eighteenth century. Scenes in Prague. They've been in our family ... a hundred years.' He hands over a glass which clinks with the sound of ice. 'Please, sit.'

Jay goes back to the chair says, 'Thanks!' and raises his glass. 'Cheers!'

'You British and your "Cheers!"' Howard shakes his enormous head.

'I'll get straight to the point,' Jay says.

'Please do.'

'Remember at your party you asked me which temple I go to?'

'Yes. I'm sorry about that–'

Jay raises his hand. 'Don't be. Since what's happened I've felt the need ... I don't know ... I've wondered whether it would help me ...'

'You'd like to try us out?'

'Yes.'

'And you *are* Jewish?'

'I think so.'

'What do you mean?'

Jay explains about his mother who had the family name Becker and how they ate only kosher food when he was young. When his father died, they became less observant until the only remaining obligation was to attend the family dinner on a Friday evening. 'There were no candles or prayers,' he says. 'But, for that one meal, it felt like we were religious.'

'Did you have a bar mitzvah?'

'No. But I was circumcised.' He blushes.

Did you really say that?

Howard merely nods. 'Any schooling of a religious nature?'

'No, I went to a state school. I joined in the Christian stuff, such as it was.'

'So you have nothing to say you're Jewish except what happened in childhood.'

'Nothing.' He's close to tears.

Howard sticks out his lower lip. It shows a bulbous bolster of tissue. 'I don't think it will trouble Rabbi Zwyck. Ours is a reform temple as I explained. Would you like me to talk to the rabbi on your behalf and see what she says?'

'I would, yes.'

Later that afternoon Jay is sitting on the azurro-blue sofa watching *Cabaret*. The MC provides a running commentary: *Can you see how my eyes light up and my grin widens so much it hurts my face? It's so good to see my beautiful girls again. They have not grown in age at all! This makes me sehr melancholisch. How naughty was I with those beautiful girls? You know I was having the bumsen with all of them? Yes, every one – all the 'wurgins': Heidi, Christina, Mausi, Helga, Inga* and *Betty.*

In the film Sally is making prairie oysters for Michael when the house telephone rings. Automatically Jay hits the video's pause button and picks up the handset. 'Hello?'

I was watching! Such interruptions!
'Is this Mr Halprin?' It's a woman's voice.
'Yes.'
'Mr Lesley Jacob Halprin?'
'Yes.'
'Of Straub, DuCheyne?'
'Yes.'
Is she ever going to get to the point?'
'I have Mr Fothergill for you. Nathan Fothergill of Baxter, Fothergill and Fauset.'

Jay resists the urge to throw the phone at the back door only because there's something familiar about the name Nathan Fothergill. He recalls a meeting in a mahogany-lined office in mid-town Manhattan at the beginning of his relationship with Francois DuCheyne and Glen Straub. It involved the diminutive Mr Fothergill producing contract after contract and each of them signing in turn. With jet-lag and the whirl of what was happening, he only understood a tenth of what he was signing but was reassured by Nathan Fothergill's Canadian stolidity, his dwarfish stature and his constant reference to the fact that Jay could have his own attorney present and check through things if he wanted.

A chill presentiment sweeps through Jay's mind like an incoming tide. Had he been naive?

Should you have been so bloody English?

Should he have had a lawyer with him?

The woman on the other end of the line was evidently waiting for the answer. 'Mr Halprin?'

'Yes. Put him on.'

There's a hiatus, a few clicks and then the woman's voice again. 'I have Mr Fothergill for you.'

This had better be worth stopping my movie for.

'I don't know what to say, Jay.'

Jay thinks: don't say anything.

'I called Mrs DuCheyne today. I had to be careful. Timing with these things ...'

'Yes, I understand.'

'As soon as I heard what happened, about the firm –' his pronunciation 'aboot' betrays Fothergill's Canadian nationality '– I had to decide who to call and how soon. I was working on the basis of no survivors.'

'I think it's only me ... who survived.'

'Mrs DuCheyne told me about you – about your call to her. So suddenly I have somebody to talk to.'

'Yes. But, I'm sorry, Nathan. What's there to talk about?'

'The firm still exists, Jay. When it's decided in law that the victims have perished, the ownership of the firm is transferred as in the terms of your partnership agreement.'

'What are you saying?'

'For the present, *you* are Straub, DuCheyne, Jay. You *are* the firm.'

'But without Francois and Glen – there's nothing.'

'This is what Mrs DuCheyne says and I have subsequently spoken to Mrs Straub about the same subject.'

'Then what's there to talk about?'

'Winding up the firm in the most equitable manner. Being guided by the partnership agreements. I think we should meet.'

'When?' There's too much to take in. 'Where?' he ventures.

'The firm's disaster recovery set-up is in Stamford – just along the road from you. We'll have an associate working from there in a few days. Can we set something up for the end of next week?'

'Yes. Tell me when and I'll be there.'

Chapter 12

In the run-off election on the Sunday after our attendance at the Nazi rally, Hindenburg won with a slightly increased vote, enough to take him over the 50% winning line. However, the National Socialists gained a further two million supporters and it was their Brownshirts who were in evidence the following week, strutting three abreast along the Kurfurstendamm so that ordinary pedestrians had to step into the road to let them pass.

For me life changed slowly. I started to give morning English lessons to a succession of young people introduced to me by Frau Guttchen, who still had connections with rich Berlin families. At the end of the lessons, during which I took every opportunity to absorb German, I would wander down to the coffee shop. Then back to the room and Dexter Parnes VC.

By now, the plot of his third adventure was falling into place. Our brave English spy was tasked with creating a formal connection between the British Secret Service and the Nazi Party in order to thwart a pan-European Communist conspiracy. Like the fictional Dexter and others of my class I was enthralled by the trappings of Nazism but I never believed that what they were doing was good for wider Europe. Even in those early drafts, I knew that Parnes would end up having to deal with Nazi betrayal as well as the more obvious Communist threat.

Within a week or so of Hindenburg's hollow victory I had been back to the canal side. This was my way of dealing with a work problem. I would try to empty my head of it while strolling from the part of the canal by the Zoo - 'Rosa's Bridge' - towards the city until I came to the new administrative building on the canal side

called the Bendler Block. After walking in the
sunshine sheltered from any north wind by its
massive stone edifice, I would cross the
Bendlerstrasse bridge and return along the other
side of the canal.

I was making my way up the stairs to my room
after one such foray when I heard hurrying feet
behind me. It was Leo. "I'm glad I caught you,
Cam."

"Are you okay?"

"Are you ready for our trip to the Nolli?"

"If it's not too much trouble."

"No, it'll be fun. What are you doing
tonight?"

I had no plans, of course.

This anonymous dive beneath a building facing the
church on Winterfeldtplatz could easily have been
Isherwood's *Cosy Corner*. There were steps down to
a basement doorway. It was open but the entrance
was blocked by a sheet of thick hide nailed to
the inside of the doorjamb. It smelt as if the
tanning process of the animal's skin had been
halted midway to completion. Or perhaps the scent
was the musk of heated men coming at me out of
the darkened room.

My heart was booming as I stepped inside. I
felt Leo stumble into my back. The buzz of
conversation was loud, drowning out the American
jazz music that played in the background. As my
eyes adjusted to the darkness I was first able to
make out the shapes of white singlets, some with
short sleeves, most sleeveless. I immediately
felt out of place in my suit and tie and I
swiftly removed my hat and held it down by my
groin. My hands were shaking.

I could now make out more. There were
alcoves with men kissing and stroking each
other's faces. There were other men dressed more
soberly like me, many of them engaged in earnest
one-to-one conversations with the younger men in
white tops. I searched out a bar and led the way
across. I saw that each young male in a singlet,

younger than me, watched me with hungry eyes. Raw
sexual tension simmered everywhere. When my gaze
crossed with another's it was like duelling
sabres clashing and sparking.

I felt a face touch against my ear and
flinched. I turned and realised it was Leo trying
to get my attention. I leaned back to hear him.

"This is the only one I know. Once you're
settled in they'll tell you about others."

I nodded.

"Shall we have a drink?"

We ordered beers and took them to a side
table.

"The guy who brought me here explained what
goes on." Leo had to place his mouth close to my
ear so I could hear him. "The young ones in the
white singlets - they're for sale. Don't worry,
the exchange rate is so good they'll be very
cheap, I'm sure. They'll do anything for you if
you have the money. There are more private rooms
at the back, he told me."

"There are so many boys."

"And this is one of many more
establishments."

"So many homos..." I was wide-eyed, shaking
my head. It was a paradise, open and guilt-free.
My sort of men.

Leo snorted. "They're not queer! They prefer
women. They do this for the money."

A pair of young men, both in the shop-window
uniform, sauntered to the table. One of them made
a show of adjusting his cock as if being in our
presence had excited him. The more restrained one
said something in German.

I stood up and immediately cursed my public
school manners, "Wie bitte? Sprechen sie
Englisch?"

His face split open in a broad smile. He had
good teeth. "A little. Have you long in Berlin?"

I smiled back and signalled to the empty
chair. "A few months but my German is not good
yet. You speak English very well."

He frowned, cocking his head to one side as he slid into the chair. "Yes, it is very well. We can be friends, Ja?"

I laughed. "Yes, of course."

The cock-shifter made to join us but Leo leapt out of his seat. He leaned on the table. "Are you happy for me to leave you now? I'm sure ..." He turned to my young man, "Wie heisst du?"

"Hans."

Leo spoke to me again. "Hans, if that's really his name, will look after you from here." He gave the cock-shifter a quick glance and made for the door. Hans waved his accomplice away and said something too quickly for me to understand.

Hans and I availed ourselves of the back-room facilities that evening. He was a very accommodating young man. It was most exhilarating and the money that changed hands was well within what I had budgeted for a night's entertainment.

We did manage to have one conversation during the hiatus.

"Where do you live?" he asked me.

I waved in what I thought to be the general direction of the west. "Towards Charlottenburg."

"But still in Berlin?"

"Yes, in the city."

"You will know the bridge at the canal in Zoo."

I shook my head - then realised he couldn't see me. But as my head was on his chest, my arm around his waist and my forearm nudging his excitingly adequate penis he probably deduced my intention from the movement.

"Rosa's Bridge. It where you meet." He stuttered and made a tight-lipped hum. Finally another word came. "Die Schwul ... Homosexuell."

"Do you mean boys like you go there?"

"No not boys. Not boys for money. No it is men to meet other men. Die Schwul."

"Homosexuals, like me. Do you mean men like me?"

"Ja. Men like you." He shifted his hips and I felt the plum-sized bulb press against my arm.

His palm moved down from my chest, gripped my
bottom and squeezed, pulling me on top of him.

So I had been in Berlin for less than two months
and my social life took off. I'm afraid I left
Leo behind as I spent time at the various clubs
in and around the Nolli, and it became my weekend
treat. I still maintained my Protestant work
ethic and Dexter Parnes VC took my undivided
attention on weekdays but I saved my Friday and
Saturday evenings for trips to the clubs.
      The boys, and there were different ones
every time, scratched my itch but they stimulated
a hunger for something more permanent. In the
Nolli I had a few beers, ogled a few boys, bedded
one of them and moved on after the grubby
exchange of notes which had attracted a soiled
state merely because of the purpose I had found
for them. In short, I had found what I thought I
wanted but I wanted more.
      It was then that I remembered the words of
the first boy, Hans - about the 'Schwuls' who met
near Rosa's Bridge. What did I have to lose from
a little cruising as night fell? I had by now
learned enough German to hold my own in simple
conversation and, let's face it, how much
conversation did I need? I resolved to try my
hand at finding one of my own kind. I didn't know
which evening was best but it was a Wednesday
when the idea came to me, so it was a Wednesday
that I went that first time.

Chapter 13

It's five days since the MC moved into Jay's head as the train carried them away from Manhattan. Without the routine of work, Jay has moments of idleness and this is when he feels the MC's presence most keenly. He's partly inured to the chatter that runs like shop-floor musak as he goes about his day but worries that when he has a new idea it may not be his alone. For instance, he wonders how he came to be reading Isherwood's Berlin novels. Whoever suggested it, he comforts himself that it will bring him closer to Ben.

The novels' unemotional tone surprises him. They're clearly autobiographical, but the narrator appears to be dispassionate about the plight of the people he interacts with – all, that is, except the boys. He truly is 'a camera' panning around the Berlin scene. Using the Internet, Jay learns that Isherwood wrote an autobiography concentrating on his time in Berlin called *Christopher and His Kind* and he decides to ask Prentice about it. Whenever he turns on his computer, Jay routinely follows the new leads about Isherwood, *Cabaret* and Berlin that *Yahoo!* throws up.

Next day, Jay plays soccer on the field behind the house. It's the usual pick-up game with his side made up of Americans and English-speaking Europeans while the opponents are locals who speak Spanish as their first language. The players arrive already changed and the game starts without any reference to the week's main event. There's none of the customary banter afterwards and the desultory conversation is, by unspoken mutual consent, steered away from Ground Zero. It makes for an awkward few minutes but Jay's happy at the respite.

Later, he and Rachel potter around the garden. Jay rakes up the early leaves, notices Bob Cochrane doing the same and strikes up a conversation during which he learns that residents make piles of the leaves in the road in front of their houses and the town takes them away for composting.

'Did *you* know about the town collecting the leaves?' he asks Rachel over dinner that evening.

'I didn't even know there was a "town"'

'I think it may be the same Burford Lakes Authority that runs the station car park.'

'I thought that was Amtrak'

'No, I have to buy the season ticket from that municipal kiosk opposite the station.'

'Seems weird that they take the leaves away yet leave us with the hassle of organising our own rubbish collection.'

'Trash,' Ben says.

'Yes, trash.' Rachel nods as if filing the word away. 'And the telephone and satellite TV. However does anyone move house in this country? And they keep telling us that they're the top dogs in customer service. I could tell them a thing or two–'

Jay pats her on the hand. 'You've had a hard time, I know.'

'You don't know the half of it.'

'Rachel–'

'You don't and there's no point to it. You have no job. There's no money coming in. Why can't we go home?'

Ben puts down his knife and fork. 'Hey! Don't forget about me. We can't leave mid-semester – I can't drop everything. What about the show?'

Your son is talking sense, Jay. Listen to him.

'The show! The bloody show. You and your dad and that bloody show.'

What about your colleagues, Jay? Your dead colleagues – are you going to abandon them?

Tears fill Jay's eyes. 'We can't leave, not yet. What about the people I worked with–'

'You didn't even know them, Jay. Not most of them.'

There has to be 'closure'. Was that me? Did I use the word 'closure', actually?

'I don't understand it myself but I have to see it through. There are going to be memorials, services, whatever. I'll have to go at least for Francois, for Glen, for Nancy. Maybe not the others. But I have to be there for them.'

'And whatever you say about the show, Mum, I can't let them down. I have to stay until the end of the semester.'

Rachel snaps her head round to face her son. 'It's a "term". Ben. It's a bloody term!'

All three are shocked into silence. Rachel's voice starts up, softer: 'How can we manage with nothing coming in, Jay?'

He tries to sound as if she has lifted the mood. 'I spoke to the lawyer guy who set up the SDC partnership. We have a meeting next week. Straub, DuCheyne still exists in some format. There'll be enough cash in the business to keep my pay going for a while, I'm sure. I'll know more at the end of the week. I'm going to the place in Stamford where they have the company's disaster recovery set-up.'

The technical talk pricks Ben's interest, 'What's that, Dad?'

'Where all the data back-ups are. There was a download of all the day's outputs onto a duplicate server in Stamford every night. So it wasn't lost when ... when we lost the servers in New York.'

'But *you* can't run the company – not on your own,' Rachel says.

'No, it'll close down. But it has to be done properly.'

'So we *will* go home.'

'Yes.'

'When?' Rachel and Ben say in unison.

101

Ben is upstairs working on an assignment or more likely sending e-mails to his classmates and his old friends in England. Jay is on the sofa with Rachel. They're reading. The boiler in the half-cellar ignites and the pipes start ticking.

Jay lifts his head. 'Have you spoken to Ben about *Cabaret* recently.'

'No, why?'

'Just wondered.' He turns to face her. 'You've seen the film haven't you?'

'Yes. Ages ago.'

'I've still got the video.'

She sighs. 'Not now. I'm reading.'

'No. I wasn't suggesting we watch it.' He had finished the movie after Nathan Fothergill's interruption but has ignored the MC's urgings to watch it again.

She lets the book fall into her lap.

'Is it okay? I'd just like to explain something.'

Rachel composes her features into the face of a person giving him all her attention. 'Go ahead.'

'I've been looking it up on the Internet – *Cabaret*. But the musical, not the film. The musical came first.'

'So?'

'What Ben is doing isn't actually in the film. It seems that the way this scene has been used in the musical is quite fluid but the song always appears twice and it's only the second time, when it's sung at a party, that it becomes sinister.'

'I thought I told you this. Anyway, is it a problem – how it's done?' Her finger is keeping her place and she flicks the book open.

'I need to have it clear in my mind.'

'Why?'

'I want to help Ben … with his part … the motivation. It's not like the film that they watched. It's entirely different. The song's in a different context.'

Rachel casts her eyes down to the page. 'Is it important?'

He sighs. 'I don't know. But there's a connection here with this whole 9/11 thing. I don't know whether there are parallels – and that the play might be more topical than the school thinks.'

'And …?'

Jay squirms. 'I don't know. But have you noticed how everybody's putting flags out?'

'I don't see the connection.'

'I'm worried about what's going to happen. Is there going to be a backlash against Muslims? Everybody seems to be flying a Stars and Stripes all of a sudden. What if it gets, you know, like Germany and the Jews?'

'You're thinking too much. Adding two and two–'

'But it's on everybody's minds. What about the guy they arrested at JFK because of his turban. He was a Sikh for God's sake. They thought he was a Muslim. It's all going crazy.'

Rachel's finger traces the words. 'I don't see how it relates to the show, Jay. I honestly don't.'

'Nationalist fervour, Rache. The parallel with the song. *Fatherland, Fatherland*, all that stuff. Is it a good thing *now*?'

She closes the book and places it on the coffee table. 'It's a school show – a tiny High School in a tiny town in a huge country.' She pats his arm. 'Have another glass of wine – you'll feel better.' She sweeps up their glasses and climbs the few steps to the kitchen.

Jay stays on the sofa. There *is* a parallel between post 9/11 America and 1930s Germany but it's not clear yet. It has something to do with retribution. The Nazis identified the Jews as having been to blame for defeat in the First World War and now the Americans – the hawks among them anyway – have a culprit in their midst to blame for the worst atrocity since Pearl Harbor.

You're on the right track, Jay. I will help you tease it out.

Is there something here that would give his survival a purpose?

You may think you have a destiny, Jay. Have patience. Your fate will become clear.

Where did that come from? At times the MC's presence is as real as if he's in the room. This is when Jay is reassured that the demon is there merely to voice his darker thoughts. But at other times, when the voice is less distinct, the things he hears sound alien – as if the MC is a discrete entity. Inside his head but detached.

Jay's heart rate quickens and his ears whoosh with blood. The voice emerges through the static. *If only I could reassure you that I have it all under my control.*

It's Tuesday, one week on. It had seemed to Jay that time would stop and yet here he is. He's waiting at the screen door when Howard's 4x4 parks next to the first feeble pile of leaves. Jay goes down and clambers into the passenger seat.

'Ready?' Howard says.

'Yes.' Jay's hands are sweaty. It's too late to backtrack.

'Don't worry.' Howard manoeuvres out of the estate. 'Rabbi Zwyck is a sweety. You'll like her.' Howard turns onto Route 22 and within ten minutes they pass through the more modern locality of Burford Station. It's seven o'clock in the evening. There are still some commuters' cars parked under the floodlights. Two have a talcum-like layer of white dust spread over them as if they've been abandoned next to a flour mill. These 'ghost cars' are present, in their ones or twos, in every station car park within commuting distance of Manhattan. They've been featured in the local television news. Families don't want to move them. It would be a sign that they've given up hope.

'So what will she ask me?' A tremor ripples in his right knee.

The bison's head turns. Howard has kind eyes, eyes that reflect a deep sadness.

They are proper *Jew's eyes.*

'Today is more about the questions you have for the rabbi, I would've thought.'

They're in one of the wooded sectors of Westchester County. The tall, orange-foliaged trees join above the road and Howard switches on the main beams. The branches toss and turn in the moving light.

Howard swings the Jeep into a drive leading to a low, contemporary building in which windows shine with colours of the rainbow. It squats like a bejewelled frog beneath its copper canopy. 'Here we are,' Howard says. 'Temple Bar Shalom.'

He leads Jay to the left of the heavy oak double-doors which, Jay assumes, open into the place of worship and heads for a smaller, side door. Howard presses a button for the intercom.

The woman's voice is sing-song. 'Hello?'

'Elayna, it's Howard Edler. We have an appointment?'

'Of course, come in.' A buzz signals that she's unlocked the door.

Howard touches the Mezuzah and Jay wonders whether he should copy him.

Ach! The terrors the Mezuzah holds for the non-Jew.

Jay freezes. He's too uptight to follow Howard's example. He decides that the visit to Rabbi Zwyck is a bad idea.

A woman dressed in a flower-patterned frock comes into the hall. Her belted waist emphasises the heft of her bosom and the shelf of her hips. She totters forward as if she's unfamiliar with high heels but Jay notices that she's in flats. 'Come in! Come in!' She shakes hands with Howard and turns to Jay. 'You must be Jacob.'

Jay nods. He can only choke out 'Rabbi' and he bows his head.

105

She smiles as if familiar with his confusion. 'Call me Elayna, please. I reserve my title for when I'm working.' She leads them into a small room off the hallway which is set out as an office. The desk faces the sidewall and there is one chair between it and the door. Rabbi Zwyck wrestles another from the opposite wall and sets it alongside. 'Come. Sit.' Her eyes sparkle as she says, 'Howard tells me you're a sinner who wants to return to the fold, Jacob.'

Jay turns to his companion. What has Howard said? He can feel the blood filling the capillaries of his cheeks and forehead. He smiles and shakes his head. His eyes fill with hot tears.

'I'm sorry,' Elayna says. 'It was a bad joke. It was meant to put you at your ease.' She stands up. Her upholstered bosom is at Jay's eye level.

You could rest a tea tray on that.

She says, 'Let's start again. Can I offer you coffee, tea?'

Howard turns down his lower slug-like lip and passes his right hand over his lap like a conjurer about to produce a rabbit. To say no would have been less bother. Jay says, 'Tapwater is just fine.'

The rabbi leaves the room and Howard and Jay sit in silence. A tower of hardcover textbooks with muted dust-covers sits on the desk to one side of the virgin blotter. A large-format diary is on the other side. It's closed. Jay wonders what's written about this meeting. On the wall in front of the desk is a year-on-show wall chart. It's set up in an unfamiliar style and its boxes are tagged with unreadable symbols.

The door opens and Elayna bustles in with two glasses. Hers has iced tea. She settles into her chair and her upper body concertinas downwards as if her backbone is collapsing. 'Now, tell me, Jay.' She talks softly while she reaches for her tea. 'Why did you want to come see me?'

This, I want to hear.

Rachel looks up from her book as Jay enters. 'How did it go?'

'Okay.'

'Well, what did she say?'

'She said I can go to services if I want.' Her wine glass needs filling. 'Want a top-up?'

'Yes please.' She holds out the glass. He goes up to the kitchen and pours one for himself. Back in the den he sits next to her on the blue sofa. 'Nothing on telly?'

'No. Is there ever?' She holds up the glass. 'Cheers! Anyway, I want to hear what happened.'

'She's persuaded that I'm Jewish. So she's happy to accept me into the congregation.'

'Is that it?'

'No, you can come as well. And Ben.'

'Are you going?'

'I'll probably give it a try.'

She turns to face him. 'You can't do this, Jay.'

'What?'

'Keep it all in. Why can't you tell me what happened?'

Because when he talks about it, his face crumples and he ends up crying. Because it's so painful, actually.

'Okay. I can – about the meeting, anyway. Elayna, the rabbi, she talked about some God stuff. She said about God being the same for Jews and Gentiles but how Jews see themselves as "chosen". She made the point this doesn't mean "better". She talked about us – Jews – being connected directly to God. And through being Jewish, through being a good Jew, maybe I could learn to be an outward person.'

This is not everything, you understand.

Rachel makes a noise, expelling air between her lips.

Tell her about God's plan.

Jay shakes his head. 'You asked and I'm telling.'

'Sorry. But what does "outward" mean.'

'Not so introspective. Not worrying so much about what happened.'

Tell her – God's plan.

'That's certainly good advice.'

'But it doesn't work.'

'What?'

'It's no good people telling me to stop thinking about it.'

God's plan!

'She says inner peace can only come to me through a relationship with God – if I want to have one.'

'And do you?'

TELL her about God's plan.

'I don't know. But if I do perhaps I'll be able to learn about God's plan …'

'What!'

'God's plan.' Jay leans forward. He presses his fingertips into his temples, making deliberate, manic circles. 'The Rabbi, Elayna, she believes in God, so of course she thinks God was behind everything that happened that morning, including me not catching the earlier train. So, if we go to the synagogue we may find out what His plan for me is.'

'Oh, Jay. I'm not sure it's such a good idea. Why don't we just up sticks as soon as Ben finishes this term and go back home? It's where we belong. Everything will look better there.'

You won't be going home until your work here is finished, Jay. The rabbi calls it God's plan. If there's a plan wouldn't I be the one to have it? I'm the MC after all.

Chapter 14

This was now July 1932 and, given that it wouldn't get dark until late, I called on Leo in his room. "Want to come for a beer?" As ever he seemed to be smoking and cleaning his brushes or tidying away his paint tubes into boxes. I don't think I ever saw him touching a brush to a canvas - painting.

"Dinner?"

I hesitated while I calculated the timings. "Why not?"

We had a few beers in our usual place on Savignyplatz and moved on to one of the many workers' cafes under the railway arches in the direction of Zoo station. Leo looked at home in his creased and paint-splattered, blue-cotton trousers and the fact that he had dressed up for me by wearing the less-stained of his two engine-driver's jackets did not make him look out of place.

I, on the other hand, had put on one of my smarter light-weight suits and a straw panama to counter the last of the sun. I hadn't worn a tie because I had one of those fashionable shirts with the mini-lapels and a wide, soft collar at the top button so it fell away from my Adam's apple. I looked rather dashing but it was too much for the rough clientele who shot me grim looks from time to time.

"You do know you're scandalising the natives, Cam?"

"I'm afraid I can't help it," I said. I was looking at him from under lowered eyelids as cigarette smoke curled up from my nostrils in what I hoped was a most alluring look. "I'm having an adventure tonight."

He leaned forward. "Do tell."

I tapped him on the knee and he flinched and looked around.

"'Do tell!' Leo, you're priceless. I shall corrupt you at this rate. I really shall!"

He assumed his gruffest voice. "Stop acting up, Cam. You'll get us thrown out." He spoke more quietly as he flicked a look over my shoulder. "Behind you, by the door, is a group of three SA guys who followed us in. If you make any more of a show they'll take an interest in us. I don't give much for our chances if that happens. They'll give us both a good kicking."

I straightened in my chair but I had the devil in me that night and because I knew some butch specimens in uniform had their eyes on me it made it even more tempting to put on the theatrics.

Leo must have been able to sense it. "I'm serious, Cam. Don't give them a chance. The Nazis have the west of Berlin sewn up. They're above the law here. Don't give them an excuse."

I nodded and took a sip of my after-meal Schnapps.

"What were you saying about an adventure?"

"Well, I'm not so sure I should talk about it now."

"Don't sulk. We'll be fine as long as we look as if we're having a normal conversation - man to man."

"Okay." I stubbed out the cigarette, grinding it into the ashtray. "I'm heading for Rosa's Bridge after this."

"Why?"

"It's where we go, apparently. Men like me."

"Are you sure? I haven't heard of it."

I gave him a look. "How likely is it you would have?"

"Hmm. I take your point."

The restaurant had windows at both ends and I had been monitoring the light. "In fact, I think it's time for me to be on my way."

"We'll go out the back way. You'll be the right side for the canal."

110

I was tempted to turn and look at the Brownshirts. "Scaredy-cat!" I said.

"I just hope you never see them in action," he said.

Our chairs scraped back across the tiled floor and we paid the bill. I looked over my shoulder as we went out onto the still warm street. The group still sat by the front door hunched over a table-top crowded with beers.

"Well good luck, Cam." Leo shook my hand. "I hope you find what you're after."

"So do I," I said.

There had been a brief shower while we were in the restaurant and the air had that metallic, wet dust and electricity smell as I walked through the streets. There were people all around me, single men and women scurrying to the station and couples strolling arm-in-arm looking as if they had no particular destination in mind. Unlike me.

I had by now discovered the short cut to the Tiergarten which followed a path along the east side of the viaduct carrying the S-bahn trains north. I was soon in the narrow shadowed strip of path between the zoo on my right and the brick wall of the viaduct which blotted out the setting sun. There were no cafes in the arches here. Instead the caves were timbered up or had low doors made up of corrugated metal sheets. There were mean artisan businesses going on here and all was quiet this late. The only sounds were the mewing and lowing of zoo animals settling down for the night.

I ducked instinctively as a missile passed close by my head before realising that it must have been a bat. More of them flew by like an escort squadron of aircraft and I reasoned that my walking along must have disturbed insects which flew up into the jaws of the swooping predators. My heart was beating faster and I looked round furtively to see if I was being followed.

111

The path opened up into Kurfurster Allee and I crossed over it, skirted to the right of the Sportplatz and joined the Ufer Garten that tracked the south side of the canal. I followed it until I could see the bridge. I reasoned that if there was a meeting place here it would be on the far side of the canal because of its immediate access to the park and its undergrowth. I crossed the bridge feeling conspicuous to be up on the skyline if there were people below. The far bank was in shadows. There was no street lighting along the Tiergartenufer.

As I turned to take the steps down to the canal-side a match flared a few yards farther along the path and two faces - men's faces partly hidden by hat brims - were illuminated. The light went leaving two red points of heat close together which then lowered and were hidden.

Looking around, as my eyes adjusted, I could see more pinpoints of red light as cigarettes were sucked into life. They would fade and I could see the shadows shifting. This was where it happened. I had found it. A man coughed behind me and I turned.

"Haben Sie Feuer, bitte?"

I smiled and reached into my pocket for matches.

So now my life was settled in Berlin. Through to the end of the summer I spent some Friday nights in the Nolli. They were for sex. On Wednesdays - I discovered that it was by far the busiest evening of the week for this sort of thing - I would go to Tiergartenufer to meet German men like me. I had hot sexy clinches with some of them in the park and with others I went further and we met away from the canal bank. Some even became students, learning English from me in a most platonic way in Frau Guttchen's apartment in the Green House.

These men would be a little bit special and customarily we would share a brother's kiss before I ushered them out onto the landing but there was nobody significant.

Dexter Parnes VC was my main man and his adventure had been rollicking along to completion - the first draft anyway. I hoped to have something ready for Peter Everley by Christmas and, with nothing to keep me in Berlin after that, I wondered where I would go next.

Leo and I still met for coffee and the occasional evening meal - never on a Wednesday or Friday - and he seemed to be happy painting still lives or portraits and sketching street scenes - beggars, strutting Stormtroopers, soup kitchens. I knew by now that Leo was an insomniac who painted mostly while the rest of the house slept.

"I need the silence," he said. "The day is for preparation. Each piece has to be delivered in the solitude of sleepless night."

"You're a poet, Leo. I should be the precious one," I said. "Instead, I'm the one churning out his art like a Wurst factory."

"But is your scribbling art, Cam?" he said as he poked me with the chewed end of a brush.

Chapter 15

The dream happens on the cusp of Jay's waking. The MC perches on the end of the bed and the only sound in the room is Rachel's regular breathing. The MC's face is bare of make-up and lined. His cheeks are hollowed out. He addresses Jay directly and every word is received clearly and imprints itself:

I make as if I'm the happy joker of the Cabaret. It wasn't always the same. I'm not here because like you I was a survivor. This is far from the truth. When the Nazis closed down the Berlin clubs it was only a matter of time for me. I was everybody's friend on the stage but in the alleyways, in the always more seedy rooming houses, I was the Jew.

It was only two days after I was arrested that they sent me on a train to Poland. And so I didn't have time to lose my fitness. They put me to work. My job was to heave dead weights from the blockhouse to the hand-pulled wagons. It was an endless toil. I was not a big man. My back could tolerate the burdens for only so long. The time came and I was too weak to work. 'Time for you to take the shower,' they said.

All I had was weary; weary of the body, weary of the mind. I stumbled of my own free will to join one of the lines for the blockhouse. I didn't tell what is going to happen as we shuffled forward. There was such darkness for me in that place. Out of such darkness no light emerges.

I'm not here for me or for you, Jay. I'm a servant of destiny.

Rachel unpacks the hypermarket shopping after a visit to Danbury. Jay has spent the morning reading a book about Judaism loaned to him by Elayna Zwyck. He has been combining his learning about how the status of Jesus

114

differentiates the two religions with the lighter prose of Christopher Isherwood describing an encounter with Mr Norris. Both texts are uninspiring.

'Aren't you going to help?' Rachel says. She heaves the third and fourth of her burdens on to the work-surface in the kitchen. 'There are only two more.'

'Sorry.' He puts down the rabbi's book and steps through the open door. The sun is low in the sky and thin, filtered through high cloud.

It's as cold here as my remembered Berlin.

The air is dry. It's not the wet cold that Jay associates with freezing bones in the UK.

'What's this?' Jay says, holding up a *Stars and Stripes* he finds in the top of one of the bags. The flag is about the size of a paperback book and its stick is six inches long. He waves it half-heartedly.

'What's it look like?'

'A flag. But it's not our flag.'

Rachel sighs. 'You said the other day about everybody having them. Their flag is everywhere. If we don't have one somebody might think we're terrorists. Let's be safe rather than sorry.'

Do you think the terrorists haven't thought of this? I would bet you that their houses have more flamboyant patriotic bunting than the apology of a flag you have there.

'We'll be regular Tony Blairs – "shoulder to shoulder",' Jay says.

'He carries on the way he's going, he could be President.'

'He wasn't born here.'

'You know what I mean.'

Jay goes out to the mailbox and pushes the stick of the flag into a gap in the metalwork so it sticks up from the rear. Up and down the street, above porches and garages, a rash of

115

similar flags – of all sizes – has appeared, their poles fixed into special brackets.

Back in the house, he says, 'I reckon they must put out flags for the Fourth of July every year.'

Rachel kneels in supplication before the freezer. She shifts packages around a drawer and pummels them into place. 'Buggering cheapskate landlord and this tiny frigging freezer. All this stuff is not going to be so bloody cheap if we can't fit it in,' she mutters through her gritted teeth.

'We'll get an English flag and put it up on St George's Day', Jay says.

'We'll be home before then.'

At dinner later the same day, the family is in wonder at the size of the prawns.

'They're incredibly cheap as well. I would have saved them for a special occasion but I had to cook some because I can't get any more in the freezer.'

'This is delicious, Mum,' Ben says.

'It's a recipe card from the shop. Tell you what, they do *some* things well here. There are free samples and recipe cards everywhere in the big stores. You should have seen it, Jay.'

'Next time,' he says.

They return their attentions to the food.

Ask Ben about the musical.

Jay turns to Ben. 'I haven't checked in with you about *Cabaret* for a while. How's it going?'

'Great!' But Ben shakes his head.

Jay and Rachel share a glance across the table.

'Really? It's all going well?' Jay asks.

'Yeah. I said.'

Rachel makes warning eyes towards Jay and he concentrates on twirling the strings of pasta onto his fork. He adds a prawn and a wedge of softened courgette and steers everything towards his mouth.

'You're not having any trouble with the song?' Rachel says.

'No.'

'The acting?'

'No!'

Now it's Jay's turn to make eyes at her as he swirls the ball of flavours around his mouth.

Rachel ignores him. 'I know you, Ben. Something's wrong. What is it? The schoolwork?'

'It's nothing.' He shifts in his seat.

Jay can tell that Ben is *so* close to storming out. But he also knows that Rachel won't let go. She's betting her cooking can keep her son at the table.

'So there *is* something,' she says.

'It's nothing.' Ben is shovelling a final mouthful of food together.

'So there *is* an "it"'

Ben puts down his fork and spreads the remaining pasta back onto his plate. He sighs, still prodding at his food. 'It's some parents. They're unhappy that we're doing *Cabaret*. They don't like the Nazism in it. Mr Costidy says he may have to cancel.'

Jay's first thought is to rail against 'PC gone mad' but instead he asks, 'How would you feel?'

Ben looks up at him. His brown eyes shine. 'I'd be gutted.'

Rachel nods.

'Then we'd better make sure it doesn't happen. What have these parents got against it?'

'I dunno, really. I think they think it glorifies the Nazis. It's some of the Jewish families.'

'But it's ludicrous. It was written by Jews – Kander and Ebb. I've looked it up.' He leans forward. 'Are you saying there's a group of them?'

'Sort of, I think.' He pauses as if preparing himself for a bad answer. 'Dad?'

'Yes?'

'Are we Jewish?'

Jay smiles. He looks at Rachel. She's wide-eyed and shrugs so dramatically it nearly lifts her out of the chair.

'Why do you ask?' Jay says.

'Because I think it's *my* song that's the problem. They think Mr Costidy shouldn't have cast a Jewish boy to sing *Tomorrow Belongs to Me.*'

Jay breathes deeply to quell a surge of anger. 'We'll see about that!'

Rachel's looking at her husband. 'It's a good question though, Jay. Are we Jewish?'

The alarm sounds in the room above and Jay stirs. Even though he no longer has a job to go to, he and Rachel still like to get up with Ben, to make sure he has a good breakfast and see him on to the school bus.

The MC's face coalesces in front of him as Jay opens a tentative eye. *Nancy! What do you reckon? Was it Nancy who jumped? Was she the one who had her shoes in her hand as she plummeted 110 floors? Where is she now?*

Jay groans and buries his face in the pillow.

It's only to let you know I haven't left you.

After Ben has left for school, Rachel is helping Jay load the dishwasher. 'What are your plans for the day?' she asks.

'I'm seeing Fothergill –' he sees her brow furrow '– the lawyer guy who set up the SDC partnership. The appointment's at eleven and we'll probably have lunch. You know what they're like.'

'And this afternoon?'

'I need to pop into the library with the *Cabaret* video. Have you got anything planned?'

'No. As if.' She flicks a dishcloth into the sink.

'Why don't you come with me? You could go to that department store – Lord & Taylor – while I'm in the meeting. I could cry off lunch so we can eat together.'

'No. I'll potter round here.'

His irritation rises like indigestion. 'I've had an idea,' he says. 'Why don't I ask at the library whether they've got voluntary work you could do? It would give you *something*.'

'If you like. But we'll be going home at Christmas, won't we? It's only three months away if we leave as soon as Ben's term ends. Perhaps I should start planning it. It'll give me something to do.'

'Let's just see how the meeting with Fothergill goes before you do anything definite.' He looks at his watch. 'I'd better get ready.'

The cross-country road from Burford Lakes to Stamford is spectacular at this time of year. The leaves are turning and it looks as if the foliage is suffused with golden candlelight. Jay tunnels under arches of flaming boughs and the tree-trunks form a guard of honour.

He's trying to recall his only meeting with Nathan Fothergill. He remembers him as an unusually small man, barrel-chested and with a twist in his upper back that some might unkindly call a hump. While his torso had seemed to be of normal length, his legs were so short that, if he sat down, it wasn't that his feet didn't reach the floor but that, when he sat back, his legs stuck out horizontally. Neither Francois nor Glen had warned Jay about Fothergill's appearance and he had spent the first half of the meeting trying to ensure that he concealed the 'sizist' puns that kept bubbling to the front of his brain. He realises now that this is another reason he can remember so little about the papers. What if he'd signed his rights away? Maybe Rachel is right and they have nothing – not even a salary to take them through to the end of Ben's term.

Would you feel any better about your dead colleagues then?

Even if the other partners had cheated him, he wouldn't have wanted them dead.

But this is the point. They are dead. Them and fifteen others. One of them Nancy. Remember her? How you were mesmerised by her cleavage?

Seventeen! What must the families think? He considers the ordeal they're facing.

You have your life. What more should you have?

He decides he doesn't deserve anything. Why should he expect? It should be enough that he's alive.

He sees the outer suburbs of Stamford through a mist of tears and negotiates the ringway to the eastbound exit. The road here is a strip-mall and passes a Wendy's burger outlet, an aluminium-clad diner, the red and white of Staples office supplies, followed by the similar colouring of the CVS pharmacy. Jay turns in by a sign for the Borders bookstore (with Starbucks) and on the right is the tawdry office block belonging to *Safa-Data Recovery*. Grey and disorderly vertical blinds sag behind streaked windows.

Jay works the automated entry system and stands inside a vestibule carpeted with loose tiles that look as if they've seen service underneath a leaky drink-dispensing machine. It isn't Nathan who approaches but a woman. She's strikingly tall and dark-skinned, possibly mixed race. Her hair is black and cropped boyishly so it fits close to her head. The fringe has been left long and is pressed flat across her forehead. This, together with her height and her conservative dress, gives her the look of a catwalk model presenting a for-the-office range. Jay's pulse quickens. Her handshake is dry, firm – satisfying.

'It's good to meet you, Mr Halprin. My name is Teri Herbold. I work for Baxter, Fothergill and Fauset as an assistant attorney. Would you like to come through?'

'Yes. Please lead the way, Ms Herbold.'

She turns to blitz a smile on him. 'Teri, please. Nathan is through here.'

This girl – Teri – she is so beautiful. I wonder what instrument she can play – for my orchestra, you understand.

They step through more sticky carpet tiles, enter double doors and Jay finds himself in an office space that extends across the building. The snaggle-toothed windows are to his left and right. Teri navigates a narrow passage between rows of unoccupied desks and empty chairs. Each desk carries a computer with a flat-screen monitor and the cables coil around like snakes in a viper pit.

'What is this place?' Jay asks.

Teri stops, turns and straightens the waisted jacket that shows off her slim build. 'Yes, this is probably new to you. The *Safa-Data* servers are in the basement. That's where the *Safa-Data* people do the day-to-day work. This is a disaster recovery floor. If one of their client's buildings was to be destroyed – in a fire, say – this accommodation would fit enough people to get the company re-started. They'd use it for a week or so until new temporary accommodation is found. It doesn't have to be pretty – as you can see – just functional.' She turns and continues walking. 'They've given us a small office at the end here.'

She leads Jay towards a cubicle that has been excised out of the main space, presumably to be taken by a supervisor for the recovery team in a disaster scenario. It's glazed from the waist up and the top of Nathan's head is progressing towards the doorway. He's waiting there when they arrive.

'Jay!' Good to see you.' He clasps his left hand over the handshake, a thick identity bracelet rattles on his wrist. 'Coffee?' he shakes his head. 'It's machine but it's recognisably coffee.' He goes back to the desk and points to his own empty cup. 'Teri, please?'

Jay turns to her and licks his lips.

Did you really do that?

'I'm feeling thirsty. Cold water would be good.'

She nods and turns out of the office and through the adjacent swing doors.

Jay is still looking at the space Teri occupied when Nathan speaks. 'She won't be long. Sit, Jay. Look, I have to start this by saying I'm so sorry. You were so lucky.'

You think so? He doesn't have the dreams, does he, Jay?

'Yes.'

'You're probably wondering what this is all about.' Nathan hops himself up into his chair and shuffles his posterior back. The toes of his panther-sheened shoes point to the ceiling. The soles are leather and not unduly worn.

Stop worrying about the shoes. There are weighty matters to be discussed. Pay attention.

'Jay?'

Jay snaps back into the room as Teri enters with two plastic cups. She gives him the one with water. She places the other on the desk before smoothing her skirt, sitting in the chair alongside Jay's and crossing her legs. He recognises her perfume as it settles around him but can't put a name to it.

Nathan lifts the cup, raises it – 'Thank you, Teri' – and sips. Jay is thinking about the way the age in Nathan's face contrasts with his boy's body.

This man's appearance is not the problem. What he has for you – this is your problem. Now, achtung!

Jay straightens his back and focuses on Nathan's eyes.

The lawyer uses the next ten minutes to repeat his telephone conversation with Jay giving the layman's explanation of the company's legal position now that the two main partners are dead. In each case the partnership passes into their estates and is dealt with as an asset under the terms of the wills. In the case of Straub, DuCheyne these wills work in concert with the partnership agreement that, he reads from a paper in front of him: 'obligates the surviving partner or partners to purchase the partnership or partnerships from the deceased partner's or partners' beneficiaries under their wills'.

When Nathan mentions that he has an obligation to Francois and Glen, Jay reaches for the water. His fingers tremble; his skin is clammy.

'Do you remember the terms of the partnership agreement, Jay? Have you brought your copy?' Nathan peers over the desk expectantly but sees that Jay doesn't carry a briefcase.

'Uh! I kept all that stuff in the office.' Jay hears Teri clicking a ballpoint pen into action.

'Too bad. Nothing to worry about, though. Teri can provide you with copies.'

She reaches down into her briefcase for a yellow legal pad. She makes a note and re-crosses her legs.

Stop thinking about her and consider the matter in the hand.

Nathan steeples his fingers in front of his face and crinkles his eyes. This draws up the corners of his mouth. It resembles a smile. 'All it means is this. Francois and Glen have family members who, until you buy them out under the terms of the agreement, own the majority stake in the company. I've met with these family members and their instinct is that, with Francois and Glen gone, the business should not continue. However, they'll respect your wishes if you want to carry on. Do you have a view at this moment in time?'

Jay is reeling from the words, 'buy them out under the terms of the agreement'. How much is this going to cost?

'Jay? Do you want to continue the business alone? Have you decided?'

You on your own? With Rachel wanting to go home as soon as possible?

Jay shakes his head. 'No.'

Nathan raises his eyebrow. 'No?'

'No – I mean I don't want to keep the business going. I think we're going back to the UK as soon as it's practicable.' Waves of distress threaten to overwhelm him as he wonders whether they will be able to go back to England once the terms of the agreement he so foolishly signed have been satisfied.

Nathan lowers his hands into his lap. Jay sees him only as a child in an outsize chair. 'Good. Good.' The lawyer nods towards Teri. 'Perhaps you can apprise Mr Halprin as to the current state of the company.'

The words 'current state' stimulate Jay's sweat glands.

She nods, says, 'Surely,' and, uncrossing her legs, turns to Jay. 'Nathan delegated me to look into the company on the day after the tragedy. I contacted *Safa-Data* and we have set up Straub, DuCheyne in this room.' She points to her closed laptop. 'This computer has been configured with Mr DuCheyne's access codes. As far as the data is concerned, I am Mr DuCheyne, if you will.'

There's a pause and Jay is the first to break. 'And what does it tell you?'

'The company's in a healthy position.'

His temperature stabilises; the pressure drains away.

'It appears that the managing partners have always kept a healthy cash reserve, equivalent to six-month's trading. But you'll know this from your due diligence.'

'Due diligence?' Jay says.

'The investigations you carried out when you joined the company?'

'I just went with assurances from Francois and Glen that the company was sound.'

Teri raises a dark eyebrow and studies the back of her left hand. The only ring is on her second finger. 'Surely. In this case your trust was well-founded. There's very little debt – mostly small invoices that we can settle. Given the circumstances, some companies may have written them off already so we'll wait for them to chase us. Payroll is the biggest obligation. Under our advisement the families of Messrs DuCheyne and Straub have instructed us to pay the employees in full this month and make a further ex-gratia payment in October. I assume you'll concur.' She raises an eyebrow.

Jay brings both hands up in front of him to signal his agreement.

'The in-service death benefits are insured and the insurers are looking at how to handle claims now. It seems certain that they'll waive normal proof requirements and work on the basis that as long as a Trade Center employee left for work that morning and hasn't been seen since the dependants have a valid claim.'

Jay is dizzy from information. His view of the room is fading; it feels as if the ground is sliding under his feet.

Teri continues, 'There's business continuity insurance in place and we're trying to find out the terms of settlement given the extraordinary circumstances here. It's likely there'll be compensation from one body or another. All in all, the current value of the business, even though it's not a going concern, is substantial. Over a million dollars.'

Jay's not sure whether this is good news or bad. Does he have to find this figure and pay it to Glen and Francois's dependants? 'What does this mean?' he says.

Teri looks at Nathan who nods for her to answer. 'Briefly, Mr Halprin – Jay – it means that, even before the partnership assurance, your share of the business is a conservative $200,000.'

Look at that. Everybody dies and you win the lottery!

125

'Sorry, I need to understand clearly. That's without any obligations. I won't owe the managing partners' families anything.' Jay turns to the small man in the big chair. The corner office in the dingy building. The sting of perfume pervading the atmosphere. Everything is surreal.

'Remember what we said, Jay,' Nathan says, 'the managing partners' families think it best to end the partnership. This means that on their say-so – which is the majority, remember – Teri is winding up the company. When she's completed this job – probably in the New Year she'll send you your share of the proceeds. Are you clear now?'

Jay does a quick calculation. He visualises their most recent bank statement. He knows what Rachel will ask when he gets home. 'And between then and now?'

Nathan steeples his stubby fingers again. 'Like the other employees you'll receive this full month's salary and an ex-gratia payment for October.'

That should be adequate to the end of the year, Jay thinks. 'Is there anything else?' This sounds mercenary. 'I mean, have we covered everything?'

Nathan's face is grim. 'You *have* forgotten all the forms you signed when you were in my office.'

'Jet-lag!' He attempts a lame grin.

'Teri? Over to you again, I think.' He shakes his head. 'Don't you remember going for the insurance medical?'

Jay recalls a modern clinic facility in Burford Station where he underwent tests. He was passed fit enough for the company's death benefit scheme. 'I don't get paid death-in-service; I'm still alive.'

'You are indeed but there's the small matter of the life assurance you took out to underpin the partnership agreement. Teri?'

Jay's questioning why Nathan can't give him the news himself. Is it so bad?

Teri reaches into her briefcase. Her manner is business-like, deliberate.

'The necessity for you to pay the managing partners' families under the partnership agreements will be lost when the company dissolves,' Teri says. 'But the policies of life insurance that you took out on each of the managing partners under the reciprocal agreements are still valid. There was insurable interest at the time the policies were taken out and this is all that counts.' She shuffles through a sheaf of papers. 'Ah! Here it is. Sums assured of $1.5 million on each life, Mr DuCheyne and Mr Straub. I have the claim forms for you to sign today. I'm sure New York Life will expedite things. I imagine you'll receive a check for the $3million sometime next month.' She neither smiles nor scowls. She's keeping her manner neutral.

Jay throws himself back into his chair. A surge of laughter rises in his throat and he swallows it down.

Because nobody in this dusty cubicle can allow themselves to treat this as good news.

Chapter 16

As the days shortened, so we Wednesday men met
ever earlier, catching the end of the daylight
before the dark hid our furtive assignations.
Soon it would be too cold and my activities would
be confined only to the clubs around the Nolli
where it was poor form to arrive or leave as a
couple.

It was late September, destined to be one of
my last nights at Rosa's Bridge, when I met Wolf.
I had arrived a little early. The bats were not
yet in the air and there was too much light for
cigarette smoking so I went farther west along
the canal towpath than was my custom. The trees
of the Tiergarten, the ones bordering the Neuen
See, were on my right as I walked along the path.
After say fifteen minutes following the canal
around the long bend, I was ready to turn back so
I would be at the meeting point at the right
time.

That's when I saw him, shoulders hunched,
hands in trench-coat pockets, scurrying towards
me. At first, I perceived him as a youth who had
put on his father's coat and hat, wearing them
more for concealment than for warmth or style. As
we passed each other he looked up at me and I saw
fear in his eyes. He seemed to be about to say
something but hesitated.

I stopped and turned. Had I let him down by
not showing some recognition of the needy look he
gave me? I spoke in German. "Are you looking for
something? Can I help you, please?"

He took a step back, his head down,
presenting me only with a side-view of the brim
of his hat. "Is there a footbridge further down
where I may cross the canal?"

"Yes. If you walk on for about ten minutes
you will find it."

"Is it by the Zoo?"

"Yes, by the Zoo."

He looked up. He was awfully young. Did I recognise him then? His face was flushed. There was a down of blond hair on his upper lip. "Thank you," he said.

I was concerned for his safety. He was an attractive boy and there was an element of 'rough trade' who met by the bridge. Did he know where he was going? "Are you looking for a *special* place?"

He put his hands into the pockets of the raincoat and shrugged. "Not particularly." He looked up into my face but only briefly before studying his shoes once again. Perhaps he noticed the small amount of kohl I had applied to my eyelids. He seemed to be on the point of making a decision that required all his willpower. "Is the bridge we are talking about sometimes called Rosa's Bridge?" he asked.

"Not by everybody," I said. "Are you looking for Rosa's Bridge?"

There were tears in his eyes. "Yes."

"And you know what happens there?"

He stepped away from me as if I was about to strike him. His head moved urgently to one side like a startled fawn that has heard a twig snap in the undergrowth.

"Can you not tell from my accent - I am British? I am not likely to be a policeman, am I? You should not be scared of me."

He relaxed but he seemed to be on the point of turning away.

I reached out my right hand and touched his forearm. "It is getting dark. You look very young to me. I am not sure you are old enough to look after yourself if you go to Rosa's Bridge."

"But, I am!" His bottom lip was jutting out and trembling.

I smiled, trying to look like a kindly older brother and I swear that at this first meeting my thoughts were only for this youth's wellbeing. Was he making the right choices when he was so young? "Why don't we go for a coffee and we shall talk about it. If you still want to go the bridge afterwards there will still be time."

"Why should I go with you?"

"Because I am worried about you. Perhaps I can help you make sure that what you are doing is right. I do not imagine you have anybody in your family you can talk to, do you?"

"How do you know?"

"We all have the same experience. By the way, do you have any cigarettes?"

"I do not smoke."

I took him by the arm and chuckled. "If you are going to Rosa's Bridge you will have to learn to smoke. It is the way you meet ... other men. So, we will have a coffee and you can buy some cigarettes – if you still think you are going to need them. Now, is there a cafe back the way you came? We do not want to carry on this way until you are sure you are ready."

When we had put our hats on the table and we were under the electric light, I became aware of two things. Firstly, that this young man was young – too young for the sort of thing that went on by Rosa's Bridge – and I recognised him but I couldn't place him. I tried to recall the attractive young Berliners I had bumped into during my three months. The review of my memory came back blank.

We ordered coffees.

"What is your name?" I asked.

"Wolfgang. My friends call me Wolf."

"Do you mind if I call you Wolf also?"

"Please do."

We waited while the waitress served the coffee. "I am sorry," I said, "I didn't ask whether you would like some cake with your coffee."

"No, this is fine." He twirled the cup in the saucer so the handle was to his left and lifted it to his lips. He took a sip and drew the cup away suddenly. "Hot!"

"You are left-handed," I said.

"Such a thing is not allowed,' he said. 'When I was a child I had my left arm tied to my side so I had to write - do everything - with my right hand."

"People do not accept difference," I said.

His intelligent eyes met mine. "Can we speak English? I have been taught English and I would be more comfortable ..." he looked round at the other tables, all with couples - men and women - looking across at each other silently, "... if we are going to talk about ... difference."

"If it pleases you," I said in my native tongue.

"Please - it would be better, I am sure." His English was heavily accented but not at all hesitant. He had been taught well.

"So you know what happens at ... the bridge." I looked round but nobody seemed to be taking any notice.

"Yes, it is well-known in Berlin. The authorities are aware but they allow it to continue."

"Not for long if Herr Hitler is elected." I made sure I said the name under my breath. A conversation in English about politics would arouse interest.

"Yes. But it would be for the greater good if the National Socialists lead Germany. This is our destiny. What is my individual ... difference ... against what is right for the Fatherland?"

It was when he said this word that I became aware of where I had seen him before. "You're in the Hitler Youth," I said.

"Yes."

"I think I saw you leading the singing at Neuen See a few Sundays ago."

He blushed. "This could be so."

"You have a beautiful voice."

He looked down at his coffee, took it up in both hands and took a long sip. "Thank you."

"Do you mind me asking how old you are?"

He counted silently. "I have fifteen years."

"Funfzehn!"

"Ja."

"Then you must not go to the bridge. You are far too young to know your mind - your sexuality." This word is similar in German and I looked up furtively again. We did not seem to have drawn attention.

"I know what I am." He sounded desperate. "I do not find girls exciting the way do other boys. I want to be certain."

I tried to think back to the way I had been at fifteen. It had been a relatively easy time. I was at public school where 'homo' was the only sex in town. Those of us who did not see it as second-best kept our feelings to ourselves while we made the most of the opportunity.

I imagined it must be very different to grow up in a regimented German environment and it was certainly contrary to everything the Hitler Youth stood for. Poor Wolf was trying to run before he could walk.

I took out a cigarette. "Do you mind?"

He waved a hand. "Nein."

I smiled sympathetically. "Wolf. I want to help you discover yourself. Do you understand what I mean by that?"

He nodded. He was blushing again.

Chapter 17

Jay's driving back to Burford Lakes. He's trying to reconstruct the events of his first meeting with Nathan Fothergill. When did they explain about the life insurance? Did he really not know he had arranged cover on the lives of both his senior partners?

Don't question it; you're a multi-millionaire. Pprrpff on being poor!

Doesn't the money really belong to the widows Straub and DuCheyne? Did they know he would make so much out of their husbands' deaths?

So you're going to give them the money? I can see you selling that one to Rachel. See how love flies out the window …

If Jay had the cover on them, presumably they had similar policies on each other. That means each family has $1.5 million each plus death-in-service – a multiple of salary. The payout will be huge. Perhaps they don't need his money. Should he ask them if it's all right for him to keep it?

You think they're going to turn down $1.5 million? The richer you are the greedier you get. You keep schtum. If you and Rachel can't use the money there are plenty of other Straub, DuCheyne families who can. Widows and widowers with children to bring up. When they discover that you survived, you'll be able to look them in the eye?

Why can't he feel good? $3 million – what is it in sterling? Something like two million pounds! Plus his share of the business – that in itself is more than enough to cover the cost of going home.

Money money money money money money – that clinking clanking sound can make the world go round.

Two million is enough to do whatever he wants! He punches the air and becomes aware that he's driving a car and he's on the outskirts of Burford Lakes. He resumes control, steers it into a space by the green and takes the *Cabaret* video from the glove compartment.

Going back so soon? Can't we view it one more time?

As he crosses the road he recalls how vigorous he felt before the plane struck on the morning of 9/11. For the first time since then there's a swagger in his step. He hopes Prentice will be on duty. Perhaps she'll detect a multi-millionaire assurance when he presents himself at her desk.

So we go back to hubris? What is it they say about pride?

Prentice *is* there wearing a lavender twinset. She has put something of the same shade on her eyelids – a thin line that merges into the darker brown that sets off her blue eyes.

'Why it's Mr Halprin. How are you today?' She gives a bob of her head that fails to dislodge a single fibre of her thickly sprayed mane. Her voice is softer.

He holds up the video and smiles. 'I'm returning this.'

She takes it from him and for a split-second her long nails tease his palm. The contact sends a tingle to his shoulder.

She's picked it up, Jay. You animal.

'Let me see now.' She studies the computer screen. 'That's fine. There's nothing more to pay. Now, is there anything else I can help you with today, Mr Halprin?'

'Jay.'

'Excuse me?'

'Call me Jay.'

'Very well.' She's looking straight into his eyes. 'There's nothing to pay, Jay.' She puts her hand in front of her mouth chuckling at her accidental poetry. 'Now, is there anything else I can help you with today?' The intonation is exactly the same as before.

'I still have the book – Christopher Isherwood.'

134

She consults the screen. 'That's right. You have it for another ten days so no hurry.'

'There's no point in renewing it?'

She shakes her head. 'Not yet.'

'Is there anything else from that period – Berlin ... 1930's – you would recommend?'

Her brow furrows. 'Let me see ...' her fingers tap-dance across the keyboard '... no, nothing comes up here ...'

'There's another book by Isherwood – *Christopher and his Kind*. Do you have it? '

'Let me see.' She taps at speed, her eyes on the screen. 'Mmm. No. Ah ...' She shakes her head. Her lips are doing that wriggling thing again. 'No we *definately* don't have it.' It's as if even to consider his request has somehow sullied her.

'What's wrong?'

'Do you by any chance know the content of this book, Jay?'

He shrugs. 'It's a memoir – about his time in Berlin.'

'Well that may be. But the library trustees have entered a black mark against this book. It's not suitable to order.'

'Does it say why?'

'Beg pardon?' She's stalling and a flush creeps up from the high neck of her sweater all the way to her ears.

'On the screen – does it say why the book is banned?'

Her lips twist as if she's attempting to tie them into a bow and her voice drops. 'It mentions content of a homosexual nature.'

Jay shrugs. 'It makes sense. He *was* gay.'

Prentice's eyes are wide. 'And they're performing this gay man's play at Jefferson High? My goodness!'

'It's a musical based on a play based on one of his books.'

'Excuse me?'

'Never mind. If you can't help me with any more books.' He turns to leave.

135

'There is one thing may suit you. I was cataloguing local-interest books a few days ago and we had something by an author who lived in Burford Lakes. He gifted some books to the library quite a number of years ago. Where was it?' He follows her and Jay can't resist the urge to watch the lilt of her hips as her heels click-clack on the parquet floor. There's an open entrance to a small back room with a card over the lintel – 'Local Interest'. The walls are solid with shelves leaving a small space in the middle. Jay is aware how close Prentice's cashmere-clad breast is to his arm.

She moves to one of the shelves. 'Let me see.' She bends at the knee with her torso precariously upright. Her skirt is restricting her movement. Jay's excited at the thought that, if he wasn't there, she would probably hitch up her skirt and squat down.

Oh! This girl has talent. Imagine her in the line-up at the Kit Kat Club. What I could make of this lady. But here, in the 21st century, in Burford Lakes Library – such a waste.

She's pointing. 'See there, Jay – *Green House* something.'

He studies the spine of the book. The author's name is Cameron Mortimer. It's a name that he thinks he's heard of but he can't recollect where. He takes the book. '*The Green House Envelope*. Hmm.' It's a hardback subscription-club edition.

'If I remember, it's set in Berlin at the time you want.'

It's not a diversion, Jay. It will speed up your process of discovery. Take it.

He turns the book to view the cover and jerks back at the sight of the film-poster style artwork that depicts a scene where a square-jawed man in a trilby hat and a trench coat is running alongside a steam locomotive. The front of the engine is decorated with a swastika. In the distance behind the running man a group of three black-uniformed soldiers are chasing him with Luger pistols outstretched. The book's flame-tinted title flashes across the sky. 'It doesn't look like a book I would normally read.'

Take the book, Jay.

He opens it and reads the blurb on the inside cover. 'It *is* Berlin and it's 1930s …'

Prentice stands behind him close enough for her perfume to fill his nostrils.

You're safe here in this little private room. All you have to do is turn and 'stumble' into her.

'He's a local author, like I said. Cameron Mortimer.' Her hand snakes across in front of him and the invasion of his space is so acute that he feels the urge to step away. She's turning the pages as he holds it. He wonders if it's because he's a lover of books that this is such an intimate move.

That soft pressure on your upper arm is her breast. Is this a green light?

A fog of lust obscures the words as he reads where her taloned hand is holding back the pages: 'Cameron Mortimer was born in England in 1905. The first Dexter Parnes VC mystery "The Silvered-Eagle Device" was written while he was a student at Oxford University and was published in 1930. There are sixteen Dexter Parnes VC books and fourteen movies. Cameron Mortimer lives in New York State.'

She takes back her hand and steps away.

Forget about her and take the book.

Jay draws a deep breath and closes the cover. 'I'll take it.'

Rachel drives carefully so as to avoid the slippery strip-carpets of leaves along the margins of Route 22. They are in the Subaru heading north after their first Jewish service together. It hasn't been as embarrassing as Jay thought it would be. They met up with the Edlers in the synagogue car park and Howard led them into the vestibule where they were greeted by Rabbi Zwyck. Jay was conscious that he was bare-headed but the rabbi was keen to put him at his ease. 'We're not stuffy, here, Jay. You and your family are welcome to observe your own ways until you decide to join our congregation. See how you feel. We have many gentiles come here for bar mitzvahs and the like and it would be silly of us to force them to do something alien.'

Jay detected a softening in Rachel's rigid stance.

'If you decide to join us you'll have to take some classes before you're accepted into the congregation. Ben, here, will have a bar mitzvah.'

'Well, what do you think?' Jay asks half-turning from the front passenger seat.

Ben leans forward. 'It's just like church really. Not scary? All that Jewish when they read from the scrolls, though.'

'Hebrew.'

'What?'

'The language is Hebrew and the scrolls are the Torah – the holy book. It's equivalent to the Bible – but the copies are treated with more reverence.'

'Yeah. All that stuff?' He sits back, puts on earphones and flicks on his music. They hear the tinny beat in the front of the car.

'Your ears, Ben! Turn it down.' Rachel twists round and signals.

'What?' He removes one of the 'phones.

'Turn it down please, Ben. You'll damage your ears.'

Ben makes an adjustment and reinserts the plug in his ear.

'What did you think, Rache?'

'It's not for me but I'll come with you if you think you're going to stick at it. If you think it will help.'

Can being a *real* Jew help? He watches the bare trees pass by but doesn't see them; his focus is internal. Why should he carry the burden of all those lives? Does this new God he's learning about have a plan?

The MC appears over his shoulder. *Why don't you let me worry about whether there's a plan. If there's a plan I'm the one who's going to know.*

Perhaps he should stop worrying about God's plan and merely try to live a better life. A religious life – a Jew's life. Uncle Hymie seemed to have the answer. Do something well and leave it behind. His religion gave *him* comfort.

Rachel interrupts his reverie. 'Do you want Ben to have a bar mitzvah?'

'What?'

'Ben – do you want him to be Jewish – to have a bar mitzvah?' Rachel says.

'If he wants it.'

'It can wait until we get back home though, can't it?'

'I suppose so, and let's face it, we can afford to push the boat out.'

She turns away from the windscreen and looks at him. 'Is that how you see us now, Jay? Are we a rich Jewish family who can put on a show? Are we going to become pillars of the community in somewhere like Golders Green? Keeping up with the Cohens?'

Jay scratches at his scalp. What is he trying to find? Will Rachel take them back to England before he has taken this religion thing as far as he can?

It's not her call, Jay. You and me – it's between us.

Jay recollects going home with the news that they were rich. Driven inside by the September rain, Rachel had been in the basement airing some washing.

'Hi! How did it go?'

All the way home from the library he had contemplated how he would tell her about their good fortune. He wanted to sound like a general who had a great victory to announce but, at the same time, regretted the suffering his troops had endured. 'Basically, SDC is being wound up. The company's sound financially but there's nobody to carry on. The business will be liquidated and we'll get my 15%.'

Rachel was attaching washing to the makeshift line and spoke through a peg clamped between her lips. 'Will it be much? How long will it take?'

'Francois and Glen are dead!' he said. Then feeling he had been too harsh too quickly, he held out a hand. 'Come up here and I'll tell you about it.'

She sighed, finished pegging up a shirt and trudged to the top of the stairs wiping her hands on the seat of her jeans. Jay felt the urge to hug her but thought about Prentice's perfume. Nothing had happened but ...

Jay guided Rachel to the blue settee. 'Yep, Francois and Glen's shares go to their beneficiaries whoever they are. Our share is worth up to $200,000. It'll come through next year.'

'How will we manage until then?'

'Everybody gets paid for September and October and it's enough to see us through to the end of the year.'

'So we go home with nothing.'

'Only if you call $200,000 nothing.'

'It's only what you're due and we don't get it for months. How can we manage until then?'

'You're forgetting the two month's pay but it's not going to be a worry anyway – because they reminded me about the life insurance.'

'Life insurance?'

'Exactly. I'd forgotten it too. Policies I took out on Glen and Francois so that I could buy their share of the partnership if one of them died.'

'How much?'

He fought to keep the mask of indifference. '$3million. One-and-a-half million on each of them.'

She looked at him and he couldn't stop the smile that infected the edges of his mouth.

'Seriously? Three million? We get three million?'

'Seriously – dollars.'

'Yes!' She threw herself at him and jitterbugged in his arms. 'Three million!'

Now his grin was wide and unashamed.

She stepped away. 'Right! We go home. Ben can start the new term back in the UK straight after Christmas. Promise?'

'Promise.'

She returned to his embrace and there was comfort for him in the familiarity of her body engulfed in his arms.

She stiffened. 'What's that scent?' she said.

He still isn't sure that Rachel accepted what he had said about how Prentice had stood close while explaining the Cameron Mortimer book he had brought home – the one with the garish cover. Jay thinks about the librarian and starts constructing the fantasy of a possible affair. The figure of the MC appears and encourages him with leers and licking lips but the vision of Rachel is there too – the vengeful wife having discovered his infidelity through some typically thoughtless lapse on his part.

But the sex. Think about the abandonment of extra-marital sex.

There's something comfortable about his sex-life with Rachel.

Comfortable? Why settle for comfortable?

But when it happens with Rachel it's better than anything he experienced before. Would he put that in danger? Perhaps it could happen more often but is this her fault or his? He wonders when to tell her that it's a mitzvah for a Jewish married couple to have sex every Friday night.

Once a week. Would you be up to it, big boy?

As Rachel steers onto their drive and parks behind the VW, Jay finds himself thinking not of Prentice but of Teri

141

Herbold, the attorney responsible for winding up Straub, DuCheyne. The idea of their weekly meetings in Stamford, a good distance from Burford Lakes, sets his blood running.

Now you're thinking straight. She's a much better candidate. I want a front row seat for that.

It's early afternoon and, as a result of an hour of vigorous activity in the 'yard' after synagogue, a second pile of early leaves sits by the English family's US-patriotic mailbox. The family is scheduled to have supper with the Cochranes but the rest of the afternoon is free. Neither the newspapers nor the television – other than their weekly ration of *The Sopranos* – holds any attraction now that their return to England is firmly scheduled … at least in Rachel's mind.

He's settled in the den. Having finished the *Berlin Novels* he's now turning over the Cameron Mortimer book that Prentice found for him. He starts reading and finds himself following Dexter Parnes VC as, using false papers, he attempts to negotiate the platform barrier of the Zoo railway station in Berlin. Members of Hitler's Brownshirts stand in his path even though they don't have official sanction. They're using the authority of their clubs and pistols and they're looking for a Jew to fool with. They gather round a dark-haired, Slavic-eyed young woman in a fur coat like ants chancing upon a grounded moth. It's soon obvious that only Dexter Parnes VC has the courage to go to her aid.

Jay's wonders whether he wants to bother with the book. There's something about the casual reference to the woman's Slavic eyes and the description of her plight that makes Jay think that he's going to be troubled by its dated values. He crosses to the computer desk and enters the *Yahoo!* web address. This leads him to a Dexter Parnes VC fan page which yields references to 16 books and 14 films. The books are out of print and he can't trace videos of the films – either in tape or the new disc format. A new *Yahoo!* search links him to a site called IMDB that describes the movies as, *'hour-long second features written by uncredited Patriotic Studio scriptwriters based on the mystery-adventure books by British writer Cameron Mortimer'*.

A further search on *Cameron Mortimer* links Jay to a specialist bookseller site that has a stock of the out-of-print books. It has a pen-portrait of the author that ends with the comment that Cameron Mortimer *'followed a number of leading lights of the English arts movement based in America by "coming out" as a homosexual. W H Auden mentions in his autobiography having had an unsatisfactory short liaison with Mortimer in 1941 when they were collaborating on a theatrical production that was never staged. Mortimer died in 1986.'*

Using *Yahoo!* Jay finds the new Internet-based bookshop called *Amazon* that allows him to search for specific books. The autobiography of WH Auden isn't easy to locate because he doesn't know its exact title but he succeeds eventually. The blurb describes how the book relates Auden's relationship with Christopher Isherwood and their time in Germany. It costs $14.99 and Jay wonders whether he should pay that much.

You're a multi-millionaire! You're quibbling about …

I'm quibbling about a few measly dollars when a $3 million cheque is in the post, he thinks. The Auden biography goes into his shopping basket. While he's in the site, he looks up Isherwood's book, *Christopher and His Kind*. He follows the link and it too goes in the shopping basket. For a second he ponders …

Tell me you're not thinking of putting the Auden book back. You're so busy you can't read two books? You're not able to afford both? You think Rachel wants you under her feet? Better that you sit in the den reading.

He can't believe he's hesitating and proceeds to the check-out. He picks up the Dexter Parnes again and within

143

minutes is following the spy's footsteps through a city that, day by day, is losing its conscience.

A city that I recognise …

Chapter 18

When we met that first time in the cafe near
Tiergartenufer was I concerned solely for Wolf's
welfare? Honestly? I don't recall. Perhaps I was
already thinking that if he was like me then I
could shape him; he could be everything I wanted
in a companion.

Of course Wolf's innocence was extremely
arousing and I vowed to keep my baser urges under
control during that meeting. "When I say I want
you to discover yourself, I don't mean in a
physical relationship. I mean I want to be your
friend. Do you know what I mean if I say mentor?"

He nodded.

"I can tell you what it is like being of our
kind. Help you see whether this is what you're
really made to be. Am I making sense?"

His blue eyes were wide. "You want to be my
friend."

"But only a friend - at least until you are
sure what you want." I knew saying this that the
thought of going further would be a fantasy for
me until it could be fulfilled or denied. "Is
this clear?"

"Es ist klar."

"What it means is that you can talk to me
about anything and I will help you." I looked at
my watch. "It's late. Where do you live? I think
it's about time I took you home."

Wolf told me he lived in Charlottenburg in a
square near the Rathaus and so we took the tram
all the way along Hardenbergstrasse. He explained
that his family owned a factory that made
enamelware. It had thrived when other factories
struggled because it had the sole contract to
supply the millions of bowls that were used in
soup kitchens all over Germany. His father, Herr
Koehler, was very rich. He supported the Nazi

Party and had encouraged Wolf to join. The boy was proud of already being fast-tracked for a position in one of the elite Brownshirt battalions when he would become eighteen – in 1935.

When we talked about our next meeting, Wolf suggested that he should propose to his father that he have private English lessons and that he had found a suitable teacher. The plan was ideal. I would meet this innocent but captivating boy weekly and be paid for it!

We left the tram at the Rathaus and crossed the road to Spreestrasse. The Koehler's house was in a side road on the right taking up a whole block. It was a tall, detached town house behind high, spear-topped railings. We shook hands at the gate. I watched as a butler opened the front door and ushered Wolf inside.

How long did I hold out? Longer than you would think. I was convinced of his innocence and I was not sure he was one of us. I had seen so many boys at school for whom it was 'just a phase' and I wondered whether this was true for Wolf. The season for Rosa's Bridge activity passed as we went into autumn and then winter. I didn't live like a monk, of course I didn't. Every weekend I would go to the Nolli for sexual release but it was becoming more seedy with every exchange of money for sex.

Wolf and I met every week and we explored, in English to fulfil my duty to Herr Koehler, what it meant to be homosexual. I became more and more convinced that Wolf was right in his conviction. At the end of every meeting we would hug and kiss on the cheeks in a chaste way and I would send him home. I'm not embarrassed to say that his presence in the room was overpoweringly erotic and as soon as he left I would have to take myself in hand to relieve the pressure.

At Christmas, we exchanged presents. It was also Wolf's sixteenth birthday on Boxing Day. Was he being ironic when he gave me a copy of Mein

Kampf? Given his convictions, I couldn't be sure.
I bought him a ring for his little finger. He
preferred to wear it round his neck on a thin
gold chain. We lingered over our hug that day and
I found myself patting his bottom in a mock
chastisement for his present. I realised
immediately that I had overstepped the mark and
apologised. Wolf merely smiled. He had long since
stopped blushing in my presence no matter what we
discussed.

The meetings continued weekly and by now had
taken the format of my other lessons. We no
longer needed to talk about sex. We discussed the
news of the day – and this meant that I was able
to keep track of the rise of Hitler which
culminated in his accession to the post of
Chancellor on January 30, 1933. Wolf telephoned
me that day bursting with pride and enthusiasm at
the news. "There is going to be a huge torchlight
parade tonight. At the Brandenburg Tor. You must
come. I will be marching. I have the honour to
carry our banner. Tell me you'll be there,
Cammie!"

Leo and I took an unusually crowded overhead
train from Zoo station to Lehrter Bahnhof. From
there it was only a short walk across the Moltke
Bridge before we found ourselves on the edge of a
massive crowd milling around the Victory Tower in
the Platz der Republik. The way south to Unter
den Linden was blocked by the crowds of seething
Berliners all in festive mood. Something had been
released with Hitler's victory. It was as if a
new spirit was passing from person to person like
a bug. People would break into applause through
sheer exuberance and the sound of clapping would
sweep across the crowd in waves.

There were policemen in evidence but it was
strange for us not to see another uniform. Leo
leant in to speak to me. "Where are all the
Brownshirts? You'd expect them to be strutting
about as if they owned the place." It was true.
Other than the police, there was not a uniform to
be seen. This was so strange in a Berlin that had

become accustomed to showing deference when a gang of Brownshirt thugs hove into view.

"This is hopeless," said Leo. If we want to see anything we have to get into Pariser Platz. Follow me."

It had been dark for some hours. We hadn't expected anything like this number of people. Wolf told me that the march was to be a spontaneous show of support for Herr Hitler. How had this number of people come to know about it?

I followed Leo as he backtracked to the riverbank where we turned right and followed it eastwards until we came to a narrow street where we turned right again, this time between office buildings. The crowd was thinner here and it was easy to hurry through to the north side of Unter den Linden. The Brandenburg Gate was on our right.

Leo put his mouth to my ear again, speaking in German. "I suggest we keep our comments to ourselves and no English - you don't know who you might be standing next to."

I looked at the people to either side of me. With their winter coats and headgear they looked no different from the ordinary Berliners we saw every day, but I took Leo's point. This was no time for British cynicism about the enthusiasm that was building all around us.

The first notes of a military band sounded far off to our left. The parade must have collected at the eastern end of Unter den Linden and the intention was clearly for a triumphal march through the Brandenburg Gate before sweeping right and towards the Reichstag. This was the route that the police were trying to clear.

The band was joined by the deep booming voices of hundreds of men singing. I recognised the Horst Wessel song, an anthemic tribute to an early Nazi martyr. Despite myself, I could feel the hairs on the back of my neck tingling. As we stood on tip-toes trying to make out how far the march still had to travel I could make out a glow

in the distance. The word 'Torchen' was passed
among us by way of explanation.

It came louder and louder still. The crowd
stiffened to attention as one - not only to
stretch for a better view - but also in a
militaristic response to the approaching army.
Men removed their hats. Leo and I looked at each
other. I took off my hat and Leo stuffed his
artisan's beret into his pocket. He gave me a
look with a shake of his head which I interpreted
to mean 'don't do anything to draw attention'.

The band came first, each player accompanied
by a lantern carrier. Then the first of the
Brownshirts appeared carrying flaming torches and
their voices swelled as they repeated the verses
of the Horst Wessel over and over. My, how they
strutted. They goose-stepped as if their lives
depended on it; this was their victory as much as
Hitler's. They were now lords and masters of all
around them.

Chapter 19

It's raining and, as on every Sunday morning, Jay's been playing in the pick-up soccer game. After a short session of hand shaking under the shelter, the players all agree to be at the same place at the same time next week. Jay sets off across the pitch towards the break in the trees that leads to the Halprin's backyard. Through the steady drizzle he can make out a tall figure shrouded in a drover's coat and baseball cap waiting on the far touchline. Jay recognises Howard Edler; he has the family Labrador on a leash at his side. They appear to be standing in Jay's path.

'Howard! Not a good day for hanging around.' Jay wears a waterproof top over his wet T-shirt but hasn't covered his legs. His thighs have broken out in goose-pimples.

'Or for soccer.'

'It's always like this back in the UK.'

They shake hands. 'You're used to it then,' Howard says.

'Yes. Did you want to ask me something?'

'I hoped I'd catch you, yes.'

'Do you want to come into the house?' He looks round. 'Out of this rain.'

Howard shakes his head and drips from the peak of his cap spin away. The dog bares its teeth and snaps at the drops as they fall past its head. 'No. This won't take long. It's about Ben.'

This can't be good. Jay involuntarily pictures Howard's daughter Leah. She has her mother's dark colouring and looks older than her 12 years. If he was Ben ... 'What about him?'

'Did you know there's some discomfort about his role in the school production?'

'*Cabaret*?'

'Yes.'

'He has mentioned it but we didn't take it seriously.'

Howard nods eagerly and the dog whines because it's too slow to pick off the falling raindrops. 'And you're right not to. We at Bar Shalom aren't concerned at all. But we understand the more conservative elements at Beth El are reacting badly.'

'Beth El?'

'It's the orthodox synagogue in Burford Station – our more conservative brothers and sisters.'

'What's the problem?' Jay worries that he's sounding aggressive but he's cold and wet. Howard merely shrugs and the water-drops from his coat set the dog dancing again. Jay guides Howard and the dog to the shelter of one of the conifers that separate the park from the Cochrane's back yard.

'They don't seem to understand the nature of the show, the meaning of the song,' Howard says.

'So they don't object to the whole show?'

'I don't think they can. It's written by Jews, after all. No it's more because the part of the Nazi Youth member – the one who sings the song – has been taken by a Jewish boy.'

'But that's nonsense. If I'd asked to join the other synagogue, they probably wouldn't recognise us as Jewish.'

'But you *are* Jews.'

Jay wipes a hand across his forehead, wiping away the raindrops threatening to fall across his eyes. He finishes by squeezing his nose as if he's wringing out his face. 'Why are you telling me this if it's not a problem for Bar Shalom?'

'I wanted you to know that we're on your side. Rabbi Zwyck saw me yesterday and asked me to make this point to you as soon as I had an opportunity.'

Jay senses there's more. 'And?'

Howard's face crumples into a wince. 'And to let you know that Rabbi Stern of Temple Beth El has started a petition

151

and they'll be taking it to Jefferson High. He'll probably see Mr Costidy.'

'The director of the show? To achieve what?'

'Presumably to ask him to cast another boy in the Hitler Youth role – a gentile boy.'

'I don't believe it. Are they serious? This rabbi …'

'…Stern. I'm afraid he is.'

Jay looks across the soccer field. The rain is easing and the grass gleams in weak sunshine. The roof of the shelter is steaming. He turns back.

'Look,' Howard says, 'you must be cold. You should get inside. I just wanted you to know as soon as I could and I knew about the soccer game.'

Jay offers his hand. 'Yes. Thanks for coming.' He turns away and cuts across the back garden of the Cochrane property. He's anxious to have a hot bath. He needs to think.

His first concern is what Rachel is going to make of it. He enters the house through the back door and into the warmth of the den. He decides to wait until dinner to find out.

Although Jay would prefer to move the focus of their weekly meal routine to Friday evening, Rachel maintains that a winter Sunday demands a roast dinner and so they're sitting at the dining table in a formal setting. A steaming dish of carrots, broccoli and peas is at its centre. Jay has finished carving the chicken and slides portions of meat onto each plate.

'Just white for me,' Ben says.

'No, you have both.' Jay picks some of the paler dark meat and flips it onto Ben's plate. 'How did the rehearsal go?'

Ben, who was out of the house for most of the afternoon, says, 'Not too bad?'

'How's your solo coming along?' Jay ignores Rachel's warning frown from across the table.

'All right.' Ben uses his fork to select a raggy-edged sliver of the brown meat and isolates it on the side of his plate.

'Have you heard any more about some people in the town being unhappy about it?'

'Yeah.'

Jay can see that his son is pretending to be untroubled.

'They're still complaining apparently,' Ben says. 'But it's not bothering Mr Costidy?'

'Good.' Jay is seeking a way he can encourage his son without alienating him.

'You just ignore them, Ben. They're ignorant.' Rachel says.

'I suppose if I'm Jewish …?'

'You are.' Rachel brandishes her knife like a fencing sword and it wavers between her son and her husband. 'It sounds wrong to say "admit it" but we have to admit it – we're Jewish.'

It's not about being Jewish. It's about Rabbi Stern and his prejudices.

'It's not about being Jewish or not being Jewish!' Jay blurts out. His wife and son look up from their plates. 'What I mean is that you being Jewish or not *should* be irrelevant.' He turns to Rachel. 'I was talking with Howard Edler after soccer today. He kept me talking in the rain.'

Rachel is nodding encouragingly, hurrying him along.

'He said that it's the rabbi of the other synagogue – the orthodox one – he's causing the stink about Ben doing the Nazi song because Ben's a Jew.'

'But we're not proper Jews. We don't do the religion thing – not unless you decide to keep going, and when do they officially make you Jewish – a Jew?' Rachel says.

Ben leans forward. 'I'm Jewish enough for the Nazis to have put me in a camp sixty years ago.'

The boy talks sense.

153

'He's got that right,' Jay says.

Rachel is serving herself more vegetables. 'But the other rabbi – the orthodox one …'

'His name's Stern,' Jay says.

'OK. This Rabbi Stern, he doesn't think Ben's Jewish enough to join his church.'

'To be fair, we don't know that. He'd want more proof than Elayna Zwyck asked for, that's for sure,' Jay says.

'So what's the point of the protest?' Rachel strikes the handle of her knife down on the table top. 'Sorry. But is it about the swastika or about Ben being Jewish? If it's the flag the whole thing has nothing to do with Ben. If it's about Ben … if Rabbi Stern doesn't think Ben is Jewish why's he making a fuss?'

'I think everybody accepts that Ben is a Jew and I think that's Stern's main problem. He sees it as Jew plus swastika – a toxic mix.' He turns to his son. 'More to the point, Ben, is how does all this fuss make *you* feel?'

All the brown meat Jay had selected for his son now forms a gravy-fringed ghetto of left-overs walled-in by Ben's knife and fork. 'You have to see how the song works in the play? The first time it's quite innocent – like a country ballad? It's only when they put it in the new context of it being sung to threaten the old Jewish couple at the party that it's sinister. It shows that context is everything? That's what Mr Costidy says anyway. It's the strongest piece of theatre in the show and I want to be part of it.' His face is flushed and his eyes are moist.

Jay leans across and puts a hand on his arm. 'Good on you, son,' he says.

'So, now what?' Rachel asks.

'Perhaps I have to go and see Mr Costidy to make sure he doesn't bow under pressure from Rabbi Stern and his people,' Jay says.

Which is exactly what you should do, actually.

The Jefferson High School campus sits alongside Route 22. Jay's holding to the 15 mph speed limit along a driveway that could have been built in a straight line uphill to the visitors' parking lot but it's deliberately kinked to pass alongside the running track and the separate arenas for American football, soccer and field-hockey that have been cut into the slope.

Jay recalls that the school also boasts indoor basketball and swimming halls with banked seats for spectators. He wonders whether it's a good idea to hurry Ben away from all this and back to the claustrophobia-inducing rooms of his previous school in England.

With your money he could go private.

He wonders whether he could muster enough arguments to persuade Rachel that they can afford a public school but decides that he should concentrate on the matter in hand. When he phoned Mr Costidy earlier in the day it was as if the teacher had been waiting for the call. 'Yes, Mr Halprin, it would be good to talk. Can you come in today – at 11.00?'

Pedestrian students, scantily dressed, considering the temperature, and with their breath clouding in the air, bustle along the walkway between the main entrances of the three buildings. They scurry like insects satisfying some unknown greater need. When one group bumps into another they exchange scents with brief touches, hand to arm. Females, the more socially secure gender of this species, hug and sometimes touch cheek to cheek. This cements their places in the hierarchy. They bustle on, each individual confident in his or her own purpose. Jay compares this with the slovenly foot-dragging of Ben and his contemporaries in the English school.

He parks in one of the visitor bays in front of the Arts Building and enters through glazed double doors into a reception atrium that, if you took away the milling students, would have graced the foyer of a Manhattan office building.

155

I know this is wicked of me – but I'm reminded of the World Trade – sorry the ex-World Trade Center. If I had a wrist I would slap it hard.

Jay registers with a receptionist. She has spectacles that cling to the end of her thin-tipped nose held in place by a chord round the back of her neck stretched as taut as the hawser on a suspension bridge. She asks Jay to wait, indicating a row of chairs.

Mr Costidy appears after only a few minutes. His arrival coincides with a bell sounding and the reception area empties of students. 'Mr Halprin?' Costidy nods towards the wall-clock. 'That's the five-minute bell for the next session. I have a free. Thanks for coming.'

'Thanks for agreeing to see me.'

Costidy clasps his hands in front of his chest and squeezes his shoulders together and upwards. 'We *have* to talk about Ben and the show, right.' He tugs at the sleeves of the expensive-looking, pale-pink sweater that's draped over his shoulders. 'Have you seen our theatre? It's empty. Let's go there. Call me Mark, by the way'. He hurries through one of the internal glazed doors and leads Jay with quick, tiny steps along a corridor. The windows on their left look out over the playing fields. It's a bright day but, in the distance, where the traffic pulls up at the crossroads, the exhausts billow white clouds. The marked-out soccer pitch is stubbled with iced ridges of turf.

There are teaching rooms to the right and when they reach the end of the corridor it opens up into a large space with two sets of doors. These are set in the wall which Jay, guided by his internal navigation system, imagines to be the end of the building. Mark opens the nearer door and ushers Jay into the back of an auditorium that falls away in rows of tiered seats down to the proscenium of a stage that juts out beneath closed curtains. Jay whistles. 'It's a proper theatre.'

156

Mark smiles. 'Not what you'd expected, I imagine. I was in the UK for an exchange in my early teacher training. This must seem very different if your only experience is a school assembly hall.' He points to the end seats in a row a few steps down to indicate where to sit.

'This is where you're staging *Cabaret*?' Jay examines the stage area as he lowers himself into the cinema-style seat. There must be room for five hundred, he thinks. A picture of Ben, alone on the bright-lit stage in front of a darkened auditorium, flashes in front of him. Would it be better for his son to not take part rather than to fail?

Mark tugs at the sleeves of the sweater and half-turns to face him. 'Your son is very good, you know ...' he tails off with an upward inflection.

'Jay – call me Jay.'

'We want him to have a significant role in the production.'

'What makes me think there's a "but" coming?'

Mark smiles 'But there has been this unpleasantness and we have to be sensitive–'

'I hope you're not going to give in.'

Mark stiffens. 'It's not a matter of "giving in" as you put it.' He turns the wrist of his right hand so he can examine his nails and sighs. 'Rabbi Stern is an influential man. He's on the Board of Trustees. Many of the parents are in his congregation.'

'More are not.'

Mark nods. 'That's true.'

Jay leans forward, his elbows on his knees. He doesn't look at the teacher but speaks in the direction of the stage. 'There are so many reasons why you shouldn't give in to the protest. Not least is freedom of speech–'

'I'm way ahead of you on this one, Jay. The First Amendment also enshrines religious tolerance and the synagogue seems to be going against this as well.'

157

'Does the rabbi know that Kander and Ebb are both Jewish?'

'I don't think it's the musical per se that the rabbi is against.'

'What is it?'

'A Jewish student wearing the swastika?'

'You know what's laughable here? You know what's making me angry? Ben isn't Jewish enough to be welcomed into Rabbi Stern's temple. But he's Jewish enough for all this fuss to be made.'

'We shouldn't demean the rabbi's position on this. His is an honestly held view. He would like us to cast another boy, a gentile, as the Hitler Youth singer.'

Jay bangs his hands against the back of the seat in front of him. 'You can't do it. Ben has set his heart on the role. The school has to stand firm. You mustn't allow yourself to be intimidated.'

'You're preaching to the choir here, Jay. I'm with you. I needed to find out how you feel about it. If the school stands up to the rabbi, we need to know you as a family are not going to back down.'

Jay draws his palms down over his face. 'We won't do that.' He sits upright. 'There is a compromise.'

'Which is?'

'That you use symbols that are fascist-style – lightning bolts, for instance – but they're not swastikas.'

Mark's jaw sets firm. 'I couldn't do it. It would compromise the integrity of my directorial vision.'

What!

Jay nods. 'Hmm. I can see it would be impossible.'

Chapter 20

How long Leo and I stood in the crowd by the Brandenburg Gate watching the Brownshirts parade I can't say. Still they came, row after row. To my right the flow swept through the Brandenburg Gate and to my left more still, voices strong. It was an overwhelming show of strength. One by one, the people around us stretched out their right arms. They were self-conscious at first but as more and more of them did it, so the arm-spasm spread like a contagion. And swept up in it, I too pushed out my hand. I could feel the flush on my face, the exhilaration of the moment as this display of manpower strutted in front of me. I felt the sex of it and I'm sure many of the women and men like me experienced it too. I glanced at Leo. His face showed no emotion. His hands were stiff at his sides.

The Brownshirts had passed at last and here came the Hitler Jugend – hundreds and hundreds of them, with each platoon divided by a gap in which a solitary leading figure carried a banner. I studied each of these individually and there he was: Wolfgang, his chest puffed out, marching at the head of his group. I nudged Leo and pointed. He nodded.

All too quickly Wolf's squadron had passed, yet more Hitler youth girls and boys marched by until, finally, the parade finished with Brownshirt officers mounted on horses. As they passed, the police cordon broke and the watchers dropped their right hands and joined the procession. It looked as if all Berlin was marching that night.

Darkness descended. I turned to Leo, careful to speak in German. "Did you see him? Did you see my Wolf?" My right shoulder was painful from having held out my extended arm for so long.

Leo shook his head and turned away.

We hardly spoke on the train back to Zoo Station. We had broken away from the crowd early - most of them had gone on, presumably, to listen to speeches at the Reichstag.

"What's troubling you, Leo?" I said.

He shook his head. "There were so many of them."

"Brownshirts? Yes, but they looked good, didn't they? Somehow, not so thuggish when you see them together like that."

He whispered even though the nearest passenger was at the other end of the carriage. "No, so many Berliners. Look, Cam, this is meant to be Germany's liberal city. This is where the communists are strongest. It's the city of Liebknecht and Luxemburg. How can there be so much support here for Hitler and his crazy gang? They're like a Music Hall turn. Did you see the hysteria? Even you were taken in."

I spluttered. "I was melting into the crowd like you said."

He snorted. "You couldn't see the look on your face. It was pure rapture. You looked like you were going to ... well, you don't want to know what you looked like."

I scratched my ear and adjusted my hat. "It was a magnificent show, though, wasn't it?"

"Hmm. That's the problem. I think things are coming to an end here for me in Berlin."

The city settled down but for only a month. The Reichstag fire at the end of February gave the Chancellor a pretext for outlawing the Communist and Social Democrat parties and this passed into law at the end of March. Leo was convinced that most of the leading communists were arrested weeks before it was legal.

All this was going on in the background. Another harsh Berlin winter was blossoming into spring and Wolf and I emerged into the streets. Our weekly 'lessons' first moved to the indoors of the cafe in Savignyplatz and, as the sun became warmer, to a table outside. There we would discuss the affairs of men airily while we both smoked my Turkish cigarettes. The only evidence of the changing political times was that the Brownshirts became even more arrogant as they strode along the pavements.

Occasionally we might see a Jewish man, one who was clearly identified by his brimmed hat and ringlets, forced to step into the gutter by a Brownshirt wielding a swagger stick but this was not a regular sight.

More regular were the collections for the Nazi Party at almost every street corner and in every bar, restaurant and cafe. It was never wise to refuse on any pretext and Berliners became accustomed to having a pocketful of change to keep the collectors happy.

It was easy to see the growing tension between the brown-uniformed SA and the sharp-edged crows of the SS. The latter, who appeared to be chosen as much for how they filled the uniform and their militaristic bearing as for their aptitude as soldiers, were generally magnificent creatures. If one came to the cafe, Wolf and I would suspend conversation and watch him strut to the table, cast an arrogant look about him as he removed his cap and gloves and sit down before crossing one extravagantly jodhpured thigh over the other. I wondered whether they had classes in deportment. The sight of this routine was usually enough to set us both drooling. These sophisticates treated the Brownshirts as their country cousins.

One of the advantages of the ascendancy of the Nazis was the colourful street scene that resulted. Every building along the Ku-damm, for instance, displayed one of the vertical pennants in black, white and red and these fluttered in the breeze of that Nazi spring.

Wolf was radiant. His father's firm was booming, having recently secured another Wehrmacht contract and his party was in the ascendant. He spoke of how he would be prepared to serve Der Fuhrer in any capacity but that, after he had served his term in an elite post in Roehm's SA, he would probably have a political role. He saw no conflict between his being of our kind and the likelihood that the Nazis would stamp out the laissez-faire attitude to 'deviancy' for which Berlin was famous.

Wolf was an enthusiastic and, as far as I could discern, leading member of his Hitler Youth squadron. If he held extreme views he kept them largely to himself, perhaps because he knew I was unlikely to be sympathetic. For instance, one Wednesday in May that year, Wolf excused himself from the lesson because there was a large demonstration he wanted to join. This turned out to be the book burning in Opernplatz off Unter den Linden. I read about it afterwards and realised that he must have taken part but we didn't talk about it.

Our relationship remained platonic even though I fantasised about taking it further. I was fixated with the notion that he was innocent of grown-up physical relations and was also conscious that, if I acted upon *my* desires, it would be an abuse of my position of trust. There was also the simple mathematical fact that he was sixteen and I was eleven years older. He could not be interested in me sexually. I knew that he enjoyed my company and looked forward to our lessons, because he told me this every week, but that was as far as it would go.

It was a Saturday in the August of that year, as I was approaching my 28th birthday, that Wolf was unwell during one of our lessons. We had been watching the people passing by at the Savignyplatz cafe when he complained of a headache. Perhaps it was the sun or the noise from one of the loudspeakers in the square. Every Platz had them, relaying one of the speeches of Hitler or Goebbels always with the same message 'Germany is awake'.

In any event I took him out of the square and we walked back to the Green House with Wolf leaning heavily on my arm and me enjoying the weight of him against me. I could feel the heft of his young body through the thin cotton of our summer jackets.

Chapter 21

On the drive back to Burford Lakes after his meeting with Mark Costidy, Jay runs through the events since the morning he missed the train. He's aware of the MC lurking at the back of his brain —- as if he's sitting in one of the rear passenger seats – monitoring his thoughts.

He's certain that he's right to defend Ben's role in the play. Somehow it has become central to the success of their time in America. If the family fails in this it means an ignominious return to the UK with nothing achieved.

$3 million?

Okay, there's the money. But it's not everything. Rachel's right, there's nothing for them here. He wants to go home – and yes it is home – with Ben's achievement ringing in the ears of their Burford neighbours.

His research into the history of *Cabaret* isn't a diversion. It's part of his support for Ben and it has led him to Cameron Mortimer – an earlier Englishman in New York. Jay's intrigued by him and senses a connection from Mortimer to Isherwood via Auden.

You have to thank the lovely Prentice for knowing about Mortimer. Prentice of the twin peaks in a twin set.

Yes, Prentice. What of her? There *is* a flirtation going on there. But if he was to go down that route …

Teri is the better option.

Teri *would* be the better option. But why would he be unfaithful?

Because you're alive and you can?

Wouldn't it be *really* living to have that sort of fling? His heart rate quickens and his palms go moist. Yes, if he was going to engineer it to happen with anybody, Teri's the one.

Hmm. Not sounding to me like a religious man, Jay.

Oh, yes. There's his Jewishness. Is this where the answer to the question 'why me' lies? All that his Jewishness has brought them is Rabbi Stern's opposition to the play and ...

And you come full circle.

Which takes him back to Ben and Rachel – the family who are in a holding pattern until they can return home. And Teri?

The thing with Teri will develop or it will not.

With Teri it's wait and see. And Rachel's right – they have to go back at Christmas.

The Holidays.

Correction – the Holidays. But can he continue flitting from one enthusiasm to the next until something concrete turns up? It feels like his life is on hold ...

Waiting.

'They need to know we're not going to back down.' Jay says. He and Rachel sit at the dining table in the afternoon after his visit to the school. They're waiting for the school bus, each with hands clasped round a mug of tea. 'If the school stands up to Stern, they don't want to be left high and dry.'

Rachel takes a sip. 'What do you think?'

'I said we'd be rock solid behind them.'

'Is it wise? Aren't we going to make enemies?'

'We already have. The good thing is we don't know anybody from that part of town.'

'And even if it does cause problems, how long do we have to live with it? We'll be gone by Christmas.'

'Hmm. Yes, the Holidays.' Jay's lack of confirmation hangs between them.

'We *are* going aren't we?'

'What if we settle here?'

'What?'

'You ought to see the facilities at the school.'

'And?'

'And – I don't know. Look at the sun shining. It's cold but it's not like the constant grey days at home … winters in the UK … the whole year … there it's like you only ever see the sun through a filthy skylight.'

'So?'

'Shouldn't we give it a year at least? We didn't see the *whole* of the summer – the bit we were here for was all sunny days, time by the pool. There'll be more of it – much more.'

Rachel looks into her mug. Her knuckles are white. 'We're not staying and that's an end to it. If we leave at Christmas Ben will have only missed one term. We can settle down again.'

Don't forget the $3million.

He leans forward and clasps her arms. 'Think about it, Rache. $3million – think what we can do here with that sort of money.'

She aims her laser-stare at him. 'I can't work.'

'You wouldn't need to – not for money. Do something voluntarily – at the school – at the library – anywhere.'

'Jay, I'd end up like one of these skeletal Burford wives. Anyway, what would *you* do if we stayed?'

He puts his palms to his forehead and drags them down across his eyes drawing down the skin of his cheeks. 'I don't know. But going back. It'll look like we're running away.'

But you decided you won't be – as long as Ben keeps the part and he's a success.

That evening, Bob Cochrane from next door invites Jay to join him for Monday night football. At a few minutes before 9pm

Jay and Katy Cochrane cross on the boundary between the front gardens as if they're characters in a Checkpoint Charlie hostage exchange. Katy carries a bottle of wine and Jay has a four-bottle pack of *Rolling Rock* straight from the refrigerator.

After closing the front door behind him, Jay stands at the top of the half-flight and looks down to where the dimmed moving light from the television appears to be the only illumination. The TV is out of sight at the end of the room but he can see part of the couch with Bob's tousle-haired blond head leaning back. He has his eyes fixed on the screen, but half-turns to throw his voice over his shoulder. 'C'mon down, buddy. Pick up a beer in the fridge.'

Jay enters the kitchen, opens the refrigerator and spies bottles of Budweiser in ranks. Is it rude to drink his own, the one he prefers? He turns and shouts. 'Bob! Can I get you one?'

'Nah! Got one on the go.'

Doing what he would have done in England, Jay takes one of his *Rolling Rock*s and puts the other three on the shelf. He steps down into the den and sees that Bob is not alone. 'Hi, Tyler,' he says.

Tyler waves a hand but his eyes stay on the television screen which is showing commercials. 'Hey, Mr Halprin. Ben not coming over to watch the game?'

'He's not really into American football.'

Both the Cochranes chuckle.

'What's up?'

'We just call it football, buddy.' Bob says. 'Tyler, you come over here so Mr Halprin can sit down.'

'Can I go to Mr Halprin's and hang out with Ben?'

'Don't you want to watch the game, buddy?'

Tyler's shoulders sag. 'Nah. Will it be okay, Mr Halprin?'

Jay nods. 'I'm sure Ben will be happy to see you. There's a TV in his room so you can watch the game there if you want.'

On the TV, a sombre flag-raising ceremony is conducted in silence. The Stars and Stripes is carried by officers from the fire service to honour their dead comrades. Jay's anticipation of the spectacle drowns under a tidal wave of despair.

The MC bows his head and wrings his white-gloved hands. *So many dead …*

The game starts and Bob watches intently but as a neutral. The teams are the Washington Redskins and the Green Bay Packers and he's a fan of the New England Patriots. He's there because it's Monday night football and every fan is in front of a screen – especially today.

'I hope Tyler watches the game at yours.' Bob swigs from his can. 'It's important to show solidarity – the first Monday football after 9/11 and all.'

The words 9/11, so often on everyone's lips, twist in Jay's gut.

'I like it that Prime Minister Tony Blair is standing shoulder to shoulder with Bush. Okay, Bush is a blowhard but he's the only President we've got. It's good to know you're on our side, buddy.'

They watch a play in silence and when it finishes Bob takes a slug of beer his eyes fixed on the screen. 'Gather your Ben has a big part in the school show.'

'Not one of the leading roles – but he's in it, yes.'

'Been a bit of trouble with the synagogue up by Burford Station.'

'Yes, Rabbi Stern has taken against the idea of Ben wearing Nazi regalia.'

'Because he's Jewish?'

'Yes.'

The action restarts but Bob speaks over the commentary. 'Think the people of Burford Lakes are happy to go along with what's decided by the school. It's not for the church – any church – to interfere.'

'Has it been discussed in your church – which is it?'

'Presbyterian – on the green.' He waves the beer can. 'Not as such. But most folks round here think that Jefferson High is doing a good job. We leave it to them.'

'So you won't be marching with Rabbi Stern?' Jay inflects his words with an irony that his English friends would have picked up.

'Hell no!' There's a commercial break and he stands. ''Nother one o' them beers?'

'Thank you.'

With one foot on the first riser of the half-stairway, Bob stops and, looking up towards the kitchen, says, 'Well, neighbor, we hold by the First Amendment in this house. Katy and me – and Tyler. We're gonna stand by Rachel and you on this. I reckon most of the people round here are. Burford Lakes folks – generally we're not the marching sort and Rabbi Stern is going one step too far. We'll be shoulder to shoulder with you crossing the picket line if it comes to it.' He nods in affirmation of his pronouncement and continues up the stairs. He shouts from the kitchen, 'Yep, shoulder to shoulder just like Prime Minister Tony Blair.'

Jay is relieved to hear him rearranging the cans and bottles in the fridge because it gives him the opportunity to take a tissue from the box on the coffee table wipe his eyes and blow his nose. 'Thanks, buddy,' he says when Bob returns and hands him his second bottle of *Rolling Rock*.

It's now Jay's custom to attend Synagogue every Saturday. Rachel stays at home but Ben joins him on the basis that this duty will lead to a bar mitzvah party when they go home.

Rabbi Zwyck is not putting pressure on Jay to do any more about becoming a practising Jew than 'see how he feels'. She's invited him to attend shul and was relaxed when he declined and said he'll take it up when he returns to England.

169

On this Saturday she asks him to stay behind after the service so they may 'have a word'.

He waits in the vestibule while the rabbi stands at the door shaking hands with the members of her congregation as they leave. She turns back to face him and Jay, sensing that they will talk about *Cabaret,* suggests to Ben that he waits in the car. 'Catch!' he says, as he tosses his son the keys.

'Elayna.' They shake hands.

'Come!' she says flicking her hand up by her shoulder. She totters ahead of him and Jay wonders whether the heft of her bosom means that her feet are always trying to catch up with her centre of gravity.

It's the counter-weight of that posterior that keeps her upright.

The rabbi sidles behind the desk and topples back into the chair. Jay sees the North Tower imploding, settling on its haunches.

It never goes. Not while you can imagine such things.

She signals to the guest chair. 'Sit!' She says it without command, as if she is talking to an aging pet with arthritis. She waits until he's in the seat with his hands clasped in his lap. 'I've met Rabbi David Stern at Beth El twice now to plead Ben's case.'

Jay nods.

'As Americans we both believe in the First Amendment.' She shrugs and her head wobbles from side to side. 'Unfortunately, David believes the First Amendment supports his right to protest at what is happening – to put his case forcibly enough to persuade Mr Costidy to change the casting for the Nazi boy.'

'So no progress then.'

'I wouldn't say that. My main argument after the school's right to freedom of expression is that your boy Ben is not Jewish enough to be part of his congregation. And I tell him this does not sit well with his concern about Ben wearing the swastika.

170

Either Ben is a Jew or he's not. Stern's response is to make a distinction between Ben's Jewish ethnicity and his religious practice. I have to say, David has an annoying certainty about him. He doesn't entertain doubt as many rabbis do.'

'So it *is* Ben's Jewishness that troubles him.'

'His Jewish ethnicity, yes. '

Ethnicity – shethnicity. Ben is doing it – end of story.

'And he's not going to shift?'

'He's implacable. It's not just a bee in his bonnet about Ben wearing the swastika, it's also where it comes in the play. He's turning this into some sort of personal crusade. As I say, I've not met many rabbis like him. Generally, we're questioning – we turn to rabbinical teaching for our guidance. Rabbi Stern is a dogmatist. It's as if his life depends on each decision he's taken and he can't turn back.'

'Well we can do implacable too.'

Good one, Jay! The MC is skipping on the spot clapping his fingertips together. The red gash of his lips splits into a wide smile revealing his off-white teeth.

'If I say that Ben's doing it, whatever Rabbi Stern says, do I still have your support?'

'I've taken soundings. The elders here understand what *Cabaret* is – it has to be seen in the round. It's a condemnation of Nazism and all it stands for. At Bar Shalom we stand for tolerance. We stand behind the production and we stand behind Ben's part in it.

She's good this one. How we could have done with her in my time.

There's an uneasy truce in the Halprin household. Rachel is making preparations for the return to England. Like Rabbi Stern she sees the distinction between the family's ethnicity and its religion. She has no intention of joining Jay and Ben in the synagogue. She accepts the Friday evening obligation to sit down to a formal family meal because it gives them an opportunity to spend time together. However, she doesn't light the candles; nor will she recite the prayers. Jay cooks the meal and his recipes avoid pork and shellfish. In return Rachel expects Jay and Ben to think of their Sunday evening meal also as a *mitzvah*. Ben grudgingly accepts both. Jay hasn't mentioned the mitzvah that married couples have sex on Shabbat. He's not sure Rachel would believe it.

It's over the family meal on the Friday following the discussion with Rabbi Zwyck that Jay asks Ben for the latest news regarding *Cabaret*. He registers Rachel's tight-lipped glance but ploughs on – this is *his* meal. 'Rehearsals – how are they going?'

Ben runs his fingers through the lank of his hair that hangs over his plate. Lamb cutlets from the kosher butcher in Burford Station swim with the vegetables in an overabundance of mint sauce that gives everything a green tinge. 'It's coming together?' He transfers his fork to his left hand, picks up his knife and cuts the next mouthful of meat. 'Yeah!' He nods. 'Coming together, yeah.' He puts down his knife, transfers his fork to his right hand and starts using it like a shovel.

Jay knows that Ben's performance with the cutlery will stretch Rachel's patience. 'What about your song?'

Ben nods. 'Yeah. Going okay?' He takes another shovel of food. It will be time for a repeat of the meat-cutting soon.

'Any news of the protest?'

Ben puts down the fork. He lets out a sharp breath as if to indicate this is his final word on this subject. 'We *know* about it – course we do. But Mr C says we should ignore it? They've asked Rabbi Stern not to visit the school until it's over. He only came in for Board meetings, so I don't think it's a problem.'

'So basically, it's all going smoothly.'

'Cept for a group of seniors. They're hardliners? They go to Beth El. They've held protest pickets at rehearsal times and

172

put up posters around the place. But there's fewer than ten of those guys. I think it's cool they're doing something about it? Most of us do. Freedom of expression and all that?' He makes to pick up his fork and Jay catches his eye, signalling with the cutlery in each of his own hands. Ben sighs and picks up both implements.

They all resume the meal and Jay asks, 'But they're not singling you out?'

'Who?'

'The Beth El protestors.'

'No, they want to ban all the Nazi insignia and the Heil Hitler. I think I'm being picked on because when my song comes it's the end of the first half of the show? Everybody will be applauding for that but the swastikas appear at the same time? So it's like they're applauding the Nazis – me.'

'So you're not taking it personally – you'll stick at it?'

'Yeah. Why not?'

'Exactly. What doesn't kill you makes you stronger.' He looks up at Rachel hoping for a sign of approval but her expression is blank.

Jay has finished Isherwood's *Christopher and his Kind* and is fascinated by the milieu. This is not driven by a prurient interest in the lives of the gays – although he's finding their rampant lustiness attractive – but something connected to the personality of the city itself which Isherwood makes more alive in the memoir than he had in the earlier Berlin novels. Now that he's a *multi-millionaire,* Jay luxuriates in the idea that he and Rachel will travel first-class by train to the city, arriving at Zoo station as Isherwood had done before.

The W H Auden biography had been less illuminating. It deals with the poet's time with Isherwood in Berlin only tangentially and gives the impression that Auden felt he had been thrown off like a worn-out coat. However, Auden did

173

confirm the existence of Cameron Mortimer and admitted a brief affair in 1942.

Jay accepts that any visit to Berlin will have to wait until their return to Europe so he puts it on the back burner. Of more immediate interest, in the acknowledgements of the Dexter Parnes mystery, the author thanks Meta Güttchen and Leo Plomer, 'the friends I made in Berlin.'

Real people from my time there. What else will you find?

Jay decides to learn more about the Burford Lakes author.

Chapter 22

Wolf had suffered a bad headache when we were in
Savignyplatz and now he was in my room. I gave
him a drink of water and Frau Guttchen fussed in
and out with remedies, pulling the shutters to on
the eccentric windows and generally making a
fuss. Finally I had to ask her to leave us alone
so the poor boy could settle.

"This is so much painful for me, Cammie."

I dabbed at his forehead with the damp cloth
Frau Guttchen had left behind. "I'm sorry, dear
boy. As soon as you feel up to it I'll see you
home."

"This is what I am talking about. I must not
stay here. I must to be at home."

"Why? Whatever is wrong?"

My parents have already left for our
holiday house on Ruegen Island. I am meant to
join them tomorrow. I haven't even packaged my
clothings yet."

"It's not midday, Wolf. You have time."

"When I have one of the headaches I must to
lie down for hours. I am on my own in the house.
The staffs went first to open up the house in
Lauterbach. I have to do it at my own person." He
looked up at me his blue-eyes flooded with tears,
his bottom lip quivering.

I knelt alongside the chaise-long and
gathered him into a hug. "You don't have to be on
your own. Let me help you, Wolf. I can see you
home and help you pack. If you are well enough we
can have supper in Charlottenburg and you'll be
ready to leave for your holiday in the morning.
Does that sound good?"

Wolf gripped my hand in his and held it to
his chest. "Would you? Would you, Cammie? Would
you do this thing for me? You are so good for
me."

He seemed to brighten up immediately and threw off the blanket Frau Guttchen had placed over his legs. "Then let us go there, to my home, now."

We sat side by side on the tram and I was aware of the pressure of his thigh against mine. It was as if Wolf was teasing me. We chatted in English about the scene as we passed along the centre of Hardenbergstrasse with Wolf pointing out the university buildings where his father had hoped he would be studying before they opted for him to have a military career.

"What made him change his mind?" I said.

"My father joined in the Nazi Party in 1929. It was not in those years a national organisation. My father had paid large monies in as gifts."

"It looks as if he backed the right horse."

"Excuse me?"

"He chose to support the right group."

"Well, yes. He is sure that the Fuhrer is the right man to lead Germany out of troubles. He sees my future in the party leadership at some time and says I must serve my time in the front-line of action, in the politics on the streets. This is why I will join the SA. Then, when it is right, I will leave and work directly in the party."

"Will you miss not going to University?" I had to speak over the screeching of the tram as it crossed points turning left onto Berlinerstrasse.

"The future of Germany is not in the hands of the intelligentials. The future of Germany is from the strength of the people." He lowered his voice even though I doubted whether the other passengers would understand him. "The country was made weak by a conspiracy of Jews and intelligentials," he laughed, "and intelligent Jews. We must not let this happen again."

We left the tram at the Charlottenburg Rathaus and crossed to Spreestrasse. We slowed after a few yards. Ahead of us a gang of

Brownshirts was loitering at the end of one of the roads on the right tapping their thighs with wooden clubs. We crossed to the left hand side and walked on keeping abreast, not touching, our eyes fixed ahead. As we drew alongside the Brownshirts I glanced down the opening. Another group was at the far end of the short street effectively sealing it off.

"Gruenstrasse synagogue." Wolf was whispering out of the side of his mouth. "The Jews have to show their papers if they attend. Many in this area have already fled. Our house, my father bought a few years ago very cheaply from fleeing Jews. It is good for all Germany that they are leaving."

We turned into Kanalstrasse and there was the Koehler's imposing house. I was excited by the knowledge that it was empty – that when we went inside this mansion we would be alone. I couldn't remember when we had been truly alone. Even when I was giving Wolf lessons in my room, Frau Guttchen threatened to bustle in at any time.

Wolf unlocked the door and held it open for me. I stopped in the hall. It was on two floors and a stairway extended up ahead of us to a landing which went round on three sides. The colours were all muted creams and beiges with plasterwork frills like icing punctuating the cornices and door arches. There was an electric chandelier.

"Are you sure everybody has left?" I said and my voice echoed as if to make the question redundant.

"The staffs went early in the week and my parents left yesterday. I stayed on the extra day because of my lesson with you, Cammie."

"You could have cancelled."

"I did not want to. But since last year I have been going to Lauterbach on my own. Come! My room is upstairs." He took my hand.

"Are you sure?"

177

"Yes, Cammie." He touched his brow. "My head
- I need your help."

"So it is still hurting you?"

He spun round like a dancer and then ran up
the stairway. He turned back at the top. "No,
Cammie. Look at me! I am completely better now we
are in my home. Come on!"

I followed him to the landing and he led me
to a room on the right. He opened the door. He
had a double-sized bed with a thick chintz cover.
Theatrical buttoned cushions rested against the
headboard. There was a bow-fronted mahogany
wardrobe and a matching chest of drawers. It was
a young squire's room in a country house. The
only incongruous item in the room was a small
leather valise on a folding stand by the dressing
table.

He opened the lid. It was almost full. "Ah!
Koelisch has done the packaging for me. I only
have to put in a few of my personal items."

"But you were worried about your packing.
Where is everything?"

"Of course, it has gone already in a ... big
box?"

"A trunk - a steamer trunk." I said it
absent-mindedly. What was this all about? Today,
I was seeing a side of Wolf that I did not find
attractive. The easy way he talked about the
eviction of Jews and their treatment at the
synagogue. The milord act he was putting on for
me in this nouveau riche mansion.

Wolf stood by one of the two windows in the
far wall. "Come and look, Cammie."

I joined him and he linked my arm with his.
This was evidently the back of the house. There
was a small courtyard and beyond it a single
floored stable-block which, I assumed, had been
converted to take a motor car. Over the tiled
roof of the low building we could see into
Gruenstrasse. The synagogue was facing us with
its Star of David in plasterwork around a
circular window. The double doors were shut and

the words: 'Juden Rauf' had been daubed across them with white paint.

I shook my head wondering what to say when Wolf turned in towards me and, at the same time, pulled a chord that released the drapes so they fell across the window. He pulled me to him and kissed me on the lips. Before I knew what was happening his tongue was in my mouth and his hands were up behind my head forcing our faces together.

He released me partly but our mouths were still together and he was sucking on my tongue. It seemed as if he was trying to tear it out by the root. There was no mistaking his intention as he steered me stumbling towards the bed.

Despite this and the level of arousal initiated by those few seconds of contact I was still unsure. I pulled away as Wolf flopped back onto the bed so that I was standing while he was sitting in front of me. "Stop!" I said.

He pressed the palm of his hand against my trouser front. I slapped it away. "Stop!"

"But, Cammie." His face was flushed and there was sweat on the fuzz of his infant moustache. "I want you. Do you see it yet?"

I couldn't bear to look at him and put my hands to my face. "You're so young. I can't be the right person to do this."

"What does this mean, do this?"

"Do this. Have sex. Be your first. It should be someone—"

He was sniggering.

"Why are you laughing? You are young - inexperienced. You should be certain."

"I *am* certain, Cammie. One of the reasons I'm certain is because I have been with the other men. You are not the first. It was my first when I was fifteen. What do you think we are all doing on Hitler Youth camps - all the boys together? I want it this time with you." He looked down at his hands which were clasped in his lap. "I love you."

I knelt down in front of him and took his hands. There was a bubble of emotion building in my chest. "I love you too, Wolf. And I will always care for you." I pushed back the lock of hair that had fallen across his forehead and, tentatively at first, I put my lips against his.

Chapter 23

As autumn is turning into winter, the days shorten but most of them remain bright. The wind is cold and cutting and Jay has to wear his overcoat and scarf for his walk to the library. Falling leaves swirl about him. Cars whip past and when an outsize SUV booms by it shoulders the air aside with enough force to make him cower by the ditch.

The library beckons from across the green with welcoming golden windows while its white clapboard sides are grey in the afternoon light. Inside, a cushion of warm air embraces him and he loosens his coat buttons. He welcomes the familiar sight of Prentice behind the reception desk. On his way to her he passes a side table displaying a copy of the October *Burford Buzz*. His spine tingles and he vows to take a detour to the grocery store to see if he can buy one there.

'Why, Jay. I haven't seen you in a while.'

He smiles and takes in yet another twin-set – this one is moss green. He tries to deconstruct the superstructure beneath her breasts as if he's capable of discerning their texture through the cashmere, their ability to withstand gravity.

No, Jay. You've already decided. She's not the one.

He nods his agreement but this doesn't stop him scanning the mossy tussocks again.

Prentice waits for him to speak. She's used to men not being capable of eye-to-eye contact.

'Look at you,' he says. 'You're working every time I come here.'

'I must be lucky I guess.'

'Don't you ever take a break?'

She cocks her head to one side causing her hair to go off-kilter like a balance with unequal weights. 'Of course.' Her eyes are wide; she smiles, inviting the obvious next question.

Stop! We agreed the risk is too great.

Reluctantly, Jay adopts a more businesslike tone. 'I've brought this back.' He holds up the *Dexter Parnes VC* book.

She nods and turns to one side, fingering a display of leaflets. 'Did you enjoy it?'

'It was lightweight – not my usual fare.'

She turns back, smiling and showing off expensive teeth. 'Oh, Jay, you have such a lovely accent.' She tries it out, 'maou usuwal ferre', and puts a hand up to hide her giggle.

His face is already hot from the heat in the room; now it's the colour of an English Grenadier's coat. 'The book?'

She wriggles herself upright and smooths her skirt over her thigh. She takes the book from him and passes it over the reader. 'Just in time. Nothing to pay. Is there anything else I can help you with today?'

'Not unless you can show me anything *about* Cameron Mortimer rather than *by* him.'

She looks as if she has to tell him that his pet dog has died. 'No, I'm sorry.' She perks up. 'I've remembered!' She points a finger to the ceiling. 'I *did* put something by that I thought would interest you.' She dips, retrieves a book from under the counter-top and holds it up.

Jay reads the title aloud, '*The British Are Coming*'.

'Something about it made me think you'd be interested,' she says. 'Let me see.' She flips it over and looks at the back. 'Yes, here it is: *an account of the pre- and post-second world war invasion of Hollywood by English writers including in their number: PG Wodehouse, Aldous* – am I saying that right? – *Aldous Huxley*,' she pauses for emphasis, '*Christopher Isherwood*,' her voice tails off for the rest of the list, '*JB Priestley, Noel Coward, Elinor Glyn,*

WH Auden, Edgar Wallace, Hugh Walpole ...' She turns it over to show the front cover and hands it across.

'If it mentions Isherwood, it's got to be worth a look. Thanks, Prentice. It was very thoughtful. I'll take it.'

She's blushing. 'I'm pleased.'

There's a moment when they're both holding the book at the same time. Eventually, Jay lets go so that Prentice can pass it over the reader. When the book's in his hands again, he starts buttoning his coat and makes for the door. He knows she's sweet for him at least a little bit, but he'd never get away with it.

And you have better fish to fry.

Burford Buzz – 11 October 2001

Melissa Rosenberg interviews the Rabbis who have disagreed over the Jefferson High production of *Cabaret*

You would have to be a hermit living in a hole in the ground to be ignorant of the spat that's dividing the men and women of Jewish faith in our fair boro. It all started when Mark Costidy, head of Theatre Studies at Jefferson High, decided that this year's school production should be the Kander & Ebb musical *Cabaret*. The two rabbis have taken up opposing positions regarding the casting of a key part in the production so I invited them both to explain their views.

I asked Rabbi Stern from Burford Station's Beth El (translated 'House of God') to state his objection.

'Let me start by saying we have nothing against the production per se but I've always been uncomfortable with the final scene in the first act. This is where the woman sings *Tomorrow Belongs To Me*. It troubles me – the audience reaction to this song. When I discovered that Mr Costidy had cast a Jewish boy in this part, it made me even more worried because it's trying more to emulate the mood of the film.'

I turned to Rabbi Elena Zwyck of Bar Shalom (translated Son of Peace) and she smiled. 'David appears to be conflating two separate things: his concern about the mood of the piece and the casting of a Jewish boy in the role of the singer. The piece has always been ironical. We see the song from the present – with our current knowledge. We understand it's an example of misguided nationalism. It doesn't matter whether the singer is Jewish or not.'

Rabbi Stern leans forward aggressively. 'Rabbi Zwyck may, with all sophistication, say that the song is ironic. But she should know that it's been taken up by neo-Nazi organisations throughout the world. It's not ironic to them.'

I asked Elayna to respond.

'It *is* regrettable,' she says calmly, 'that these despicable people have adopted the song but this shouldn't mean that we censor the production.'

Rabbi Stern reacted angrily to the accusation of censorship. 'I'm not asking for the song to be cut. I'm asking for the part to be re-cast. It's wrong for a Jewish boy to sing this song that's so open to misinterpretation and which is greeted so positively by audiences because it's the end of the first act. It's wrong for a Jewish boy to be one of only a few cast members to wear the despised Hakenkreuz – the swastika.'

What did Elayna have to say to this?

'The boy in question is ethnically Jewish but he hasn't been brought up in the religion. So I'm not sure David's outrage stands scrutiny.'

Rabbi Stern is resigned in his response. 'Ethnicity is everything here. Was it not for ethnicity that 6 million Jews were sent to death camps? Is it not for our ethnicity that we have our own Zionist principles? Is it not for our ethnicity that we founded the only democracy in the Middle East and defend it against the hordes who would have it destroyed?'

I remind the rabbi of the topic and Elayna's calm voice intervenes to close the discussion. 'One of the greatest blessings of being an American is that we all believe in free speech. I believe in Mark Costidy's right to put on the production in the way he sees fit. But I also believe in Rabbi Stern's right to make his case against the way it's cast.'

With that I closed the meeting and the two rabbis shook hands. Rabbi Stern left for a pressing engagement and it was so nice that Elayna was able to stay behind for more tea and a relaxed discussion about all the positives we enjoy by living in the fair town of Burford Lakes.

The grocery store has a *Bedford Buzz* counter display and Jay reads the article while he walks along the road's verge. Rabbi Hiller's views trouble him and he wonders whether he wants to be part of a religion that tolerates such a hard line. But he's struggling to focus. His encounter with Prentice has put the idea of extra-marital sex forefront in his mind. For the last few hundred yards, with the *Buzz* stowed in his pocket, Jay's thinking about his weekly one-to-one meetings in the eerie, empty office with Teri Herbold. Her frostiness at the outset has thawed. She still wears the tailored jackets but leaves them unbuttoned. Softer blouses with lower necklines have replaced the collared, white shirt she wore for their first meeting.

Should he make a move? The idea of adultery doesn't carry the anguish that Rachel would expect or hope for. This has always been in his character – the part that allows him to be flipped from point to point like a pinball. If Teri makes the move, so what? He's alive. It would be an adventure, an exciting experience ...

A life-affirming experience.

... and he would find it impossible to deny himself. The only negative would be if Rachel found out.

And who's going to tell her?

He resolves that he'll stick to the business necessities during the meetings in Stamford but if Teri gives him an opening he'll make a move. If she doesn't, nothing is lost – he won't have made a fool of himself. He needs to progress the life insurance claim. Rachel has urged him to pursue it so they can have the money in the bank. Teri has told him that it's only a matter of time. He's relaxed about it but he knows that Rachel is on edge.

After each morning's work in Stamford it has become Jay and Teri's custom to go for lunch at a trattoria in the same strip mall as the office but further out of town. They could walk but Teri prefers to drive them in her Lexus. It's a two-seater with a hard, fold-down roof that stays on so that they're cocooned in an atmosphere clouded by Teri's Issey Miyake perfume. Drawing Jay's eyes like a magnet, Teri's skirt rides up, as her right foot works the pedals. If she wasn't looking ahead she would see his gaze mark every millimetre shift as it exposes more nylon-sheathed leg. In the minute or so of loaded silence, the exposure is no more than when Teri sits in the office. But this is not the point. The effect is such that he has to cross his forearms on his lap.

At the lunch in the week Jay picked up *The British Are Coming* he and Teri discuss the inrush of clients volunteering to pay for work that will never be done. 'SDC's plight has elicited a lot of sympathy,' she says.

Jay admires her use of the word 'elicited' – he always falls for a woman with an expansive vocabulary and well-formed bosoms.

She's ripe like the apple on the tree. But leave it to her. Wait to see if she makes the time and the opportunity.

'We were good at what we – Straub DuCheyne – did, weren't we?'

'Surely.' She breaks off to study the menu. 'I think I'll take the crab and avocado salad.'

This is no surprise. Every time they've lunched together, Teri has 'taken' the same salad. She'll eat the leaves and use up their calories by prodding the scraps of crab and the slices of avocado backwards and forwards across her plate.

He's working his way through the risottos and has come to 'crushed pea and lemon'. He'll try it out. 'No, I mean SDC has built up a durable brand. It's sad to let it go.'

Teri leans across the table like a Mafia don ordering a hit. But unlike a Mafia don the upper slopes of her bosoms converge and the cleavage winks at him. 'It's a strange coincidence you should say so, Jay. It's something I wanted to ask you about.' She pauses as the waiter approaches. They order their meals and each has a glass of Chardonnay. Jay would like to ask for a jug of tap-water to watch the horror it provokes but instead asks for their customary bottle of San Pellegrino.

Jay is wallowing in the intimacy of the implied conspiracy. 'That sounds mysterious,' he says, raising an eyebrow.

'The salad?' Teri says.

He's not sure whether she's joking. He sniggers just in case. 'No, the coincidence you want to talk to me about.'

'Oh yes. Do you remember Heroes of the Alamo Mutual?'

'Of course, I was negotiating with them when ...'

'Exactly. We sent them the same letter as the others. You know – sad loss of the company blah-blah and the paragraph about the partnership beneficiaries and the surviving partner – you – winding up the business.'

'And?'

'Did you send them a contract for the project?'

'Can't remember – maybe a draft?'

'Well, they would like for you to fulfil it – on your own.'

He leans back. It was a major rebranding project. He had factored in a lot of support from the team in SDC. 'It's not the sort of thing I can do alone.'

Teri put her hands flat on the table. 'They say they'll provide you with an office and administrative support from their marketing department. They're adamant – they *want* you.'

Jay contemplates what Rachel would say if he went back to Burford Lakes to tell her that, instead of returning to the UK, he'll be spending two months or more in Texas. They lean back in unison as the waiter comes to the table with their wine.

'Cheers!' Jay says as they chink glasses. He observes the way her fingers curl round the stem of the glass and his imagination runs ahead. 'No, I can't do it.'

187

'That's what I told them. But they're playing hardball. They say they sent back a signed contract on September eight and SDC is obliged to complete the work.'

'Except SDC doesn't exist ...'

'Not strictly true – not for the next few months while we wind it down.'

'They can't force us to.'

'Not in any way that I can see. But I think I shall have to go down there – to San Antonio – to smooth them out. I need to know you're comfortable with it – there'll be expenses to pay – flights, accommodation.'

'Of course. If you think it's necessary ...'

Here it comes. What did I tell you?

Teri takes a sip of wine. She lowers her eyelids and regards him over the rim of her glass. 'I think ... we should go together. They'll understand your situation better if you're there. I'll deal with the legals while you explain on a personal level. I'm sure they'll come round if we both go.'

Jay lifts his glass. He's recalling something a friend in the UK once said to him, 'As far as extra-marital activity is concerned – opportunity is everything'. 'Yeah,' he says. 'We should go. We need to get it sorted.'

Teri is sitting alongside him on the flight to San Antonio, Texas. Jay has explained everything to Rachel – the necessity of the trip to extricate Straub, DuCheyne from a difficult contract – but has omitted to tell her that Teri is going as well. It's a detail that will only cause misunderstandings.

Having been aware of the horror stories about the new security measures, Jay had arranged for them to have two hours in hand when they met at La Guardia. They were through in half that time and had spent an hour conversing while they watched the passengers collecting at each gate. Jay discovered that Teri lives with her boyfriend, Eduardo, in New Jersey and

188

that he's an attorney whose work mainly involves defending Blacks and Hispanics in the local criminal court system. He sounded like a saint.

When a full-bearded man appeared wearing an ankle-length shirt with a jacket and a white cotton cap, Jay sensed the people around them tense. The man passed them heading for another queue.

'What would you have done if he'd been on our flight,' Jay asked.

Teri shook her head. 'Taken a later one?'

'What if we all did that?'

She smiled. 'Dressing like that – it's one way of making sure you get a row to yourself.'

She's trim and fit looking, don't you think?

Jay nodded and blurted out, 'How do you keep in such good shape?'

Teri smiled – did she mean to encourage him? – and said, 'Why thank you. I work out most days in a gym near the office in Manhattan.' On one level, the one that his body responded to, Jay saw the exchange as loaded with promise. But *had* something happened between them? If she'd brushed him off with, 'it's none of your business' at least he would know.

Now they sit companionably in the stale air of economy class; they've used up their small-talk. Teri is reading *Corporate Law* magazine while Jay has his copy of *The British Are Coming* open on his lap. He's struggling to concentrate because the nerve endings in his left arm are tingling – making him aware of the contact with Teri's right arm. She isn't moving away. He's read the first paragraph of the book five times. He's reached the bottom of the page twice but hasn't retained enough information to turn over to the next one. He sighs.

Admitting defeat, he turns to the index and fingers through to the 'Ms'. There's one reference to Cameron

Mortimer and he turns to page 233 in the chapter on Auden. Here the book's author is describing the Brit's hectic love life:

It is not known for certain whether Auden and Isherwood continued the sexual side of their relationship in America. Isherwood was in a stable relationship and Auden seems to have respected it – perhaps he had no choice. He has documented some affaires de coeur in his diaries and one that interests us here is with another British writer, Cameron Mortimer. Mortimer came to America in 1935 and sold the film rights of his *Dexter Parnes VC* mystery thrillers to Patriotic Studios. Strictly speaking, Mortimer does not fall within the purview of this work because Patriotic employed its own team of US writers to turn his thrillers into hour-long B movies.

Auden and Mortimer collaborated in creating a stage play, 'The Few who Dare' about an English fighter squadron in the Battle of Britain. It failed to make it even off-Broadway and they hawked it around Hollywood as a screenplay before giving up on it. According to Auden's diary, the partnership with Mortimer was a failure on both the writing and the intimate level. He was clearly embarrassed by the relationship and his diary of this period ends with some catty remarks about 'Mortimer living off the proceeds of his penny dreadfuls knocking about in a Connecticut mansion with his pool-boy, Willy Keel.'

The hair on the back of Jay's neck pricks up as he finishes the section but he doesn't know why. In the confines of a personal diary it's reasonable for Auden to have been so negative about Mortimer's talent even though the latter had written a very popular series and made money from the film rights. On another level, Jay is puzzled why Auden should have made the point about Mortimer's 'pool-boy'. This relationship wasn't unique. Hadn't Isherwood had a similar one in Hollywood? Perhaps Auden was so specific about Mortimer's boy's identity because he was emphasising the accuracy of his knowledge – and at the same time showing disdain for his ex-lover's choice of new partner. Even as these thoughts churned over in his mind Jay knew he wasn't close to the real reason for the unease stimulated by Auden's words.

They're in the cab from the airport to the hotel. All that Jay knows is that Teri has booked them into the Homewood Suites – the destination she gives the driver. Jay's revelling in her closeness. It's late afternoon and the appointment with Heroes of the Alamo is tomorrow morning. Teri has left the rest of the day after the meeting open – 'in case we have to see them again to finalise a deal'. She has booked a second night so the homeward flight is an exciting 40 hours away.

She turns to him, 'When you saw Heroes, where did you stay?'

'I didn't. I flew into San Antonio, saw Heroes and then went on to Houston to see Lone Star. I stayed in Houston.'

'So you didn't see the Riverwalk?'

'Riverwalk?'

'Hey! Great! I'll be able to show you round. San Antonio is *so* fun.'

'Good.' He relaxes into the seat.

'The hotel I booked – it's on the Riverwalk, not far from the Alamo.'

'*The* Alamo – Davy Crockett, Jim Bowie, Laurence Harvey. That Alamo?'

'Didn't you know?'

He shakes his head. 'I must have made the connection somewhere but–'

'Laurence who?'

'Laurence Harvey. No … hold on. He was the actor. He played … Colonel Travis?'

She pushes his arm. 'You Brits. It was real, you know – part of America's history. Not just a movie. You've gotta lot to learn, boy. I'm gonna show you some things.' A flush breaks out on the dark skin of her throat.

'Okay, folks. You arrived,' the cab driver calls.

Teri has a Hilton loyalty card and organises everything at the express check-in. As they make their way to the elevators, she holds up a single key card. 'We have a two-bedroom suite. Suites here are no more expensive than standard rooms in other places but you have more space. We can use the living room to work in.'

This is it. She's throwing you together.

Jay's breathing quickens. Or is this really the most cost-efficient and business-like approach? In the lobby waiting for the elevator they study the floor indicator in silence. The air fills with Teri's perfume. His nostrils flare as he breathes it in.

She's studying his face. 'You okay? You don't got an elevator phobia, do you?'

He forgives her use of English. He'll do nothing to diminish their familiarity.

The bell tings, the lift doors open and he follows her in. They turn their backs to the mirror and, standing alongside each other, they watch the lights as they change. He wants to brush the back of his hand accidentally against hers but holds back. What if it's the wrong move?

Teri turns her head. 'It has two en-suite bathrooms – his 'n hers. What say we freshen up and go down for the manager's reception? We can plan tomorrow over a drink, leaving the evening to explore the Riverwalk.'

'You're the boss.'

She stops in the open doorway. He nearly bumps into her bag. 'Actually, you're the boss, Jay.' She turns away and leads him to their suite.

Look. I swear she's putting extra juice into the swing of those hips.

Chapter 24

I became obsessed with Wolf and as summer turned
into autumn and then winter, he would spend his
weekdays at school but on Wednesday evening each
week and on Saturday morning, on the pretext of
English lessons, we would have ninety minutes
together in the my room in the Green House as
lovers. Frau Guttchen knew everything and was
discreet. I no longer felt the desire nor need to
frequent the clubs in the Nolli on a Friday night
- I had to conserve my energy to keep up with
Wolf.

When the weather turned warmer in March we
started venturing out. Wolf would come to the
Green House straight from his Gymnasium and we
would walk together along K-Damm to Kaufhaus des
Westens, the department store. After passing
through the Nazi picket, because KaDeWe was owned
by Jews, we would wander through the exotic food
halls before sitting down to coffee and cake. I
can picture Wolf now offering me a finger covered
in whipped cream in a moist suggestive way, which
I had to take in my mouth.

It was strange what I had become inured to
by then. All along K-Damm and Tauentzienstrasse,
the shops, even the smaller emporiums owned by
Jews, sported the long Nazi regalia hanging from
their upper stories like Christmas bunting. It
was so normal that we only noticed its absence.
The facades of KaDeWe, stretching for a block in
each direction, were among those few that
remained naked and unadorned. "It is only time
and this monument to Jewish greed is taken over,"
said Wolf as he tucked into his pastry.

It was during one of these afternoon forays
in May that Wolf sat uneasily opposite me. I
could sense from his squirming that he had
something on his mind. Like any older, less

attractive person in any pair of lovers I felt a sense of dread. "What is it, Wolf? You are sitting there as if you have ants in your pants."

He laughed. "Yes, ants in the pants. It is very good. A good idiomatic saying, no? I will use it. Ants in zer pants."

"Ants in *your* pants. I think you are trying to avoid answering my question."

He fiddled with the paper that had been used to separate the pre-cut slices of the torte he had chosen. "I have a confession, Cammie."

This did nothing for my wellbeing. Had he grown tired of me already? Was he seeing someone else? "What is it?"

He sighed. "I have confess for something."

"Do you mean own up to something?"

"Ja, own up. I have been very bad for doing something you will not like for me." Wolf's English was always more ragged when he was emotional.

"I'm sure it can't be that bad. Tell me."

"The day after today —"

"Tomorrow."

"Ja, tomorrow — is the anniversary of when we burned the books in Operplatz. It was May 10."

I looked at my watch in reflex and then shook my head. "So it is." I looked around and put my hand over his for a second before withdrawing it. "So much has happened to make me happy since then."

"Yes, me also. But you are not so happy to hear what I have to say."

"Go on."

"On that night my job with many other Hitler Youth boys was to take the piles of books from the Humboldt University to the Opera House for the SA men to throw them on the fire."

"Yes, it is a terrible thing to burn books but I understand that you were only doing what your leaders had told you. I don't blame you for it. You were following orders."

"It is not the main thing. The main thing is that I put your books on the pile."

195

"What?"

"Do you remember early you gave me copies of your Dexter Parnes books one and two? You wrote a very nice thing in each one."

"Yes, of course."

"Well, I am now ashamed to say that because Dexter Parnes is a hero against Germany of the Western Front that I must burn this books as well. So I took them to the Opera House that day and added your books to the pile. I burned your books, Cammie. I am so sorry."

His eyes were downcast and I knew from the way his face was flushed that he was close to tears. I could feel a huge guffaw of laughter building inside of me which I knew I had to control.

"This is terrible news," I said, trying to swallow back my amusement. I put my finger in front of my lips as if I was trying to take in the enormity of his confession. "Are you telling me that my books were burned alongside those of Ernest Hemingway, Jack London and H G Wells?"

"Yes, it is true. I am so sorry."

I took my hand away and released my widest smile. "Don't you see what this means, Wolf? In other countries when they denounce the burning of the books I can say *I* was a victim too. In England I can boast that my books were burned alongside HG Wells and some of the greatest writers in German literary history. This can be very good for me. Are you sure my books were burned?"

"I took them to the fire, myself." Wolf's brow was furrowed.

"My books were destroyed in the infamous Berlin book-burnings. It has a wonderful ring to it."

"So you are not angry with me, Cammie."

"How can I be? You have put me on a pedestal with some of the finest writers in Europe. Hurry up with that cake. I want to take you home!"

196

Within a week or so of Wolf's 'confession' he
told me we were only two weeks away from the
final Hitler Jugend weekend camp and his
recruitment into the SA. I joked about how I
preferred the SS uniform but he was adamant that
his future was with the Brownshirts who were,
after all, the true holders of the National
Socialist flame and that this was his father's
chosen route for him. He was a privileged young
man to be able to take up this apprenticeship on
the fast-track officer course in the SA which
would be a stepping stone to a career in the
party hierarchy.

   "But this weekend we have the rally at the
Neuen See Biergarten. Will you come to see me
again, Cammie?"

   "Of course. Will you be leading the
singing?"

   "Yes."

   "Then I'll be there."

   But on that Sunday morning I woke with an
interesting plot development for Dexter Parnes VC
in my head. I sat at my desk and wrote and wrote.
Lunch time came and went and it was only when I
ran out of steam that I realised that I was late
for the rally in the park. I washed and shaved
hurriedly and took the short cut alongside the
overhead railway to Rosa's Bridge. As I passed
the cafes in the arches the smells of cooked meat
and vegetables reminded me that I hadn't eaten
anything. I resolved to have some Wurst when I
arrived at the Biergarten.

   The rally was in full cry. I passed under
the Nazi flags catching in a quiet breeze from
across the Neuen See where boaters were rowing. A
band played oomphah-oompah music as I made my way
to a space near the front. Wolf was there seated
on the stage and we nodded in recognition.

   I had my first beer while the band played on
and the second while they relayed a Goebbels
speech over the loudspeakers. Finally, it was the
turn of the choir and I decided to put off
ordering some food until they had finished.

197

The choir went through its repertoire of traditional songs and ended with the one where Wolf stepped forward and sang the solo. His voice was clear and strong. As he sang, members of the audience stood to join in and for the final verse, when the choir joined in as well, there was a strong feeling of camaraderie between everybody in the Biergarten which culminated in a flurry of Nazi salutes as the song finished. I stood to applaud and a cold clamminess broke out on my skin. Then it all went blank.

Wolf told me later that I had been unconscious for only a few seconds. I had fallen sideways and was lucky not to have banged my head on the way down. Wolf had been the first to reach me and, as I regained consciousness, he came into my blurry vision. His strong left arm cradled my neck and the swastika on his right arm was prominent in my view.

Most of the crowd had dispersed by the time I recovered, and Wolf and I were able to leave the park together. We crossed Rosa's Bridge and made our way back to the railway arches where we found a cafe to give me my first meal of the day. Then we went back to the Green House and made love in my room.

The following weekend Wolf arrived at my door having escaped from the massacre at the SA Barracks.

Chapter 25

Jay is wearing a polo shirt and chinos as he emerges from his room into the suite's shared living space. He hopes he's striking the right note. The room is empty and he crosses to the window. The view looks down on an artificial waterway – a shallow canal that winds its way beneath him. A couple is promenading arm in arm on the far bank. This must be the Riverwalk. He visualises Teri and him in their place. What has the evening in store for them?

Don't think about it. Your shirt isn't long enough to cover what's going on down below. What's she going to think?

The intervention prompts Jay to consider the stalker standing at his shoulder. It doesn't worry him. He's managing his wayward thoughts. He knows this; he's not insane.

A pleasure boat glides along the shallow canal. It's loaded with women of a certain age in red hats and purple dresses. Two of them are involved in a good-natured tussle and one tosses the other's hat into the stream. The boat's crewman wields a long-handled boathook to retrieve it and Jay imagines the women's ribald observations. He decides that he can jettison the MC as unceremoniously as the woman dispensed with the hat. On the family's journey home he'll give him a parachute and order him to jump out of the Jumbo somewhere over the Atlantic.

Hold that thought …

Jay looks at his watch. He turns back to the room seeking further distraction and …

Achtung! She's coming. Stand up straight.

The door to Teri's room cracks open and she emerges.

You're 45. You've been 'round the block' – a few times. You remember from when you were a teenager: if a girl wears a 'button-through' dress on a date it's a green light. She's as ripe for it as my lovely Orchestra girls: Heidi, Christina, Mausi …

Small white buttons start at the neckline of Teri's dress and go all the way to the hem. The top one is undone.

And the others are aching to be free.

It's a classic 'Audrey Hepburn look' – crisp, smooth cotton in dark blue with white spots, sleeveless and nipped at the waist with a narrow white belt. The skirt flares over Teri's bare legs.

Say something.

He can't think of what to say. It's either going to be too forward or too lame. His face is overheating.

Don't be a schmuck, say something.

'How do I look?' She spins with a white clutch purse in her right hand. Her heels are high but she makes the complete turn without a misstep.

Gott im Himmel! Bring that slack jaw under control and say something.

It's a moment of inspiration but already he thinks it's misguided. He tries a poor imitation of a Confederate gentleman. 'Thank heavens you're not in rags. I'm tired of seeing women in rags!'

She peers at him from behind the fringe. 'Excuse me?'

Jay! That film was at least 30 years old by the time Teri was born. She may not even have heard of it.

'Sorry. It's from an ancient film. Way before your time. Sorry.'

'*Gone with the Wind*! My momma talked about it.' She shakes her head. 'Not the kind of film people of colour are likely to use as a reference.'

Blood rushes to his cheeks. 'Oh God! Sorry! What was I thinking? Look, Teri. I didn't think.'

Her laugh tinkles like a cat tripping along the right-hand end of a piano keyboard. 'I only said it to make you squirm. You English!' She turns to the door. 'Let's hit the bar. We have to loosen you up! I'll fetch my wrap and you'll need a jacket. The evenings are cool here.'

The manager's complimentary cocktail reception is a feature of the deal Teri has made with Homewood Suites. It's crowded but there are still one or two vacant tables. Male heads turn as Jay leads Teri to a place next to an ornamental fountain and asks what she's drinking.

'There's only one choice. You should take one yourself. Long Island Tea – it gives you most alcoholic bang for your buck.'

There's a crush of bodies at the bar but training from English pubs has sharpened instinctive techniques in Jay that Americans, used to being served at the table, don't understand. These, plus his accent, do the trick and, abracadabra, two Long Island Teas are delivered over the heads of the people in front of him and into his hands.

This success puts a spring in his step and he places the glasses with a flourish.

'Oops! Should have told you. You order up double-bubble – saves you going back again.' She closes her lips – they're painted in a dark, purplish gloss – around the straw. 'Mmm! I was watching you. I can see how you got where you are in business. You're quite an operator.'

Jay takes a sip – nearly poking himself in the eye with the straw. 'It's good! It tastes like a cross between cold tea and Pimms.'

'Pimms?'

'A very alcoholic drink they serve at Wimbledon with strawberries and cream.'

'You been to Wimpleton?'

Her pronunciation tickles him and he vows that if they end up in bed he's going to ask her to name the home of British tennis while they're doing it. They talk about England and compare the places Teri wants to visit with those he thinks she would like.

Jay repeats the process at the bar and, when they've finished their second Long Island Tea, Teri announces that it's time for her to show him the Riverwalk. It's cool but not cold in the pedestrian traffic and the walkway, lit by fairy lights and bordered by restaurants, bars and gift shops, has a quality that is no less romantic for being synthetic. Had Jay seen this on TV in England, he would have adopted a superior tone and droned on about the American obsession with the ersatz.

His delight in the surroundings has something to do with the fact that Teri has linked her arm in his and, from time to time as they squeeze through the crowd, hugs close into him. He looks down at her arms where they emerge from the edges of a fine-knit shawl. Her dark skin glows in the lights. It looks smooth and dry – a texture that he anticipates in the tips of his fingers. Her hip is nudging him rhythmically.

'Crabs!'

'What?'

'We'll go to *Dick's Last Resort* for crabs. You haven't tried *Dick's* before?' she says.

'No.' He can't stop himself grinning. Teri doesn't notice. She's navigating them through the crowd.

Yes. Crabs at Dick's, Jay. It is what they call humour in Texas.

'I better warn you. You do it for the experience – absolutely not the food. That's to say it's not cordon blue but it is good.'

'Why? What experience?'

'You'll see.' She hugs hard against him to steer them as a single unit further into the bustle.

He's unbuttoning the dress. He is, really – this isn't Jay's fantasy. His fingers are fumbling. His lips are still wet from the kiss – a kiss that went on and on, where her lips and his tongue had a discussion about penetration and passionate acceptance. She's holding his head in her hands.

He's slow, delighting in the sight of her skin as it's revealed in the opening he's creating. He can only glimpse the front clasp of her bra but it's enough to see that it's white and that the contrast with her skin is stark – exciting. He kneels to complete the task. Her fingers are teasing his hair. Now, only now, does he part the material and his eyes feast on her bare thighs, the white-covered junction, her navel set in a softly padded, hard-ridged belly. He runs his fingertips up the back of her porcelain-smooth legs until he's able to pull her to him and press his face against her pubic bone. He wants her to know that, for him, nothing is off limits. It will be all for her pleasure.

It was so much easier than he had anticipated. They had finished slurping on crab claws and their glob-covered plastic bibs were thrown aside. He had demonstrated his skills in swapping corrosive banter with the waiting staff. They had drunk their third beer of the night. She had pinioned him with those dark eyes and said. 'We'll use your room.'

'What?' He wasn't sure he'd heard correctly because of the noise coming from inside the restaurant – they were on the deck outside.

'You know. It's a classic "my place or yours" move. I'm telling you it's yours. You have the king-size bed. My room has two queens.'

The MC giggled.

He shook his head to dispel the laughter. He'd forgotten him. He reminded himself that there was no third person at their table. Teri could have taken his delay the wrong way. 'You mean–'

'I *mean* –' she pronounced it meeyan '– it's your place not mine.'

He decided to play it cool. 'Okay.' He took a swig at his empty beer glass. Teri laughed – an extended stifled bray ending with a snort that Jay found weirdly alluring.

They had tumbled into the elevator and had it to themselves. It was she who had reached out so that they were able to come together for an exploratory kiss. Their lips touched and it was like his first kiss ever. She ground her pelvis against him. Their lips parted.

'Please don't say anything about guns and being pleased to meet you,' he said. For once, it was the right thing at the right time. So it seemed natural that they should enter the suite hand in hand and he should lead her to his room where they had sucked at each other's faces until he helped her out of her dress.

'You're going to stay, aren't you? Tonight, I mean.' Jay says.

She's naked, lying in the bend of his arm. 'Sure. Do you have a cigarette?'

Her hand rests on his belly. He wishes he was in better shape. 'You don't smoke.'

'I gave up. Now I could use one.'

'Sorry.'

She slaps her hand down gently. 'You Brits and apologising.'

'Sorry.'

She slaps him harder.

'Ow! Seriously I can think of nothing nicer than waking up with you here with me.'

'That's sweet. You're sweet.'

'Hmm.' Should he tell her that he knows she's way out of his league?

'You know, Jay. We never really talked about it.'

Oh-oh! 'Let's talk about our relationship' already?

204

The MC's right. Surely she's not going to talk about commitment. 'What?'

'9/11. How come you weren't in the office?'

The 'relationship' conversation would have been preferable but saying he'd rather not talk about it would spoil the mood. 'Simple really. I missed the train.'

'How?'

'I dunno. Vanity I suppose.' He explains in as few words as he can how he had made the decision to stay in his car reading the *Burford Buzz* article.

'That's quite a story. Just imagine if the magazine hadn't been there.'

He shivers. 'I do imagine it.'

'The stupid magazine saved your life.'

'Don't I know it,' he says. 'I carry it round with me like a sort of talisman. It's in my briefcase now.'

Jackpot! You know what she's going to ask.

The shaft of realisation stabs him in the kidney. Please don't ask to see it.

'Wow! Can I see it?'

Double jackpot!

He shuffles himself down until his face is opposite her breast and he closes his eyes as he nuzzles against it. 'I was thinking …'

She's not going to fall for that.

She pulls his hair. 'No, I'd like to see it.'

The MC is skipping around the room clapping his hands beneath his chin. *It's going to be such fun when she reads about Rachel and Ben.*

He gives it one more try. 'Later?'

'Now!' She's smiling.

The act of walking across the room appals him – she's able to study his flabby musculature for the first time – but it also excites him so, by the time he returns with the magazine, he's hopeful she'll be distracted by his penis which in its erect expectation resembles a begging dog.

Teri wafts a hand in its general direction. 'Later!'

She starts reading.

Hmmm. The Halprins play happy families.

His heart falls as, over her shoulder, he views the picture of domesticity that Melissa Rosenberg describes.

'Exclamation marks!' Teri says.

But Jay's eyes have strayed to the article below describing the wedding of an old man and an old woman in a White Plains old people's home. It's the man's name, Willy Keel. Cameron Mortimer's pool boy! This wizened creature. The one and the same.

So now you have it. A connection from Mortimer to the present.

She lowers the magazine. 'Fascinating!'

But Jay's mind is still not in the room. If he can find this Willy Keel he can ask him about Mortimer. Will it lead to Isherwood? Would the teacher Costidy and the people of Burford Lakes be interested to learn that he's connected the town to the great man?

Hey! You're in bed with a beautiful woman.

What *is* he thinking? 'Sorry about all the family stuff,' he says.

'Don't be silly! It's not as if I didn't know. We're having fun. What goes on tour stays on tour.' She's reaching down. 'Hey! What's happened to Mr Pleased-to-see-you? Now what do I gotta do to have him perky all over again?'

If you stopped talking like that it would help.

The room is dimly-lit when Jay half-wakes. He tries to calculate the time based on the height of the sun and the weight of the curtains. He doesn't have sufficient information and relaxes. It must be too early to get up and risk waking Teri. He's on the point of closing his eyes when the MC's chalk-white face appears. He's asleep and Jay watches him stir into life.

Quite a night last night, the MC says.

Yes. I'm not sure …

Stop worrying. She called the shots. Blame her.

But …

This is no time for guilt. Listen, Jay; guilt is for the officer class on the back row of the chessboard not the pawns who serve them.

You're saying I'm just a pawn?

The MC nods and smiles sympathetically. With the greasepaint and the sides of his mouth turned down he resembles a sad clown. *Emotion is futile in a person who is only a bit player in another's destiny.*

Nobody in my life is as important as me, are they?

It's a point of view.

When Jay is wholly awake nearly three hours later the conversation with the MC is no more than a trace of a memory lurking below the surface. Teri is there beside him and he must focus on negotiating the erotic possibilities and matutinal intimacies that mark their first waking as lovers.

The meeting with the marketing management of Heroes of the Alamo later that day passes in less than an hour. In that time Jay's subjected to an initial painful condolence for his loss, the embarrassment of congratulations on his survival and a brief enquiry as to whether he could see his way to completing the project on his own. When he declines, it appears that the offer was made more out of concern for his wellbeing rather than any need on the company's side.

In the cross-town cab back to the hotel he's scrutinising Teri who's wearing a grey nip-waisted trouser suit. He's imagining the body beneath. 'That was hardly the struggle to extricate ourselves from their clutches I thought it would be.'

She smiles and places her hand in his lap. 'It leaves us the rest of the day to explore.'

'The Alamo?'

I think she has something else in mind.

'I gotta get out of this suit first,' she says.

After an early, energetic siesta, they visit the Alamo and watch the IMAX film, which, Jay tells Teri, is good but not a patch on the John Wayne version. He explains that the film made him cry when he was a boy. It's a cynical ploy to score points on the emotions index and it's not a surprise when she leads him back to the hotel. Later they dine in a Riverwalk trattoria.

They're silent on the plane back to La Guardia. He's thinking about how they should say goodbye when they leave each other and go in opposite directions – she to New Jersey, him to Westchester. Should they hug and kiss? What if somebody's meeting her?

Consider the possibility that Rachel cancels the limo and makes for the surprise greeting at the airport. She comes at you with a big sloppy kiss? What if you and Teri walk hand-in-hand into the arrivals hall like you were still on the Riverwalk?

He has this picture in his mind when he asks, 'You know what you said – what goes on tour, stays on tour?'

She turns and her eyes seem darker, more intensely brown than they've ever been. 'Yes?'

'Does it mean it's over?'

She smiles and leans her head on his shoulder. Her lips are close to his ear; her breath is on his neck. Her signature perfume stings his skin. She links an arm into his and hugs it against her chest. 'We still gotta have our weekly meetings, don't we? It may not be the most romantic bug hutch in Connecticut but it's our bug-hutch. Just us alone.'

Knowing this makes Jay certain that they won't cling to each other as they walk from the plane. They'll shake hands in farewell.

Chapter 26

I had vowed to smuggle Wolf out of Germany. The only way I could envisage doing this would be to disguise him as my younger brother or cousin. He would need a British passport. For that I would need to go to England.

The first priority was for Wolf to have somewhere to live. What was to stop him staying in my room? Only Frau Guttchen need know. The other tenants in the other rooms would realise in time that there was somebody there but, if he kept himself to himself, Frau Guttchen could pass him off as my younger brother who was recovering from an illness. It wasn't inspired but it would do.

I went in search of Frau Guttchen and explained the bare bones of the problem.

"So he will stay in your room, Herr Cameron."

"Yes, and I would like you to feed him."

She sucked air between her front teeth. "This is a cost to me. How long will you be away?"

"I don't know yet. Two weeks at the most?"

She went to a bureau and took out a letter pad and a pencil. She wrote down figures and did some multiplications all the while working her tongue-tip along her lips. Reading the numbers upside-down, I couldn't see any mathematical progression. She was stalling while she calculated how much she could sting me for.

Finally she wrote a number totally unconnected with what had gone before and underlined it so heavily that she broke the pencil's lead at the end of the line. She brushed the dust away with the back of her hand. She said the number out loud.

It was my turn to suck in air but I had no choice. "It's a very fair figure, Frau Guttchen. I will make arrangements to leave for London tomorrow."

Wolf and I dined in my room that night on food I brought back from one of the cafes. We slept in my bed, neither of us in the mood for sex. In the morning I combed Wolf's hair and forced him to put on one of my white shirts and a striped tie. I posed him in front of the blank wall and took some head and shoulder photographs with my Leica. I removed the film and put it with my small carrying case.

"I must go now, Wolf," I said. I was standing with my case at my side, my raincoat over my arm.

Wolf, who was still wearing my pyjama bottoms beneath the shirt and tie, came and hugged me. The tears were dripping from his nose and chin. He smelled of a combination of bed and fresh laundry from the shirt. "Will I be safe here, Cammie?"

I pulled back and looked him in the eye while I held his forearms at his side. "As long as you stay in this room. You will have to go to the bathroom but do not linger on the landing. I'm sure Frau Guttchen wouldn't mind emptying a chamber pot of ... you know ... liquid only ... if you could bear to use it."

He made a face.

"It is most important you do not go out. When I come back I hope to have a British passport for you and we will travel back to England as brothers."

"Tell me how this will happen."

I shook my head. "I don't know exactly. I'm hoping my agent may know someone who has contacts. I can't see any other way."

"Can I tell my parents I am safe?"

"No. Have you forgotten? The SS have your papers. They may already have been to your home. Your father can't afford to protect you. He mustn't know where you are until you're in

210

London. You have to stay here secretly. Promise
me you will."

"I will. Cammie?"

"Yes?"

"I love you, Cammie. Thank you."

We embraced again. Then I turned and left.

When the Golden Arrow pulled into Victoria
Station after a difficult crossing, I took a cab
the short distance to The St Ermin's Hotel in
Westminster. After my frugal existence in Berlin
I felt I deserved to be looked after properly.

My problem was how to make contact with the
sort of people who could produce a forged
document for Wolf without opening me up to all
sorts of risks. I remembered my last visits to
pubs in Whitechapel. I was a Fresher at Oxford
and was looking for the types of men on whom to
base my Lefty MacGregor character. I had been
comfortable in none of the dives that I visited
and on more than one occasion had discerned that
the other customers thought I was there on the
lookout for 'rough-trade'. This had made for all
sorts of unnecessary complications that I find it
distasteful to recall.

There was a telephone in my room so I asked
the operator to put me through to Peter Everley's
number. "Evers, it's Cameron Mortimer. I'm in
London."

"Is it finished, Mortimer? I thought you
needed until the end of the year."

"I'm well, Peter, Thanks for asking. No, I'm
not here to deliver the book; I'm still working
on it."

"Oh! Well, look, welcome back. Have you left
Berlin for good?"

"No, I'm here for a few days to sort
something out."

"Can I help?" His voice was hesitant -
reluctant.

"It's research."

"About the exciting life of a literary
agent?"

I chuckled. "No. Parnes has to organise a false British passport for a contact abroad. I need to know how he'd go about it. Any ideas?"

"What's up with Lefty MacDonald?"

"MacGregor."

"Sorry — MacGregor. Normally, you'd have Parnes send Lefty off with a five pound note and a day later he'd come back with the job done. No questions asked."

He was right. It was exactly the job I'd have Lefty do. "Ummm. Lefty's being held hostage. By the guy who needs the passport so Parnes is on his own." I was conscious that the manuscript when it finally appeared on Everley's desk would have none of this in it but I'd deal with it later.

"Hmm. Sounds like you've written yourself into a bit of a corner there, old chap."

I was beginning to wish I hadn't made the call. "So you can't think of anything?"

"I didn't say that, did I?"

"Well, can you?"

"I've got a new author. Female. Exciting talent. She has a detective book - policeman's called Alleyn of the Yard - and she researched it closely. Shall I see if she knows somebody?"

"Who is she?"

"She's from New Zealand. Funny first name, Nyo, spelt with a "g" in it. Last name's easy enough — Marsh. I placed her first book with Collins. It's out later this year - *A Man Lay Dead.* That's why she's in London now."

"Could she help?"

"Don't know, frankly. But I could ask. As I say she's hot on the procedural stuff. She must have some contacts in the police."

"OK. See what you can do, Evers. Thanks."

He called back within the hour with a lunch meeting fixed for the next day. All night I hardly slept with worry for Wolf. I hoped he was keeping out of sight in my room. At the same time I worried about this meeting with the other writer. How could she help me? This was not

merely a matter of impersonal research. She could
easily fob me off with the name of a policeman at
Scotland Yard. I could hardly say I wanted to
find a contact who knew how to forge passports
because I needed one. I had to have a plan I
could put into practice and quickly.

     We made a strange threesome next day sitting
round a table in the Grill Room in The Café
Royal. I was wearing a linen summer suit which
flowed off my spare frame in a particularly
louche (and I thought attractive) way. Everley
was his usually oleaginous self, his black hair
slicked back with oil and his dark looks
brooding. Then there was Miss Marsh, as Everley
had introduced her, who was taller than both of
us and loomed over me like a presentiment of some
dark and evil future.

Chapter 27

So much has happened to him during his two-night absence in San Antonio that Jay expects there to have been big changes at home as well. Rachel hears his obligatory cry of 'Honey, I'm home!' and greets him civilly enough before making tea. He goes upstairs and unpacks. He sniffs his shirts looking for any sign of Teri's scent before putting them in the wash-bin. If it's there he hopes the trace is faint enough not to alert Rachel unless she's looking for signs of duplicity. He realises that he's not used the T-shirt and shorts he packed for nightwear so he puts them back on the shelf in his wardrobe. If Rachel says anything he'll tell her that it was too hot in the hotel to wear them.

Over tea, he describes the meeting with Heroes, making more of the company's need for his help and their request for Straub, DuCheyne to execute the contract. He feels bad about painting the decent people he met in San Antonio in a poor light but he has to justify a whole day in their company.

Feeling that his story holds up better with a good seasoning of truth, he tells Rachel about the Riverwalk and his meal alone at *Dick's Last Resort*. He describes seeing the women in red hats and purple dresses and his brief visit to the Alamo. He declares that he would like to take Rachel to San Antonio someday. He says much less about a fictitious visit to a second company the next morning. 'It was only a courtesy call 'cos I was in the area.'

"Cos"? Where is that coming from? She'll suspect.

He's talking too much. The circumstances in which he was able to connect the English thriller writer Cameron Mortimer with the old man in the nursing home flash into his head. Having made the connection to Willy Keel, he'll follow it up as soon as he can make the time. He's desperate for it to lead to Isherwood. He retains the vision of Teri reading the article naked in bed.

Focus on now, Jay. Look at the way your wife's brow is furrowed.

He asks Rachel for her news.

She sighs. 'Nothing much here. I've arranged a quote for the removals back home and I'm looking at flights. The best deal is if we fly on Christmas Day itself. How would you feel about that?'

$3 million and she's worried about the cost?

'One answer, Rache, is to mention $3 million. Do we *really* have to find the cheapest flight?'

'We haven't got our hands on the money yet. I'll believe it when I see the cheque. Until then …' She sips her tea.

'Okay, but we *are* going business class.'

Her eyes widen. 'Is there any other way?' She puts her hand flat on the table between them. 'As far as Christmas is concerned, we're Jewish aren't we? It means nothing to us.'

'Mmm. Got me there. But somehow Christmas should be special–'

Won't the cabin staff be drunk?

Jay ignores the interruption. 'It doesn't seem right. Why not do Christmas here and leave on the day after Boxing Day? Perhaps we could have a little celebration before we leave.'

She shrugs. 'I'll look at the deals for December 27th then.'

He puts his hand over hers. 'Good! Any news on Ben?'

Rachel tells him that they've increased the frequency of rehearsals for *Cabaret* to every lunchtime. Ben's nervous about his performance because of Rabbi Stern's activities but he's determined to do his best in the role. He's also trialled for soccer and is training with his year-team.

'Have you told the school he's not going back?'

215

'No, not yet. I'll wait until we have a date.'

'Be best if you don't tell them. He may not be picked for the team if they know he's not permanent.'

Rachel nods.

At the synagogue next day, during the community announcements, Rabbi Zwyck departs from the usual rota of studies, shul and youth groups. 'I've asked for God's guidance in the subject of the Jefferson High School production, *Cabaret*. As you know a visitor member of our community ...'

Jay sees heads turn towards him and the heat rushes to his face. He knows that Ben alongside him will be blushing, looking down at his shoes. The harder Jay tries to maintain a mask the more a tic develops in front of his right ear. All the eyes in the building are burning into him.

However, for me it's good to be the centre of attention. It's like old times.

'...Ben Halprin is taking an important role in the production. Speaking personally, I'm relaxed about this. I've talked to Ben and his father and both of them understand the spirit in which the musical was written – not to glorify Nazism but to emphasise its bigotry and hatred. The song Ben sings is a pivotal moment in the play's narrative. The second time Ben sings his song, the dominant theme shifts from the decadent light-headedness to a darker, chilling portent of the future. What at first hearing was a charming folk song becomes a rallying cry for the resurgent country behind banners that we all find distasteful and shocking, and which are, to some of us, terrifying.'

A low murmur of assent gathers pace like the rumble of faraway artillery.

'But I say this, members of our Bar Shalom community: we should support the production. Don't be afraid to go. We must not be scared to confront the past. Rabbi Stern over at

Beth El disagrees. I respect his right to do so. But I think he's wrong. I pray for Ben and his family – that they have the strength to see this through.'

At the end of the service Jay hangs back and shakes Rabbi Zwyck's hand. 'Thank you for what you said. It was kind.'

'I was only speaking God's truth as I see it.'

He nods. 'Well thank you anyway.'

'Mr Halprin – Jay, you'll know better than most here that Americans are not good at irony.' She shrugs. 'Jews? We *do* irony. The way those boys wrote that song into the play, it's subtle and this is what gives it so much power. I hope Mr Costidy understands this. If the school and your Ben can pull off this song half as well as they do in the film it will bring a lot more force to the message of the play. I hope he can do it.'

'I'm certain Ben can – and will,' Jay says.

It's on the drive home from the temple that Jay decides to visit Rabbi Stern and put his point of view.

Beard the lion in his den. I like it.

Rabbi Stern has agreed to see Jay and they're meeting in a coffee shop close to the orthodox synagogue in Burford Station. The rabbi is drinking hot chocolate and Jay, who has already had his strong coffee for the day, has taken a decaffeinated long black. The rabbi's not as Jay expected. He'd anticipated the large-lensed spectacles correctly, but his other imaginings – that the rabbi would be round-shouldered and wizened – are well wide of the mark. He's tall and broad. His hair is tight with salt-and-pepper curls.

'My mother was a Jew in Berlin,' he says in answer to Jay's opening question about what's wrong with the school play. 'She had a policeman friend who told her about Kristallnacht the day before it happened. She took refuge in a hotel but the SS arrested her husband and all the Jewish men in their street and took them to Sachsenhausen. The SS tortured him there – he had heart trouble – he died.'

'Your father?'

The rabbi smiled grimly. 'Kristallnacht was in 1938, Mr Halprin. How old do I look? I was born in 1949 after my mother married a second time.'

'I'm sorry.'

'No matter. The point is that the Hakenkreuz was then and still is a symbol of oppression for my family and my people. Under it, my mother had to do unspeakable things to survive. Jews betrayed Jews. We were forced to be Judas-goats leading others of our kind into their so-called showers …'

Join the shuffling line. Keep schtum. Take the shower.

'On pain of immediate death, Jews had to wrest the gold teeth out of the mouths of the dead. Jews had to throw the emaciated bodies of other Jews into mass graves.'

The burdens … so many.

Jay's confused by the MC. Where's this stuff coming from? He needs to calm the rabbi down. 'But your mother survived.'

'She stayed out of the camps. Her police friend organised false papers. She lived through the war as an Aryan.' He uses a paper napkin to dab a line of chocolate from his lips. He takes a deep breath. 'Anyway, back to your son.'

'Yes. You know the show isn't pro-Nazi – far from it.'

'I know all this, Mr Halprin. The show is anti-Nazi. The writers were Jewish.' He's counting on his fingers. 'The song, your son's song chills the audience and ushers in the darkness – I know all this.'

'So why–'

'The things I described earlier, they happened while the swastika fluttered over most of Europe. How can our town's school ask a Jewish boy to wear that awful insignia? The holocaust is still a personal thing for so many Jews, Mr Halprin.

We lived with our parents' guilt that they survived. We knew the people who died in the Shoah. They were our grandparents and their parents. To see a Jew wearing the Hakenkreuz and have the audience clap and cheer, it's not right.'

Jay shrugs. 'We don't know for sure that Ben qualifies as Jewish. We won't know properly until we go back to England. Rabbi Zwyck tells us that the families' synagogues will have records. These together with our birth certificates …'

'Rabbi Zwyck may be correct in this. Who knows? But with your names and background I would say you'll be confirmed as Jewish.' His twisted smile appears again, accompanied by an exaggerated shrug. 'Why would a gentile claim to be a Jew?'

'What if he isn't?'

'Who knows? Have you seen the show? The audience is very wound up as the first half closes with your son's song. There is an ambiguity – are they cheering the flags? Do they applaud the swastika that they see for the first time? We're not happy. Mr Costidy doesn't understand that our preference would be for the school not to put on this particular production. If it has to be *Cabaret* – why not some other symbol?'

'But he will do it. We have Rabbi Zwyck's support … and her congregation's.'

'Rabbi Zwyck is a fine woman but she's not …' he tails off. 'Look, Mr Halprin. I'm proud to have become a citizen of this great country. I'm proud that we have freedom of speech. Mr Costidy should have the right to put on the production. Your son should have the right to play this part. I don't agree but wasn't it a British politician who said he would defend such rights with his life?'

It was Voltaire – he was French.

'I think it was Voltaire – French.'

Stern sticks out his bottom lip and nods. 'Voltaire? I must look it up. But I and my congregation – we have the right to say it shouldn't be so. We have the right to disagree.'

Jay nods. 'I can understand what you're saying. I can't argue with it. As long as it doesn't affect my boy.'

'In my experience teenage boys can stand being the centre of attention better than we realise.' He steeples his fingers under his chin. 'We can agree to disagree on this then, Mr Halprin? '

'Jay. Call me Jay.'

'You know, Jay, you're an interesting man.'

'Why do you say that?'

'I'm referring to your escape from the towers.'

Here it comes.

Jay examines the bottom of his coffee mug.

'God has given you a new start. What an opportunity!'

Butt out, Rabbi! This is Elayna's job.

'What do you mean?' Jay stretches his neck to alleviate the tension building around his collar bones.

'You're already some way along the path by returning to the faith.'

Jay spreads his hands. 'I'm confused more than anything. We're going back to the UK. After that …'

'Perhaps there you'll find the opportunity to dedicate your life … fulfil your destiny.'

'I have no sense of destiny – I don't know what it feels like.'

I've told you. I know enough about destiny for both of us.

'You'll know it when it comes – a sign from God perhaps.' Stern stands and offers his hand. 'It's been good to meet the enemy, Mr Halprin. Unbridled antipathy of a personal nature is seldom warranted.'

Jay takes the hand and shakes it. 'I agree, Rabbi. I agree.'

When Jay arrives home, Rachel tells him there's a phone message: Prentice Chervansky has set aside some books for him.

Chapter 28

The most striking thing about Ngaio Marsh, a woman in her late thirties, was that she had absolutely no bosom. The jacket of her blue woollen suit was buttoned low revealing a plain blouse which she wore with a feminine version of a cravat. The blouse was devoid of any protuberance whatsoever.

I have to confess I found her androgynous appearance and mannish bearing quite stimulating. I'm ashamed to say that, even while we were chatting, I was distracted by the unique – for me – thought of what this woman would look like with no clothes on. When later I read that Miss Marsh had denied being a lesbian despite having a succession of female 'companions', I found it hard to credit.

But, I digress. After Everley had introduced us he sat back and rather let us get on with it. Ngaio, as she asked me to call her, went through the tiresome business of praising the Dexter Parnes books. She said that she understood I was taking Parnes to Berlin for the third book and this was creating a difficulty for me. She picked up her empty cigarette holder - an ivory stub with gold banding.

I took my cigarette case out of my pocket.

"Everley here tells me your book is sure to be a best seller. He's very taken with the veracity regarding police procedure. 'It's what marks it out,' he says." I offered her a cigarette but she looked at it, wrinkled her nose and turned to Everley, who offered her one of his Senior Service.

Ngaio inserted the cigarette and put the holder to her lips. Everley had his lighter ready. She only let the cigarette end touch the flame for a second before she pulled away, her cheeks hollow as she drew in the smoke. She tossed her head as if to flick away the cloud of blue which accompanied her exhalation. "Sorry. I don't smoke Turkish."

I waved the apology away.

"I do my research," she said.

"That's what I'd like to talk about."

Twenty minutes later I left Ngaio and Everley to have their conversation about her Alleyn sequel with a name and address in my pocket. It was of a man who lived near Clapham Common. He was a reformed old-lag who was introduced to Ngaio by a policeman she had nurtured at Scotland Yard. The man - Victor Simons - made a precarious living on his wits and, if anybody knew anything about false passports, it would be him. There was no telephone number so I had no alternative than to hail a cab and ask to be taken to Clapham Common.

The cab-driver gave me a second look before saying, "Bit eager aren't yer?" and it took the rest of the journey before I understood he was commenting on my appearance and the fact that I was very early if I expected an assignation. I decided to ignore his impertinence and withheld my customary tip as a punishment.

The house was in a run-down street. It had been a smart terrace once, built probably for the people doing the work I had done, it seemed so many years ago, in that insurance office in Cheapside. But something had marked this area out for near-dereliction. The paint was cracking on the window frames and the front doors were peeling. The windows were obscured with filthy net curtains or grey sheets. Children played in the dust that collected in the cobbled gutters. I went along the terrace counting the houses to number 19, pulled back the knocker and let it fall.

The woman who came to the door had rags in her hair and a loose none-too-clean housecoat that she pulled together across her bosom which was exposed inside a cotton slip. Her legs and

223

feet were bare. "Whaddyer want?" She eyed me
suspiciously.

"I'm looking for Mr Simons ... Victor?"

"He ain't 'ere."

"Do you know where he is?"

"Yeah. What's it worf?"

"A shilling?"

"Let's see it."

I took the coin out of my pocket and laid it
on the flat of my right palm. I was ready to
close my fist if she made a move.

"See that pub on the corner. Saracen's
'ead?"

I looked in the direction of her pointing
finger and could see a pub sign swinging at the
end of the road. "Yes."

"E's in there."

I looked at my watch. "But it's not open
yet."

"Never shuts. Nah, piss off." She took the
shilling from my hand and closed the door.

The entrance to the pub was on an angle to
the street corner. I pushed the door but it was
locked. I could see the blurred outlines of
figures sitting at tables through the etched
glass. There was no noise. Nobody moved towards
the door. I turned round and retraced my steps.
There was an alley behind the pub and I went down
it, stepping carefully over broken glass. There
was a strong smell of stale beer. I knocked at
the back door.

A shout came from inside. "S'open."

I turned the handle and found myself in a
hallway with stairs leading up on the left. There
was a passage alongside it with two doors on my
right. The first was ajar and I could see steps
down into a cellar. The other open door led
through to the bar - in the far corner was the
frosted glass of the entrance I had tried
earlier. I stepped through and it was as if the
clock had gone back to the lunchtime licensing
hours - each round table had a group of men with

224

pint glasses in front of them. There was a woman
behind the bar. "Can I 'elp you?" she said.

"I'd like a gin and bitters, please," I
said, anxious to get into the way of things.

"We're shut. Want me to lose my licence?"

I looked round me.

"They're friends. We're 'aving a private
meeting."

"I see. Well, I'm looking for Victor
Simons."

She surveyed the room. "E's not 'ere."

There was a movement to my right. It was a
man standing. "S'all right." He looked me up and
down. "Looks like a man could put a bit of
business my way." He was now alongside me. "Am I
right, Mr ..."

I said the first name that came into my
head, "Everley."

"Why don't we step into my office, Mr
Everley?" With that he led me back the way I had
come and we stood alongside each other in the
back alley.

I took out my cigarette case and flipped it
open. "Smoke?"

His hand snaked out and he held my wrist.
"Gold, Mr Everley. You don't want to be flashing
it round here. Yes, I will avail myself of your
generosity." He took two cigarettes. In a well-
practised movement, he swung one up behind his
ear and the other into his mouth and then stood,
chin jutting forward, waiting for the light. I
fumbled a cigarette between my lips and then
flicked my lighter into life. We both blew out
smoke noisily while I returned the case and
lighter to my pocket.

"Shall I start ... here?" I said.

"Yeah. What seems to be the problem?" He
smiled, revealing black, broken teeth. His face
wasn't stubbled but he was clearly a man who
needed to shave twice a day. He was hatless and
his hair was combed across to hide the baldness
on his crown. His dark blue suit had a faint
chalk stripe and his shoes were not clean. His

neck was scrawny inside a collarless pale blue shirt.

He held up a hand. "Just so's you know I'm not as stupid as I look, I know your name's not Everley, is it Mr Everley? Else why would you have the monogram CEM on your smart gold cigarette case? But then maybe it's best for both of us I don't know your name. Is that what you're trying to tell me?"

I stammered. "Yes. It's probably best."

"'Cept you know mine and that might put me at risk. And we have to put this fact to the account, don't we, Mr Everley? It's a question for the account." He put his hands out as a signal for me to tell him my story.

"I am a friend of Miss Marsh, the writer. I'm afraid I told her an imperfect version of the truth ... my reason for wanting to see you. But, as you put it, this was a matter of mitigating risk. You see, I am a writer too. But I'm in a spot where I need to obtain a false passport. I don't just need to know how it's done, I need to do it."

Victor Simons screwed up his eyes, studying my face. "And if I wanted to contact Miss Marsh, she would back up that she referred you to me?"

"Yes. Up to a point. She thinks I want to know the theory of getting a passport."

"Is it for you?"

"No, a friend ... a brother." I looked down and shifted some of the broken glass with my toe.

"Hmmm. A passport to make somebody seem to be your brother."

"Yes."

"British then."

"Yes."

"Do you 'ave a photograph?"

"Yes."

"Good. Positive or negative?"

"Undeveloped film."

"Better. Here?"

"Yes."

"Better still."

I had lost any semblance of authority. "I'll want it to have some entry and exit stamps for countries in Europe - just a few to make it look genuine."

He nodded. "No problem."

"But it's important it has an open entry stamp for Germany. One that hasn't been counter-franked."

"So he's in Germany now - your brother."

"Yes." My face flushed. I was telling him too much. "How quickly can it be done?"

"Very quickly. Coupla days."

Before we parted, I had handed over the film spool, five pounds and the details for Wolf's passport. I realised that the surname of my "brother" on the passport gave mine away but assumed this wouldn't trouble Simons as long as he received his cut of the deal. We arranged to meet in the Saracen's Head three days later when Simons would hand over the passport and I would give him another £20.

"How do I know you won't go off with my five pounds and I'll never see you again?" I asked.

"You don't," Simons said, dropping his butt to the floor and grinding it into the glass with a crunching sound.

I had no trouble getting the cash together next day and I sent a telegram to Frau Guttchen to let her know when I would return. I hoped all was well. I received a reply to say that my brother sent his love.

On the appointed day I was outside the Saracen's Head shortly before evening opening time. I heard the door bolts being drawn back and stepped inside. Although there were four or five men inside already with drinks in front of them, Simons was not one of them.

I asked for a glass of mild beer and took a seat on the bench below the window. Almost immediately a spotty youth in a cloth cap and muffler sidled up. "You Everley?" he said.

I had forgotten the subterfuge of the first meeting and nearly shook my head. I recovered in time. "Yes."

"Vic says don't worry, he'll be here. Just sit tight. He said to check you've got the rest of the money."

I nodded.

He sat beside me and I was engulfed in a fug that carried the odour of mouldy bread. "Show me," he said.

I took out my wallet and, hidden by the table, fanned out four five-pound notes.

The youth swept out of the pub leaving the sour smell behind and I wondered what part he played in what was happening. Had the passport not been finished until they knew the money was assured? Were they only now pasting Wolf's picture to the document and placing the all-important stamp across its corner?

In any event I had to wait with increasing nervousness for two hours before Simons sidled in with his elbows tight to his sides and his hands inside his jacket pockets, stretching the seams. He headed directly for the rear door and beckoned me to follow him by cocking his head.

He was sweeping a space clear of broken glass with his shoe when I reached him.

"Have you got it?" I asked.

He looked to left and right and held out his hand. "The money, Mr Everley."

I stepped back; my heart was racing. Was he double-crossing me? How I wished I had Dexter Parnes VC alongside me at that moment. "Not until I see you have it."

He fished into the inside pocket of his jacket and produced what looked like a passport. "Hand over the cash."

I was determined not to be made a fool of. "Show me his photograph and the details."

Simons opened it and turned the pages towards me. As far as I could tell, the style of the script, the way the picture was stamped, all appeared genuine. "And the entry stamp?"

He sighed and glanced up and down the alley again. He flicked through the pages and turned it to face me. The stamp was there and the date was written exactly as on my own. It all seemed to be as I had asked.

"Satisfied?"

I took out the four notes and we made the exchange hurriedly, anxious that neither lost control of their side of the bargain.

"Good to do business wiv you, Mr Everley." He put a finger to his eyebrow.

I ignored him and as I stood studying the passport page by page, I heard the scrunching underfoot as he swivelled away and disappeared through the doorway. Hoping that what I had in my hand would do the job for Wolf, I went along the alley, out into the street and headed up to the main road where I hoped to hail a cab.

Chapter 29

Prentice Chervansky is wearing a caramel-coloured twin-set on this occasion and Jay wonders whether her choice is based on a rota or depends on her mood. Perhaps she has an infinite supply of these cashmere garments and once worn, each set is discarded.

She sees Jay come in and dips to reach a pile of books. She stands waiting while he unwinds his scarf, undoes his coat and removes his gloves. Her smile widens as he approaches. 'Hi, Jay. I've searched our non-fiction catalogue and these are all about Berlin and the rise of Hitler.'

He raises a hand in greeting. 'Biographies of Hitler?' Jay's not sure he wants to read them.

'No!' She glances up as if to check whether he's teasing her. 'We wouldn't carry material like that.'

'So what *have* you found?'

'Well, these are based on personal experiences of people in Berlin.' She hands him three hardbacks.

He reads the titles: *Before the Deluge, The Past is Myself,* and *What I Saw* and turns to the blurb wordings: 'the tawdry, dangerous and undeniably exciting story of the sickness which overcame Germany in the '20s'; 'immortalizing the everyday life of 1920s Berlin'; 'an unforgettable portrait of an evil time'. 'I'll take them. Thanks.' He hands over *The British are Coming*.

While she scans the barcode, Prentice asks, 'Did you enjoy this one?'

'Yes, it mentions Cameron Mortimer – the British author who lived near here.'

'Oh! Does it say anything about Burford Lakes?'

He decides it would be too cruel to shock her with an account of Mortimer and his pool boy.

It would have been fun to see her mouth curl in distaste.

'Just that it's close to the border with Connecticut.' He wants to offer her more. 'It mentions another Burford resident, Willy Keel. Do you know him?'

Prentice is bar-coding his new books against his library card and she rotates her lower jaw as if a fruit pip is caught between her teeth. 'Willy Keel, you say?' She shrugs. 'No I can't say I have.'

There's another customer waiting so Jay picks up the books. 'Thanks for these, Prentice.'

'You're welcome, Jay. Have an iced A.'

Jay visits the grocery store and picks up a *Snickers* bar to eat on the walk home. Another month has passed – there's a new *Burford Buzz* in the dispenser.

Burford Buzz - 08 November 2001

Melissa Rosenberg interviews Rabbi David Stern of the synagogue Beth El in Burford Station.

We met over cups of delicious hot chocolate (with marshmallows!) at *Deborah's Coffee Shop* in Burford Station. The meeting came about after many readers – not only from Rabbi Stern's congregation – contacted the *Buzz* to comment that last month's interview with the rabbis about the Jefferson High production of *Cabaret* had been skewed in favour of reform synagogue leader Elena Zwyck.

I started by asking Rabbi David whether he agreed that I had been biased. He declared me innocent of the charge. 'I thought the article was fair,' he said. 'You gave both arguments equal prominence. I have no complaints.'

'And you still feel the same about *Cabaret*?' I asked.

'Nothing has changed. When the production starts next month, members of *my* congregation will go on the Thursday

---

and Saturday evenings to picket it and try to persuade the audience not to go in.'

'But many of the audience will be relatives of performers.'

'And I would expect them to walk through the picket. We all have equal rights here. This is what I love about America.'

'So you don't think you'll actually disrupt the performance.'

He smiles and I feel encouraged to know more about him. He explains that disruption is not his intention. He merely wants to make his point forcibly and persuade the people who go in that it's important to think about their reaction when the swastikas are on stage. 'I would not like to think that the applause at the end of the first act is for what is happening on stage – but is rather for the players.'

Now, let's find out more about David, the man. How long has he been rabbi at Beth El?

'Three years.'

Does he see himself staying in our fair boro?

'I'm not sure. I have a strong sense of my calling, Melissa. There's an urge inside me to do more for my faith. God is expressing in me His will for my future.'

So is the rabbi experiencing doubt?

'No! I've always had a strong sense that God has a plan for me.' He took out his wallet and showed me a photograph. It's of a youth standing on a hilltop with what looks to be a desert landscape behind him. 'This is me. I ran away from home not far from here when I was sixteen and went to Israel. I tried to join the army but they wouldn't have me. When I returned to the US I went to Rabbinical School – my family has no rabbinical tradition. I'm the first. This – being a rabbi here in Burford Station – this isn't my calling. I will make my name as a leader but it won't be here.'

I leaned forward, all thoughts of chocolate and marshmallow forgotten. The rabbi has a fire in his dark eyes and it's unsettling. 'So Burford Station is a stop on the way (no pun intended!) to bigger things.'

'More momentous things, greater things. This is God's plan. It's not for me to know the detail – yet. But I have a strong sense that God will tell me when He wants me to go to our spiritual home – Zion. 'This is God's purpose. I'm marking time here ... waiting.'

'Zion?'

'Israel. It's my destiny to be a leader of men in Israel.

'Waiting for what?'

'God's sign that the time is now.'

'Why not go to Israel and wait for His sign there?' As I ask the question I begin to feel that I'm being too personal – I'm getting too close.

'Because God hasn't opened that door for me yet. The situation there is in flux. Israel is stronger – it's expanding. Politicians here and in Europe talk glibly of "The Palestine Question" and "the two-state solution". Jews are God's chosen people and He chose our land for us – Zion. He does not envisage two states – only Zion. It's not for man to obstruct His will. We must make all the people in our land accept this.' He's warming to his subject and I sense a caged energy in front of me.

'We must subjugate so-called Palestine. I have been there; I know. There is only one solution: drive the Palestinians out. Deport them. Eliminate them. That's the solution.'

'Are you sure you want this to go on the record?' I ask. 'Deport them? Eliminate them?' This is what you want me to write?'

'Why not? We must do what is necessary to deliver God's will.'

'You sound very certain, Rabbi.' I hear myself say.

'I prefer to use the word clarity. You too can have clarity, Melissa, but first you have to attach yourself to God. Judaism is the true sun and you must fix your orbit to it. Then you, like me, will know God's purpose.'

We have finished our drinks and it's time to pack away my notebook and digital recorder. As always, *Deborah's* excellent coffee shop is full and customers are waiting for our table. I thank the rabbi for his time and his candid answers.

'Now you worry me, Melissa. Perhaps I have been too forthright.'

'It's not for me to say, Rabbi,' I answered.

No, this, dear reader, is something for you to decide.

A light sleet has started and Jay is thoughtful as he folds the *Buzz* and stuffs it in his raincoat pocket. Jay finds the rabbi's sentiments disturbing. A man of the cloth shouldn't use those words – 'subjugate', 'eliminate'.

And 'solution' – so misjudged in this context.

Jay turns into Ponds Lane and spots Melissa Rosenberg ferrying hypermarket carrier bags from her car to her house. Skipping the puddles, he runs across to help. As he places the final bag on the kitchen table he asks about the interview. 'You started out being positive but it all went downhill. Did the rabbi really say those things?'

She purses her lips. 'Afraid so. He kept going on about his destiny – about going to Israel.'

'Doing what?'

'He wants to be part of the settlement movement – expanding territory on the West Bank.' She's putting the tins and jars away as she talks.

'Isn't it illegal?'

Not as far as America's concerned.

'It depends on where you stand. The United Nations thinks it is.'

Melissa is stowing two jars of peanut butter with grape jelly into the cupboard. Jay shudders. He tried it once – never again. 'What about the people who lived there before?'

'The Palestinians? They try to resist but what can they do? Look I'm being very rude, Jay. Can I offer you a drink? Tea? Coffee? Soda?'

Jay shakes his head.

The Palestinians do fight back. The settlers surround themselves with walls and barbed wire. Make the settlements like ...

'Ghettos.'

The MC laughs. *You said it – literally!*

Jay swears to himself. Perhaps Melissa hadn't heard. 'Pardon?'

'I was thinking that the settlers, having to barricade themselves in, must be like living in a ghetto,' Jay says.

'I suppose it is. But if it keeps them safe …'

It's not always the oppressor who builds the wall.

Jay nods.

'But if Rabbi Stern has his way the Israelis will keep encroaching further into the West Bank. I'm not sure …' Melissa frowns and shrugs.

And if Israel leaves only a small space for the Palestinians, on which side then is the ghetto? On which side then is the oppressed?

They stand, one each side of the table, shaking their heads. Jay's wondering whether the men flying the Jumbo jets were Palestinian. The one they say masterminded it – Usama Bin Laden – is he?

Don't try to work it out, Jay. It will only make your head hurt. Remember to ask Melissa about the old man – Willy Keel.

Jay asks if Melissa has kept the details of the old man she wrote about in the *Buzz* who married in the White Plains senior home. She consults a *Filofax*, flipping through the address section and jots down the name of the care home and a telephone number on the back of one of her *Buzz* business cards.

Later, when Jay phones the McDougall Lawns Senior Resort, he's surprised that the switchboard operator offers to put him straight through to Willy's room. A croaky voice answers and, even before Jay can finish explaining that he's researching Cameron Mortimer and would like to meet, Willy Keel suggests the next Sunday for his visit.

During Friday dinner, Ben talks excitedly about the show. Mr Costidy has seen off the pressure from Rabbi Stern and everything's looking set for three evening performances from the 13th December – a little over a month away.

Jay has noticed that ornaments and other household items are missing and asks Rachel what's happening.

'Packing has to start some time. Anything we don't need for the next six weeks is going in a box. They're all labelled-up in the spare room.'

'And the flights?'

'We need to make a final decision.'

'Better wait until we have the money?'

'If you say so. But the sooner the better.'

At the end of the meal Jay retreats to the den and skim-reads the books on pre-war Berlin. He worries that he's developing an obsession about the Nazis and what they did with power. Is he accreting more guilt because of his previous naivety about the Holocaust? As a Jew should he have cared more?

He expects an interruption from the insistent voice in his head and there it is. *Jews who suffered and survived, and the children, and the children's children, they carry the burden of guilt. Look at you. The guilt for seventeen is too much and now you want to take it on for the whole of our tribe?*

The Sunday of Jay's visit to the McDougall Lawns Senior Resort is exactly two months after 9/11. Willy wants him to be there at 9am and, as he makes early-morning tea, Jay watches a magazine programme that features the terrible images of that day followed by shots from live cameras at Ground Zero showing the extent of the clean-up. The twin towers are no more than twisted remnants resembling filigrees of spun sugar 20 storeys high. The presenters choke as they recount the numbers of dead and missing. The latest estimates are nearly 3000 fatalities, 17 of them employees of Straub, DuCheyne.

Merely so much ash – spread to the four winds. Like from the smokestacks of the death camps. Just as Willy and I remember. Like we can never forget.

A few minutes before his appointment, Jay strides along a flagged path that leads to the canopied entrance of Willy's retirement home. It's a converted mansion in one of the better off suburbs of White Plains originally constructed to house grand apartments. As Jay anticipates meeting the old man, the MC's comments about death camps repeat like a catchy tune and his stomach is churning as he anticipates what Willy will have to say. He shakes this from his mind. He's here to talk about Cameron Mortimer.

Once Jay's signed in, a receptionist leads him to a meeting room and a black care-assistant in a blue uniform brings in a tray bearing a pot of coffee with cups, milk and sugar. She places it on the coffee table positioned in the centre of a square of patterned carpet. Jay stays standing despite having a choice of three faux-leather easy chairs set round the table. Each chair has a high seat.

He walks across to the unscreened window. It looks out on the gardens behind the building. The flower beds are bare earth – the grass is faded. Grey clouds are pressing down. He finds himself thinking that many of the inhabitants here will never see the grass regain its colour; the bulbs will push up shoots but not for their eyes. After about five minutes the same assistant who brought the coffee wheels Willy in.

He is but a husk of a man. The only spark of life shines from his rheumy blue eyes which reflect the blue of his denim shirt. His shoulders slope and his wrists and hands are mottled with dark spots.

This is what you have coming to you – if you're lucky.

Willy points to the coffee pot as soon as the door closes behind him. 'It's gonna be decaffeinated.' His voice cracks with phlegm. He shrugs. 'They gonna give t'you the strong stuff so you can pass it to me and get me hyper-ventilated or whatever? I don't think so.'

'They've left two cups, Mr Keel. Would you like some?'

He waves the idea away. 'Willy. You call me Willy.'

237

Something in the way he pronounces his name, with the stress heavy on the first syllable and a soft 'v' sound, emphasises Willy's caricature Jewishness. Jay checks his head for the yarmulke – nothing.

It's not the Sabbath – why expect it?

'You wanted to see me – to ask about Cameron?'

Jay pours a coffee. It looks strong but the aroma has a shallowness that confirms Willy's doubt about its composition.

As if he knows what Jay's thinking, Willy puffs out a breath through pursed lips and says, 'Coffee without caffeine – like a dog without mustard!'

Why make a fuss? He will have drunk acorn coffee. Once tasted, never forgotten.

Jay laughs. 'That's a good one.' He takes a gulp, nods and smacks his lips as if the hollow taste is hitting the spot. 'I read about Cameron in WH Auden's autobiography.'

'Ach! Auden. He was before I came to New York.'

Jay looks round as if there are others in the room. 'But you and Mortimer – you had a relationship.'

'Before, but not after New York. I was married.'

'And you married again. I saw the cutting in the *Burford Buzz*. It's how I found you.'

'Dead.' He shakes his head. '*Both* of them dead.'

'I'm sorry to hear that. But your latest …'

'Mrs Selvaggio – Mary …'

'You only married a few months ago.'

Willy folds even lower into the chair. 'She was dying when we married.'

'I see,' Jay says. But he doesn't. 'Can we start at the beginning? How did you know Cameron?'

'Did you know I was born in Germany?'

'All I know is what I told you. You and Cameron … a relationship.'

Willy wrings his bony hands. 'I'm ashamed to say that I was a Nazi when I was young. I swallowed all their lies.'

'But you *were* gay, weren't you?'

'My name then was Wolf, Wolf Köhler. Wolf was homosexual. I don't use the "gay" word. There was nothing gay about it in those days. Cameron and me – we were together in Berlin. But the war … he went back to England.'

'You were on opposite sides.'

Willy snorts. 'I was on the wrong side that's for sure. I was in the army when war broke out and we were earmarked always for the first assault, the most dangerous front-line work.'

Jay shakes his head. 'You were lucky.'

'Pfff! My comrades didn't know whether I was a lucky charm or a curse – so many died around me but always I was the survivor. In Russia I escaped from being captured with the 6th Army at Stalingrad. I came back to Germany in the great retreat from the Eastern Front. In the end Americans took me prisoner in the Ardennes. Because I could speak English I was wearing a GI uniform. They should have shot me.'

'How did you get to America?'

'When it was all over I made a marriage of convenience to get out. She was a good woman. It was easier for us to travel as man and wife always with the plan to get to America and meet up with the famous writer who could give us employment.'

'And in America you became Willy Keel. How did you track Cameron down?'

You're pushing too hard – going too fast – missing so much. Slow down.

'We needed to have jobs so we could stay in the US. I thought Cameron …'

Jay picks up his coffee cup and holds it to his lips, waiting.

239

'Did you know Geraldine, my first wife, died in 1960?'
Willy says. 'We only had 12 years together. Ten of them in
Cameron's house. She was cook-housekeeper, I drove and
looked after the garden, jobs around the house. Then she died.'

'I'm sorry. When did you come here to the home …
resort?'

'Resort! Pfff! Let's see …' He studies the ceiling with
those blue eyes. 'I was still with Cameron at the end in '86. His
so-called friends deserted him – Aids but also old age,
pneumonia.' He spreads his arms and shrugs.

Looks like a caricature Jew.

'What was he?' Willy chuckles and coughs. 'Oh! He was
four years younger than I am now.' He pauses as if he's
recognising this truth for the first time. 'He was 81 or maybe
80.'

'And you came here after he died?'

'He left me the house, you see. There was nobody else.
No cash or income. It was all in the house. So I had to sell up in
1998 and came here and met Mrs Selvaggio. She had nobody as
well. So, when she knew she was going, it was either marry me
or leave her money to a charity. I've been lucky.'

I thought you wanted to know about Cameron and Berlin?

'Tell me about Germany. How did you and Cameron
meet?'

'So, it's a long story. How long you got?'

Chapter 30

I think my heart has never recovered from the
trip back to Berlin. For the whole day I was
conscious that the notebook in my suitcase
contained an old envelope concealing a fake
passport. Even if it was such a good forgery that
it could pass as genuine, how would I explain
that it was in my possession rather than my
'brother's'? My only story was that I had taken
it out of Germany by mistake when I left to visit
England and now, equally innocently, I was taking
it back. But I knew my limitations. Would they
believe me?

In any event, I reached Zoo Station without
any mishaps despite a close interrogation of my
motives for returning to Germany from a border
guard who called over a plain-clothes Nazi
official to double-check my credentials. He waved
away my papers proffered by the guard whose hand
was shaking visibly. "You are welcome to Germany.
Will you stay in Berlin for the Olympic Games?"

I answered in German. "No. Perhaps this may
be my last visit for a while."

He continued in English. "It is a pity.
Germany will put on the finest Games since they
began. The Fuhrer has decreed it shall be so."

I nodded. "Then I'm sure they will be,"
still speaking in German.

The party man nodded to the guard, clicked
his heels together and saluted. "Heil Hitler!"

I nodded in response knowing how sheepish
and weak I must have looked. Exactly the
discomfiture his display intended, I felt. I
turned to the guard who was writing the date
across the immigration stamp. He raised his
eyebrow almost imperceptibly as he gave me back
my passport. I often wonder whether he survived
it all.

I jumped on a tram outside the station and before I could pay had demounted at Steinplatz. I went through the porch into the Green Building and raced up the stairs. The door to my room was hanging on its hinges.

My heart dropped to my shoes. I knew it had to be Wolf. "Frau Guttchen!" I called.

She appeared, bent over wringing her hands. "I'm so sorry, Herr Mortimer."

"What happened? Where is Wolf?"

"It was the Nazi police - the Geheime Staatspolizei. They have taken him."

"Where?"

She cradled her face in her hands, her nails digging into her forehead. Her voice was muffled. "I don't know," she wailed.

Leo appeared on the staircase by the stoved-in door. "I'm so sorry, Cam." He took my hand which hung limply and shook it. "This new lot, the Gestapo, have informants everywhere. Somebody in the house must have told them. You can't trust anybody."

Hot tears filled my eyes. "When did it happen?"

"This morning," Leo said. "I heard a commotion as they bashed down the door. I rushed down but we could only watch. There were five of them. Brutish looking men in heavy leather coats. They had pistols."

I looked round for somewhere to sit down and backed towards a hall chair beside Frau Guttchen's manically polished sideboard. "How did he look?"

Leo and Frau Guttchen exchanged glances. "He wasn't hurt, if that's what you mean," Leo said.

"I have his passport. I'm that close to getting him out. If only I'd been here yesterday."

Frau Guttchen rested a hand on my shoulder. "You must be brave, Herr Cameron. Perhaps they will question him and let him go. He has not done anything wrong, after all."

I was tired after the journey and confused
listening to Frau Guttchen in German and Leo in
English, translating my questions so that both
could understand. I was sobbing. "Where have they
taken him?"

Frau Guttchen looked at the floor. Leo
studied the hat that he was twisting in his
hands. "It's said that, when the Gestapo arrest
you, you're taken to a place in Oranienburg." His
voice cracked. "It's run by the SS."

"I must go and see him."

Leo shook his head. "His fate is in their
hands now. You can't take on the SS."

It took me nearly a week to ascertain Wolf's
whereabouts. Every morning I would join a queue
at the police headquarters in Friedrichstrasse.
When I reached the front, an officer behind the
counter told me to fill in a new form giving them
Wolf's details and the time and place of his
arrest. Each day I was instructed to return for
information in 24 hours. Finally, after five days
of this I was informed that he was in Oranienburg
and that it was not possible to visit him.

I decided to ignore the instruction to stay
away. The journey north took less than an hour
and all the time I could only think of what my
Wolf must be experiencing. In my imagination the
black-suited thugs held him in solitary
confinement in a dark, damp cell scarcely big
enough for him to stand. He would be starved and
frightened. An SS guard would visit to beat him
up for his own sadistic satisfaction. I had to
get him out.

It was only a short walk from Oranienburg
station to the red-brick buildings which had once
been a brewery but now boasted the words
'Konzentrations Lager' over a ten-foot high
wooden gate. Two SS sentries posted there stood
at ease with rifles at their sides while
residents of the town hurried by on the other
side of the road. It was makeshift and insecure,

not what I had expected. Surely, Wolf could have escaped by now?

I approached the gates. I could hear my blood pulsing in my head. The blades of the rifle bayonets glistened in the sun and I imagined one of the sentries stepping forward to slice open my stomach rather than bother challenging me.

In German I explained that I hoped to find out if my friend was being detained there and demanded to see the officer in command. To my surprise, they stepped back and one of them turned to the gate and simply pushed it open. It was unlocked. He smiled as he showed me through and pointed out a building next to a loading bay that might at one time have been a weighing office. "It's the administrative block," he said.

I walked across the yard as purposefully as I could on trembling legs. To my left, between two identical brick-built factory buildings, I could see a group of prisoners drawn up in rows. There didn't seem to be a uniform – they were in their civilian clothes. There was nothing about them to say they had been abused.

I knocked on the door I had been directed to and stepped inside. The small office contained two desks at which two SS-uniformed women worked at typewriters. Neither looked up. I coughed.

Finally, one of them sighed and stopped clattering the keys. She looked up and stood. "Heil Hitler!" She shot out her arm.

"I'm English," I said in German by way of explanation for not responding. "I have come to see whether you have my friend in this place."

"Prisoners here do not have visitors. Don't you know this?" She looked at me as if I had asked her to dance naked on her desk singing *God Save the Queen*.

"I am a visitor to Germany. I came from England and found that my friend has been arrested. I have been to Friedrichstrasse. They told me there that I could visit him." I was now so used to lying that I didn't even blush.

The second woman had stopped typing and was smirking.

"His name is Wolfgang Koehler. He lives in Charlottenburg."

"We do not have anybody of that name here." The first woman picked up a number of sheets of paper and began sorting them.

I tried to smile so she would think I was not as anxious as I felt. "How can you know? You can't know the name of every prisoner here."

There was a door to an inner office between the two desks and I heard the sound of boots on the other side of it. The second woman shot to her feet and both stood straight-backed to attention as the door opened. A small man who reminded me of Victor Simons, the provider of Wolf's illegal passport, walked in, his boots echoing on the floorboards. "What is going on? Why have you stopped working?" he demanded.

The first woman pointed at me. "This Englishman wants to visit one of the prisoners."

The officer looked me up and down and smiled. I tried to respond in kind but only managed a lop-sided grimace. There was a pause while he examined my linen suit, the same one I had worn to the Grill Room in London. He seemed to be suppressing a laugh as he asked me, "Can I help you, Herr ...?"

"Mortimer," I said. "I know my friend is here." My mouth was dry and I swallowed to try to stimulate a flow of saliva. "I would like to visit him."

"Your friend? What do you mean *friend*?"

"An acquaintance I have made since being in Berlin."

"A German?"

"Yes."

"How long have you known your *friend*?"

"Two years."

The women were watching him like faithful Labradors waiting for an order and he waved a hand so they could sit. "Carry on with your work!" He held out his arm indicating that I

245

should go into his office. "Let us see whether I can help you, Herr Mortimer." As I passed him he touched my back gently as if to reassure me. "What is your *friend*'s name again?"

"Koehler, Wolfgang" I said.

He barked an order over his shoulder, "Check if we have a prisoner, Koehler, Wolfgang, and if we do bring me the file."

He closed the door behind him and gestured me to a chair in front of a desk. He went round behind it and sat down. He leaned back with his elbows resting on the arms of the chair and his hands clasped level with the SS lightning-bolt insignia on his collar. "Let us wait and see whether Herr Koehler is indeed one of our guests."

I tried to hide my nervousness but found I couldn't look the officer in the face and, despite knowing that every movement of my head made me look even shiftier, I couldn't settle my gaze on anything.

There was a knock at the door. One of the women came in carrying a thin brown file.

"Ach! So it seems Herr Koehler is here." He took the file. "We are not to be disturbed."

For the first time I saw a gleam of hope. The officer seemed to be implying that he and I would have a rational discussion about whether I could visit Wolf.

He opened the file and started reading the papers. He shook his head and tutted. He frowned. It was very amateurish play-acting and he seemed happy for me to believe it to be so.

"Your *friend* Herr Koehler has been mixing with some unsavoury people. The order for his arrest was issued some weeks ago. He was part of an SA troop that was planning a treasonous coup against the Fuhrer."

"He wasn't in the SA," I said, still happy to conduct the conversation in German. "He wanted to join them, yes. He even went to a camp with the troop he was going to join but he didn't actually become a member."

246

"What do you think we are? Do you think our laws are any less straight than in England? Of course he was not a suspect in the case against Roehm and his conspirators. Do you know the charges he faced? The ones he was found guilty of in the Oranienburg Court House only yesterday?"

"No."

"A homosexual act. Namely mutual onanism, which he admitted. His sentence is forty-two months detention and minimum two years military service."

I felt myself blush when he mentioned onanism but then the blood seemed to drain out of me at the severity of the sentence. "That's six years."

"Five and a half to be exact."

I decided I had to broach the subject. "Is there anything I can do? Perhaps a fine as an alternative to prison? I could pay it here at this office at your convenience." Now that I had the passport even a day of freedom would be enough. I hoped he would see my meaning.

He smiled. "Sadly not. Once the court ..." He opened his hands as if to say, what can I do?

"What I mean is, perhaps a fine to commute his detention and then a few days grace before the military service starts? I am sure an officer with your influence ..."

He stood up and walked round until he stood directly in front of me. He perched his rump on the desk and used both hands to tease out the wings of his jodhpur-style trousers.

"I know you mean well for your *friend* -" the emphasis was now annoying and he delighted in it "- but you must not think that this country's judicial system is any less ... correct ... than yours in England."

"Of course, not," I said. "If I gave that impression-"

He held up a hand. "However your timing may be propitious. This facility is closing down on Friday. We have already sent prisoners to our new centre not far away. It is called Sachsenhausen.

I see from Herr Koehler's file that he is due to be transferred tomorrow. Now it is a sad fact that when we transfer prisoners we are not always in total control of events. Something can occur that means a prisoner could escape." He shifted all his weight onto one leg and crossed them at the ankle. His boots shone.

I chose my words carefully. "As Wolf's friend I would dearly wish that if a prisoner were to escape because of an occurrence it would be Herr Koehler. If I could make this happen I would."

He nodded. "I think we understand each other Herr Mortimer. But we have to make something come up. It is a problem." When he said, "come up" he brushed his hand across the front of his trousers. This was directly opposite my face no more than twenty inches away. Did he mean ...?

"It is a problem, Herr Mortimer. Don't you see? Can you think of something? Use your head, now. If you see a problem comes up in front of you, do you not use your *head* to make it disappear?"

So there it was. The price of Wolf's freedom. I leaned forward and tugged at the silver death's-head belt buckle.

In the days before Wolf, I would have chewed any man's foreskin if he was cute but this was betrayal. Also, this ugly little toy-soldier wanted it to be the nearest thing to assault. He held me by my hair and used me. As Hobbes said about life, it was nasty, brutish and short and the last adjective, luckily, is a measure appropriate to both length and time in this case. So the experience was degrading rather than painful.

As he buttoned his trousers, he asked me whether as an Englishman I enjoyed being fucked in the face by a strong German.

I still had the taste of his semen in my mouth and I longed for a glass of water and to brush my teeth that were coated in his slime. "It's a price I'm more than willing to pay. Now

how will you let Wolf go? Where and when do I
have to be?"

"Let him go?" He looked at me as if I had
reverted to English.

"While he's being transferred. Where should
I be? When?"

"You are being very stupid, Herr Mortimer.
You have been *fucked*." He used the English word.
"There will be no escape."

"But the transfer ..."

"Yes. We are closing here. We are moving the
prisoners to Sachsenhausen. It has already
started. In fact your Herr Koehler went there
directly from the courthouse. He had the honour
of being one of the first batch of prisoners
there." He laughed more raucously. "You have been
fucked and you English better get used to it.
Germany is on the rise and if there is war, which
I think there will be, you and your Wolf will be
on opposite sides, Herr Mortimer. And as your
friend is serving a sentence he will be in a
punishment battalion. I would not hold out much
hope that he will survive even the short war we
shall win. Now let me show you out."

His laughter followed me as I left the
office and walked to the gate, a feeble and
foolish queer.

Chapter 31

Jay looks at his watch. He doesn't want to tire Willy out but on the other hand he's anxious to know about as much of his story as possible. If he can connect him to Isherwood in a meaningful way he'll be able to tell Mark Costidy that he's discovered they have a contemporary of the *Cabaret* originator in their midst. 'Can you go on a little longer?' he says.

'Pfff! I can talk a blue streak until Christmas you want to listen.' He strokes his chin. 'Where to start?'

'I asked about Germany – before the war.'

Willy looks out of the window, into the distance. 'Sachsenhausen!'

Jay remembers the *Buzz* headline. 'That was the death camp?'

'Death camp! Pfff! Sachsenhausen was never a death camp – not like in Poland. This was a Concentration Camp. Important difference. Yes, people died under torture but no systematic killing of everyone who arrived.'

Willy and I understand this distinction, Jay. Most prisoners in the concentration camps in Germany survived. In the death camps in the east – we were all meant *to die. Every single one.*

Jay's replaying the MC's last intervention. This is not in his memory. Where did it come from?

You must have read it somewhere.

He's only half-listening while Willy explains how he was arrested and charged with treason and being a homosexual.

'Why treason?'

'Because Wolf was involved with Ernst Röhm and the Brownshirts.'

Try again. Cameron before the war.

'Tell me about Cameron – how you met. Did you ever meet Christopher Isherwood?'

Too eager!

Willy shakes his head. 'Isherwood? No, not then. He could have come to one of Cameron's parties here in New York. Is it important?'

'I was hoping … no, not really. Tell me about when you were together – in Berlin.'

But Willy's eyes are closed and, as he breathes in, the sound he makes is like a cat purring.

As Jay strides to his car with his hands in his pockets and breath clouding ahead of him he thinks about Willy Keel's story. He's frustrated not to learn more about what happened before the war but what he's heard is far more interesting than many of the lives he's read about since he delved into Isherwood and the Nazis. He wonders if Willy would let him write up his biography. It's only something he could contemplate with the Straub, DuCheyne millions behind him.

Two days later Jay is with Teri in Stamford. She's slipping on a replacement thong and tosses the torn one into the waste basket. Their weekly meetings are now all about sex that increasingly involves a degree of humiliation for her. They bang away in the dusty cubicle as if they're actors in a porn movie and she appears to get pleasure from the pain. On the drives home, Jay feels remorse but the MC urges him to channel his disquiet into even more inventive excesses. *It's too late for me. Exploit what you have – your sensual body. Live it! Feel it! No limits!*

Teri thumbs through papers in a file and presents Jay with a counterfoil. 'Perhaps I should have given you this before – then maybe you wouldn't have been so rough. It's the check.'

Jay thinks she's presenting him with the bill for her torn lingerie. But it's a banker's draft payable to him for $3m and change. He clasps a hand over his eyes and a smile spreads across his lips. 'Shit!'

Money Money Money Money Money Money – that clinking, clanking sound. It makes the world go round.

'Well, what do you say?'

'Thanks,' he says.

'I reckon you can do better.' She tucks in her blouse and smoothes her skirt.

'What do you mean?'

'I think I deserve another trip. Maybe we could go see clients in the city for the day. Next Tuesday you can spend some of that money on *me*. What do you say?'

On the way home the only thing occupying Jay's mind is how to make it look as if the cheque is for $3m straight so he can lash the accrued interest on the day in town with Teri. He's left it to her to book the best possible place for lunch and a suite in a hotel of her choice. It isn't going to be cheap.

The second meeting with Willy, on the Sunday before Thanksgiving, takes place at the same hour, in the same room with the same coffee things served by the same assistant. The same sullen sky hangs over the drab garden bordered by skeletal trees. It's as if time stood still.

As soon as Willy is wheeled in, Jay asks him if he'll allow him to record their meetings. 'Your story would make a great book.' He's ignoring Rachel's intention for them to go home before the start of the January school term.

'You really think so? I'm not so sure.'

Jay knows him well enough now – he's waiting to be flattered. 'Think what you've lived through. The rise of Hitler in Berlin–'

Willy interrupts. 'Wolf was in the Hitler Youth …'

Jay holds up the digital recorder. Willy nods. 'I think it was his uniform that excited Cameron in the early days.'

252

Jay smiles. He's not sure how to answer.

For the next 40 minutes Willy needs only intermittent prompts to recount the story of his upbringing in Charlottenburg, his family's involvement with the Nazis, and his meeting with Cameron. He's frank about how he initiated the sex. 'Cammie was such a stuffed shirt – so English. He was so scared of Wolf when he knew how he felt. I swear Cammie would have run away if Wolf hadn't pinned him to the bed.' He chuckles and for a moment Jay can see a younger man.

'Wolf was singing once and he fainted, you know. In the Neuen See Biergarten. The scene – me singing, not Cameron fainting – it was the same as in the film ...' he clicks his fingers, '... you know, the one with Judy Garland–'

'Liza Minnelli. It was her daughter, Liza Minnelli. *Cabaret*.' And as he says the word, Jay hears a buzzing in his ears and he has to steady himself because he feels a trembling through the floor.

It's like the plates of the earth are moving together ...

'Are you all right?' Willy says.

'Yes. It's just the coincidence of that scene.' He tells Willy about Ben and the school production.

'It was a fine film,' Willy says.

'But because I'm – we're Jewish – there's a rabbi who's been trying to have the show stopped. He doesn't like the idea of a Jewish boy singing that song – you know *Tomorrow Belongs to Me* and wearing the uniform and the swastika armband.'

Willy nods. 'It's understandable. They went through so much.'

'They? You're Jewish too, aren't you?'

Willy waves his hand. 'Pfff! No. Never. You think they would have had me in the army? I *definitely* would have gone to a death camp. No, it was my wife, Geraldine, she was Jewish. Not that you'd know.'

Concentrate on this, Jay. This is important. Listen ...

253

Jay ignores a fleeting tingle of déjà vu. 'The synagogue I go to supports Ben – but Rabbi Stern, he's trying to have the whole production stopped. He doesn't think it's right for my Ben to play the part.'

There's a silence while Jay thinks about the man who's causing them trouble.

Willy has his eyes shut and Jay worries that he's gone to sleep.

'Willy?'

'Sorry. So what does Rabbi Stern intend to do?'

'He says he'll bring his congregation to the school theatre and picket the show.'

Willy sighs. 'This seems so bigoted from a man who suffered from prejudice himself.'

'I hadn't thought about it like that.'

Willy shuts his eyes again. 'I'm tired, Jay. But you can come again and we'll do the book. But first you must do me a favour.'

'Of course.'

'Will you take me to see your son in the *Cabaret*?'

Later in Ponds Lane, Jay draws a deep breath. It's not only to appreciate the aroma of coffee fresh from the grinder. 'There's been a hitch with the money.'

'What do you mean – "hitch"?' Rachel pours hot water and the scalded grounds foam as they surrender their essence.

He tries to sound casual. 'Oh. Nothing major – a couple of forms. Formalities.'

'What does it mean?' She shoos Jay in front of her like a farmer herding an unruly bull. 'Move! This kitchen! I'll be glad when we get back to the UK. A bigger house – what a relief.'

Jay takes his place at the table which is set with coffee cups. The side plates each have an English muffin, split, toasted and spread with margarine and Marmite. The Marmite comes from a Brit ex-patriot shop in Ossining where Rachel also buys Cadbury's chocolate.

'Tuck in.' Rachel presses down on the cafetière's plunger.

'Mmm!' Jay licks some stray Marmite from his lips and savours the salty tang. It's a taste from home. 'I was saying about the money?'

'Yeah, forms.'

'Formalities – but Teri says it can all be done in a day if we go and sort it out face-to-face.' He's studying the smeared surface of the half-muffin that he's taken a bite from.

'When?'

'She's organised it for Tuesday so as to not use up more than our usual time.'

'That's thoughtful.' She pours the coffee.

Jay looks up. Was that irony? Perhaps he's being paranoid.

'Is it the insurance company?'

'Yes. New York Life.'

'Why don't I come too? We could do a bit of shopping; have a celebration. What time's the meeting?'

He shrugs and screws his face into his I-can't-help-it look. 'Sorry. No can do. 'Cos Teri's arranged some more appointments while we're in the city. Closing down the last few accounts – do the glad-handing. You know how it goes. I probably won't leave until after the rush hour. Home for eight or nine? Sorry.'

'Pity. I would have liked to have come.'

'We can do it anytime after we have the money. Go into the city; stay somewhere grand. A suite at the Ritz-Carlton – that sort of thing. We're not tied down. Let's wait until after Thanksgiving. They say the shops really turn it on for Christmas after–'

'Who says?'

He shrugs again. 'I don't know. It's something I've picked up. Macy's – Father Christmas – *Miracle on 34th Street*, you know. We could sort out your Christmas present – once we've $3m in the bank. How does that sound?' He lifts the cup to his lips and the coffee's heavy bitterness lays over the salt-taste from the Marmite. 'Good coffee.' He smiles.

They had arranged to meet in the lobby of the Marriott Marquis on Broadway. Jay arrives first. He's blowing heat into his hands and cursing himself for not remembering his gloves and for not wearing his scarf up over his exposed ears. He's still stamping his feet as Teri swirls through the revolving door. She's wearing white fur earmuffs that match her faux fur coat. It has a nipped waist that accentuates her figure and its length shows off her boot-encased calves. Jay's imagination stirs his body's reflexes into action.

Layer after layer for you to take off. Make sure you take your time.

Teri links her hand around his arm and leads him to the VIP reception desk. 'We have an early check-in? Under Halprin? Jay Halprin?' she says.

Neither their before-lunch arrival nor their lack of luggage disturbs the deadpan expression of the woman behind the counter. Her 'Have an iced A!' trails after them to the bank of elevators.

Alone inside the lift, they throw themselves at each other.

As soon as they're inside their room, Jay spins her round and undoes the buttons of her coat and blouse. While they chew at each other's lips, Teri scrabbles for his belt and zipper. He hooks her breasts out over the cups of her bra and then works her skirt up. He has his mouth clamped to her nipple as he grapples her panties far enough down for her to step one leg out. Then he is in and the back of Teri's head bangs against the heavy door.

I told you to take your time. This is more like the bathroom scene at the start of The Godfather. *You know, where Marlon Brando's newly-married son has sex in the bathroom with a bridesmaid while the wedding feast continues in the garden outside. You know the one … Jay?*

Jay presses his face into Teri's neck. His eyes are screwed tight shut. He needs to banish the MC from his mind if he's going to make this happen before his knees give way.

At the casually chic French restaurant recommended to Teri by Nathan Fothergill, Jay asks whether the meal is on expenses as he's such an important client. The room is tiny and the top of their round table is no bigger than a dustbin lid. A floor-length white cotton tablecloth hides their legs. 'Oh no,' she says, '*you* are not the client. Straub, DuCheyne is the client. When we wind it up we're billing them. Perhaps I can find a way of putting the meal on their account.' She smiles. 'Yes, that'll work – but only if you treat me *really* well this afternoon.'

'I'm excited thinking about it.' Jay slips his right foot out of its shoe and runs his socked foot along her calf. Her smile emboldens him so he goes higher. She separates her knees. Higher still. By the time the waiter asks for their order Jay's cotton-encased toe is pressed into her groin. He admires Teri's sang-froid as she orders oysters for both of them.

Teri mentions that Nathan is at one of the memorial services.

'Which one?' His foot is still wedged in her groin. He tries to remove it but she reaches down and pulls it in. She closes her thighs around it – her face flushed. The tendons at the back of his knee complain.

Keep it there. D'you think she'll do it right here?
'Sure you want to know?'
Watch her eyes … she is. She is!
He keeps his voice even. 'Why not?'

257

'Your assistant – Nancy Chandler.'

His stomach lurches and he pulls his foot away.

Nancy – and you promised you'd be there for her.

'Why didn't Nathan tell me? I would have gone.'

'Did you go to the others?'

'Which others?'

'That's what I mean. Nancy's one of the last. Nathan and I decided we shouldn't tell you about any of them. It would have been uncomfortable for everybody.'

She's right. Imagine it. 'Oh look, there's the only survivor. Did you know he made $3million out of it? No wonder he's smiling.'

'But for Nancy – I should have ...'

It's over. Forget about it. Now get those toes back in there. I want to see whether she does a Meg Ryan in When Harry Met Sally.

Later, in the hotel room, their lovemaking is more leisurely but Jay's need to dominate, to punish, is even more marked. His passion takes on a darker side.

It's because of Nancy, isn't it?

He starts to slap Teri's butt – playfully at first – then harder. She wriggles away. He's laughing as he grabs her waist. She giggles and shakes her head. 'Stop it!' Her voice is light. He pins her down and uses two fingers to enter her, roughly.

So you're going to take it out on her.

'Stop it!' Her voice is sharper. 'No! You're scaring me.'

He grunts.

Go on! What's the worst thing you can do?

He flips her over. 'I know what you want.' His left hand is on the small of her back to hold her down. His knees pinion the back of her legs and stop her kicking. He slavers on his right hand and wipes the slime over his cockhead. He drools on his fingers again and prods one of them against her anus.

'NO!' She struggles under him. 'Not that. Not ever that.' She hisses it with her head arched back.

He positions himself for a thrust forward but this gives Teri the opportunity to squirm up the bed. She kicks out backwards. It's harmless but the impact on his thigh is enough to bring him fully back into the moment.

She sits up with her back to the headboard and pulls the duvet up. Her mascara is spread across her face. 'You'd better go home,' she says between sobs. 'I don't know what's got into you. Go home!'

What's this? She was up for it, trust me.

'I wasn't going to. Not if you didn't want it.'

Don't whine. You've nothing to apologise for.

'How many times did I say "no"? How many times?'

But we get it, don't we? No can sometimes mean yes.

He bangs his fist against his forehead. The MC's interruptions make it impossible for him to collect his thoughts. 'I won't try it again. I made a mistake.'

You're grovelling. What did I tell you? She may say she didn't want it but she would have lapped it up.

'You bet you did. You been getting weird. Like this is some power trip for you. Like I was getting off on you hurting me. Well, that's not me, Jay. You can crawl back under the rock you came from. I'll put you down to experience. Now get the fuck outa my life!'

That went well then. Better get dressed.

'You're early. How did it go?'

Jay has walked through the front door without his usual greeting. 'Huh?'

Rachel stands at the opening to the kitchen. Ben hovers at the top of the stairs down to the den. 'You said you'd be late.' She wipes her hands on a tea towel. 'Doesn't matter. Has the money come through?'

He nods as he puts down his briefcase and removes his overcoat. 'Yeah. It's sorted.'

'Mmph! You don't sound like a man who's just been given $3million. I've got Champagne.' She turns back into the kitchen.

'Can I see it?' Ben's crossing towards him.

'What?'

'The cheque – $3million. It's not often you see one of those.'

Jay smiles. 'Huh. No. They paid it straight into our bank account.'

Ben turns away and sits at the table. 'Spoilsports!'

The fridge door slams and Rachel comes in with a tray bearing the bottle and three glasses that clink together as she walks. '*We* are multi-millionaires!'

'It's not pounds, Mum – only dollars.'

She puts down the tray and ruffles his hair. 'Even in pounds it's two-plus – still multi–'

Sit. Forget Teri. Forget why you have three million bucks. Enjoy the Champagne.

He joins them at the table.

Rachel proffers the bottle. 'You open it.'

He removes the foil and eases out the stopper. It 'pops' but he holds the cork to prevent it flying across the room. He pours the three measures, taking care lest the drink foams over the rims.

They each take one. 'Cheers!' he says.

'To $3million!' Rachel responds.

'£2million plus!' Ben says.

They all drink.

'Tell me how it went,' Rachel says.

Jay takes them through his fictitious day. He explains that more paperwork was necessary and, how, after he signed it, Teri, Nathan's assistant took it to the offices of New York Life. In the meantime, Jay and Nathan went through the formal process of winding up Straub, DuCheyne. They visited some insurers after lunch and by the end of the day the company ceased to exist and here they are $3million richer.

'What about the rest of the money?' Rachel asks.

Oops! You let the lies run ahead of you.

Jay looks into his Champagne. 'Yeah. The company's wound up on paper. But it's not finished. 'Cos it's still a legal entity. When all that stuff is legally filed ... that's when we get the money. Like I said before – probably in the first couple of months next year.' He feels Rachel's laser beam stare on his face.

You always do it. Run off at the mouth.

'Hmmm. Well those attorneys better not be jerking us around,' Rachel says.

She's using American slang, Jay. That has to be a danger signal.

'I'm sure they're not.' He knocks back the last of his drink. 'Now, I think I'll take a shower before dinner. What are we having?'

Rachel is frowning. 'Ben and I are having pasta. *You* said you were going to be late.'

'I didn't say I'd eat out.'

'You inferred it. Anyway, why have a shower, why now?'

Ben stands up. 'I'm going to my room.'

'Homework?' Rachel says, barely glancing in his direction.

'Yeah.' He's already half-way up the stairs.

Rachel turns back to Jay and his heart lurches. She carries Ben's homework schedule in her head and normally wouldn't allow him to get away without a detailed account of what he intends to do. Jay scrapes back his chair.

'Stay!'

He jerks a thumb in the direction of the bathroom. 'My shower.'

'Stay!'

Jay remains seated. 'What's the matter, Rache?'

'You smell of her.'

'Who?' A trapdoor is opening beneath his feet.

'What's-her-name – Teri.'

'What do you mean?' It's a hopeless rearguard action and he knows it.

No way out of this one. Take it like a man.

Her voice cuts like a scalpel. 'You stink of her perfume and you stink of stale sex. How long has it been going on?' Now the blade is ice-cold. 'Don't even try to deny it.'

He looks down at his hands and sees that he's unconsciously clasped them together and is wringing them in an incriminating way. He pulls them apart and straightens his shoulders.

Best come clean.

'It's over. It started when we went to Texas. But, believe me, it meant nothing–'

'I bloody knew there was something fishy about San An-fucking-tonio.'

'Like I said, it's over.'

'It's bloody over all right.' Tears are brimming. Her voice is a sob. 'How could you?'

'I'm sorry.' He reaches out but she shrugs his hand away. 'She was there … she–'

'Don't!' Her eyes are wild. Her voice is still low but each consonant carries a fury. 'Don't blame her. It better be over. It better be fucking over. Because, if you ever do anything like this again, I'll cut your balls off before taking you for every fucking cent of your fucking three fucking million fucking dollars.'

It's as if her venom enters his blood. His head buzzes and his chest is constricting. Is this what a stroke feels like? A heart attack? He manages to mumble, hoping that if he talks long enough he'll become coherent. 'Never … I'll never … it was a one-off … I didn't mean to hurt … I'm sorry.' His tears are falling now.

'You'd better have that shower. *You* make sure you load the washing machine with your stuff. *You* get that suit dry-cleaned tomorrow. You get *her* stink out of *my* house. And you can fucking-well sleep in that sodding den tonight.

Jay slinks away from the table and makes for the bathroom, undoing his tie.

We're not having the best of days.

It's not funny. It's your fault.

How do you make that out? You're the one with the penis. Put it all behind you. Rachel will come round.

I love her. I wish I'd never …

Don't we always. Teri's toast. She's served her purpose.

Jay stands motionless beneath the shower jet, his head bowed. You're right I can deal with Fothergill for what's left.

Not only that. She's done what was needed. Stamford is over. We move on.

And Rachel?

What you told me about love – tell her. Any barriers she puts up … she'll regret them. She will. Trust me.

The next morning it's frosty both inside and outside the house. While Ben's at school, Rachel makes clear that Jay's behaviour means that she alone will decide when they return to the UK. She sits at the computer booking their flights on Christmas Day. She views rental property near their UK house and instructs the agents to give the tenants notice to quit. They have the money. She will get them back on track.

The following day is Thanksgiving and the Cochranes have invited them to their house to share their meal. Bob is keen that Jay joins him for the traditional American football game. By the time Thanksgiving night arrives, Rachel and Jay

have reached a truce and share the marital bed. She allows him
to cuddle against her back but her body is rigid.

Jay visits Willy Keel on the first two Sundays in December and
at the beginning of the second meeting, Willy announces that he
would be happy for Jay to publish his biography as long as it
doesn't happen until after his death. They agree to work on it
together and to overcome the problem of Jay's return to the UK
as and when it presents itself.

They're in Willy's room. An old-person fug hangs
around them. Jay is in the guest chair – the same plastic-
covered, high-seated institution furniture as in the meeting
room. He's swung the bed-table across in front of it so there's a
surface to write on and a place for his recording machine. Willy
is not in the bed which is crisply made. He slumps in his
wheelchair wearing a zipped shell-suit – blue with white stripes
down the sides. His feet are in slippers. There are two books
and a spectacles case on top of the bedside cabinet. The books
are piled with their edges squared. The spectacle case is set
parallel. Jay wonders whether this precision is the effort of a
nurse or the remnants of Willy's military discipline.

'I'd like to talk today about your escape from Germany,'
Jay says.

'Well, first I had to make it back home – to Berlin. This
was long before the Wall, you understand. The whole east of
the country was under Russian control. There were ways to get
into Berlin if you were resourceful enough. I went through the
sewer system. My home from before the war was destroyed.
My family was gone. All dead.'

*They were Nazis from the beginning, Jay. The worst sort – the
believers. No need to mourn their passing.*

As Willy talks, Jay glances to check that the recorder light
is on and tries to recall when Willy had told him about his

family background. How can the MC know that they were early sympathisers unless he does?

Willy mentioned it before.

'It looked as if the Russians had deliberately set out to flatten every single building in the city but a few survived and by some miracle the house where Cameron lived was one of them. The Green House we called it.'

'Which sector was it in?'

'The British. This was very lucky for me. It made it easier to get out later. It was there virtually unscathed, overlooking a burnt out Russian tank on the rubble that used to be Steinplatz. Even the wooden tobacco kiosk – it was still there.' Willy's eyes look out into the past.

'What happened?'

'Another miracle. Cameron's landlady still lived there. Frail and so old. But not too old for the Russian soldiers to have ignored, she told me. She was so ashamed. And she had hidden my passport. She still had my passport.'

'Why was it there – at the Green House? '

'It wasn't my German passport. It was English.'

'A British passport. How?'

'Questions!' He waves a hand as if swatting away a persistent wasp. 'It's a story for another time.'

'But it meant you were able to leave?'

'It wasn't that easy. I still needed money to bribe my way out. You have to understand in those days there were very few honest people in Berlin. One of them – a good man – Bernie Gunther helped me. He'd been a Friedrichstrasse 'bull' – a police detective – before the war and had served on the Eastern front with the SS. He'd come back to Berlin to be a private investigator – lots of work for him with so many missing. He found me a widow with money. Her husband had been a big player in the black market – after the occupation the Western sectors were rife with corruption. He was killed and left her a

265

stash of US dollars. Her money, my passport – we could escape.' The 'w' in 'we' sounds like a sibilant 'v'.

'So what happened?'

'Bernie Gunther took us to Osnabrück and Brits there smuggled us into Holland. We married in Enschede and ended up in Ostend where we waited for a boat.'

'But now you were out of trouble.'

He shakes his head and tears appear. 'It was still a lawless time in Europe – like the Wild West. Some GIs passing through attacked us. I was beaten up and they held me down while they …' his voice broke, 'my wife … I couldn't help her.'

'I'm so sorry'

'It didn't end there. Geraldine was pregnant. She had the boy. We brought him with us.'

'To America?'

'By the time we got to England her money was nearly spent. We couldn't afford to stay hidden – on the run. We decided to own up to who we were. So we went to the British Red Cross. We changed our names to Keel before we came to New York.'

'It's an amazing story. What happened to your son?'

'We lost touch after Geraldine died.'

'That's sad.' Jay turned the pages of his notes. 'This Bernie Gunther, the policeman. What happened to him?'

'I don't know. Maybe the authorities caught up with him. If the Russians found out he was SS …' he drew a finger across his throat, '… kaput.'

'It was amazing you got through the war.'

'Yes, I was the great survivor … Geraldine too.'

'It's funny we're talking about the past – about the Berlin you know at first hand – and you're going to see it in the musical. How will you feel?'

He shrugs. 'Who knows?'

'You were part of all the things that Rabbi Stern is protesting about. You were there.'

Willy sighs and shakes his head. 'Don't remind me. I was young. I'm older and wiser now. I was in Oranienburg. The same prison they shot all the communists. I hated the Communists. I hated their flag but now I would stand for their right to parade it in the streets.'

'And back then?'

He nods. 'Maybe not so much, I admit it. But I wouldn't have wanted them to be arrested and executed without trial. I don't think so.' He studies his slippered feet wedged in the stirrups of the wheelchair as if they hold an answer to thoughts that trouble him. 'Yes I was in the Hitler Youth but after what the Nazis made me go through nobody hates the swastika more than me. How can you defend wrapping yourself in a flag? You must be able to laugh at any flag – yes, even the Stars and Stripes.' He looks round as if he could have been overheard even though they're alone. 'And I only say this because you are English.' He sniggers and wheezes.

'So you're coming to see my son on Saturday?'

'Try and keep me away.' He smiles and pats Jay's hand.

And he's sure the picket won't put him off?

'And you're not worried by the picket?'

'I'm old. I'm going to be scared away by a bigoted young rabbi who doesn't know shit from Shinola? Now get out of here. I'm tired; I need to sleep.'

The first performance of *Cabaret* approaches and Ben is involved with rehearsals every afternoon after school and at weekends. His progress is the only subject that keeps Rachel and Jay communicating, this and the interference from Rabbi Stern's congregation. The family feeds on the rabbi's opposition. Rachel's frost softens as the weather outside grows harsher.

The denizens of Burford Lakes go about their business with hardly a glance in the Halprins' direction. The gentiles, Presbyterians and Baptists, Evangelicals and Episcopalians, stand alongside Rabbi Zwyck's reform Jews in respecting that the family is taking a stand against prejudice – the prejudice of Nazism in the play and that displayed by the rabbi.

Their neighbours are anticipating the school's Holiday production as never before. The Edlers and the Cochranes have their tickets. In the house opposite, Melissa Rosenberg sits at her computer setting up the review she'll write for the *Buzz*. She's already written the headline: *Jefferson Joy*. But she has a backup *Cabaret Calamity* just in case.

Ben comes home after the first performance with a make-up tide mark above his collar. There's cuddling and congratulation while he assures his parents that it went well. They settle around the table to hear him tell his story and let his nervous tension subside. Rachel and her son have mugs of Cadbury's drinking chocolate. Jay has a crystal glass with a finger of single malt whisky.

Ben is explaining that some cast members asked why his parents weren't there. Rachel rests a hand on her son's arm. 'Maybe we should have booked tickets for *every* night as well.'

Ben dips his spoon into his drinking chocolate and licks it. 'No! I think it's real strange that they go every night. And Kimberley Arnott who plays Sally is going to get a bouquet from her parents every show.'

Jay snorts. 'Let's get this straight. What you're saying is that all the parents of the cast members go to the show all three nights and that Kimberley's parents take along a bouquet each time?'

Ben nods. 'That's what it looks like.'

Do they bring the same bouquet?

'The same bouquet?'

Rachel laughs. 'Jay!'

'What d'you mean, Dad?'

'Is it a new bouquet every night or do they put the old one in water when they get home and bring it back next day?' He's accentuating his dead-pan voice to emphasise that he's being ironic but it doesn't seem to be working.

Ben sighs. 'I don't know, Dad. I'll check it out for signs of droop tomorrow?'

'The point is, Jay, that they expected us to be there tonight. They think we should go tomorrow as well as Saturday. But I'm a Brit and I don't care what *they* think.' She straightens her back and lifts her chin. '*We* will show restraint.' She nods in affirmation. 'We'll stick to our plan – Saturday only.'

'Good,' Jay says. He turns to Ben. 'How was Rabbi Stern's demo?'

'We – the cast – didn't see anything. They were only there for later – when the crowd arrived. They'd gone home by the time we left. It'll be worse Saturday, though.'

'What do you mean?' Jay asks.

'Well, they're not going to be there tomorrow because it's Friday?' He lets the implication of this sink in. 'But Saturday they reckon to stay outside all through the performance chanting so they'll be heard in the auditorium.'

'How do you know?'

'One of the Jewish kids in our year has an older brother who's in Stern's crowd.'

'But it went well tonight – your part?' Rachel asks, not for the first time.

Ben nods. 'Yeah. Like I said – it was good. My song ends the first half and the audience whooped and hollered – like it was the *Letterman* show on TV? There was a standing ovation at the end. You're gonna have to let go when you come – not stay in your seats clapping politely like English people.'

Jay and Rachel look at each other and smile. Can they fake it – American exuberance? 'We'll see what we can do,' Rachel says.

Jay stands and tousles his son's hair. 'Sounds like you did well, son. We're proud of you.' He tosses back the last drops of his whisky. 'I'm for bed.'

Rachel takes the two cocoa cups to the kitchen. She calls out over her shoulder. 'I'll be up as soon as I've rinsed these.'

Next day Jay is on the telephone to Willy Keel. 'I can pay for the taxi.'

'You think I can't afford a cab from White Plains?'

'It's not that–'

'I make sure the car takes my wheelchair, no problem. Order it special.'

'If you're sure. I've reserved you a wheelchair space at the end of a row so you can stay in it for the performance.'

'I could have walked to a seat.'

'I know, but it's easier this way.'

'Okay. But you don't have to worry about me.'

'I won't. We'll see you at the school then, Willy.'

'One more thing, Jay.'

'What's that?'

'I've sent you something in the post. It's something written by my old friend Cameron – Cameron Mortimer. It's a kind of life-story … Berlin. It will help explain everything.'

'What do you mean everything?'

'I'll tell you after the show.'

Jay puts down the phone and thinks about his new friend. Willy will be alone again when they go back to England. He'll have only the other residents in the home for company and half of them are gaga. He wonders whether he should offer to track down Willy's stepson. Perhaps the boy – although he'd be a man now – would like to be in contact again. After all, he should be grateful that Willy was able to give him such a good start in life.

You should interfere? Your daydream could be Willy's nightmare.

Jay dismisses the MC's negativity and nods. Yes, he'll visit Willy on the Sunday after *Cabaret*, and ask him for more details. He should have thought of it while they were on the phone. Willy could have held on to the Cameron papers – whatever they are – and handed them over on Sunday. Or why not Saturday at the show?

Maybe it would be too ambitious to aim for father and son to be reunited for Christmas but even after he's gone back to England, with them collaborating on Willy's life story, it's the sort of thing he could do on the Internet. It's a project for after the show.

Chapter 32

I trudged up the stairs to Leo's studio when I returned to the Green House. He opened the door holding four brushes that he was cleaning with a colour-stained cloth. He looked at my face. "It didn't go well, Cam."

"So humiliating. The commandant was one of us - mine - you know. He gave me the impression ..."

He sighed wearily, "What did you do?"

"Enough to feel very stupid and abused when he laughed in my face - just after he'd done something else in it."

"Poor Cam. Come here." Leo held out his arms and hugged me close to him. It was the most unselfish act I had ever experienced. He knew what I was but he was able to comfort me. And it *was* comforting to lay my head on his shoulder sobbing, taking in the scents of paint and turpentine with each wracking breath.

"What will you do?" he asked.

"I can't stay here with these dreadful people in charge."

"You're right. I haven't given up on Berlin but I rather think that Berlin has given up on us."

A tight feeling of dread invaded my chest and wrapped itself around my heart. "I can't abandon Wolf."

I think you'll have to, old man," he said, as he patted me on the back. "We'll see Frau Guttchen and tell her we're leaving.

That was July 1934. There was a tearful goodbye to Frau Guttchen at the end of September and Leo and I travelled back to Blighty together. I put Wolf's passport in an envelope with a letter giving my London address and entrusted it to Frau

Guttchen. When Wolf returned he would know where to find me. Torn apart by the feeling that I was abandoning my love, I returned to life in London. Leo and I went our separate ways.

The *Glass Madonna Codicil*, the Dexter Parnes I had written in Berlin, was published in 1936 and while I was waiting for it to come out I was approached by Associated Talking Pictures to write the screenplay for a film based on *The Silver Eagle Device*. All the while I pined for Wolf and I sent Frau Guttchen regular telegrams but I never heard news.

As Europe sped to war Peter Everley suggested that he could secure me a publishing deal in America and at the same time Warner Bros asked me to go to Hollywood. They liked what they had seen with the ATP's *Eagle* and wanted me to develop a string of Parnes pictures for release as B-movies on both sides of the Atlantic.

Writing for Warner Bros was not a happy experience and the contract was rescinded by mutual consent. I entered into an agreement with Patriotic and with their scriptwriters doing the work there was no need for me to stay out west. I moved to the East Coast where I found the climate and artistic scene in New York much more conducive to my well-being and accepting of the sort of man I am. I kept Frau Guttchen aware of my whereabouts.

Then the war came and I couldn't go back to Britain. How could I have fought against Germany? If Wolf was still alive, how could I even consider it?

So I hunkered down in New York for the duration and with Dexter Parnes VC books and movies proliferating I was able to consider moving out towards Connecticut. I had sold my brownstone and was waiting for the movers when Wolf, his wife and her son arrived on my doorstep.

Wolf never blamed me for deserting him nor for what had happened in Germany after I left. He didn't like to talk about it but from the snippets he did share, I understood that he had been released into the army in 1937 and had reached the rank of Oberleutnant in a punishment battalion by the time war started and he had to stay in. He fought in Poland, France, Russia and France again. His survival was a miracle.

At the end of the war Wolf went back to Steinplatz and found Frau Guttchen living a life of total privation in the ruins of West Berlin where she was lucky to be in the British Sector. The Green House had survived largely intact and she had spent most of 1945 and '46 cowering in the cellar with her neighbours. She was able to pass my letter to Wolf. The passport had expired but a wartime renewal endorsement was forged and it played a part in his escape to England.

The story of Wolf and his wife's flight through Europe is essentially the plot for my book *The Green House Envelope*, which became the biggest grossing Dexter Parnes VC movie of all time, so there's no need to rehearse it here. Suffice it to say they were able to travel with the boy to the United States using legitimate papers as refugees.

I owed Wolf. I had never lost the guilt about leaving him in Sachsenhausen. Giving him, his wife and stepson a secure place to live was the least I could do. So Mr and Mrs Willy Keel worked for me until Geraldine died in 1960.

The son went away to school and Wolf and I stayed together. We were never intimate in this second life. In fact, we never discussed our love. We always had Berlin but the war had damaged him.

"I have seen so much death," he once said. "Some deaths in the camp and so many more in the war. I must have held the bodies of hundreds of comrades as they slipped away. I would sit there in the frozen mud of the Eastern Front feeling the displaced air stinging my face as the bullets or shrapnel fragments zinged close to my head, passing me but blowing apart the man next door."

"There came a time when my comrades didn't know whether to try and crowd into my invincible space or keep away because it was always the man next to me who took it. They all died."

I asked him why he had married.

"She was a Jew. Did you know? God knows what she must have done to survive in Berlin."

"Didn't you ask?"

"Why? Why would I want to listen to her shame? I have enough of my own. I didn't need her to tell me how much being a survivor damaged her. It was the same for both of us."

Since that conversation with Wolf I often thought about what keeps us together - why we live the way we do. Now, now that I'm dying of the plague that has descended on my kind, it has become clear. The reason Wolf married the Jewess? The reason she married him? The reason I took Wolf, later Willy Keel, back into my life? We all had our guilt. It was the cement that kept us together. It was the guilt.

Chapter 33

It's a cold Saturday evening. New York is expecting snow soon but today's clear skies encourage the temperature to drop and Jay and Rachel are well-wrapped up as they cross the jewelled tarmac of the High School car park. As they negotiate the narrow spaces between the cars, their windscreens dressed with fingers of frost, they become aware of a rumpus around the entrance to the school theatre.

The dark silhouetted figures are like Brownshirts.

It becomes clear that they're Rabbi Stern's pickets and Jay estimates that there are around thirty of them. Most carry placards but they're unreadable at this distance. Each individual is swaddled against the cold. They have thick ski coats and pants with snow boots. Their heads are covered with tight-fitting bobble hats or fur-lined Mountie headgear with earflaps. All have gloves. Their breath clouds around them as they chant in rhythms that make it difficult for Jay to determine the words.

As an audience member jostles through, some break off the chant to jeer. A feeling of trepidation rises in Jay's chest. If someone in the group recognises him – Rabbi Stern himself perhaps – it could turn ugly. They may receive special treatment. How will Rachel cope?

A group reaches the crowd and the chanting increases in volume. The pickets thrust their placards aggressively. Jay sees that Rabbi Stern is standing to one side. He isn't shouting. Nor does he have a placard. Somehow, this infuriates Jay. It's worse that the rabbi, having instigated the demonstration, sees himself as above it.

A taxi draws up and inches forward into the crowd. The demonstrators turn on it and the placards jostle with each other to gain the driver's attention. The window slides down and releases a cloud of blue cigarette smoke. The chanting breaks up and Jay is now close enough to hear a voice emerge from the car. 'Getaddadeway! I gotta disabled man here. How he gonna geddin wid you inda way?'

With the car as the centre of attention, Jay is able to lead Rachel round behind it to the passenger side. As he hoped, it's Willy Keel. 'You slip in and wait for me,' he tells Rachel. 'I'm going to help Willy.'

She leaves him and is inside even before the demonstrators recognise she's there and now Jay is merely a man helping the disabled person out of the taxi; he has no identity in his own right. The demonstrators turn away and re-form between the taxi and the car park. Jay smiles. He's made it inside their cordon without a mishap.

Don't think it's over.

He opens the passenger door. 'Hi, Willy. Welcome. What good timing. Rachel and I have only just arrived.'

Willy swings his feet out. 'I can walk in.'

The driver has left his seat and stands by the open boot. He points at the chair accusingly. 'You gonna take dis ting?'

Jay nods, leans in and grabs the chair by the stays securing the side panel and, as he swings it round, it opens to provide the seat.

Willy waves a shaky hand. 'Lock it, lock it.'

Jay wants to tell him that it's the first time he's done this but sees a locking clip on the top bar and presses it into place. He wheels it so that the chair is parallel to Willy. 'Can you manage?'

'Check the brake – make sure it's locked down.' Willy's tremulous hand points to the brake lever by the chair's push handle.

277

Jay follows the instruction and tests that the chair doesn't move. He helps Willy transfer from one seat to the other. All the time the driver is standing by his door snatching glances at his watch.

'Have you arranged for the cab to come back?' Jay says.

'It's all arranged.' Willy is now in the seat and has lifted his feet onto the rests. 'Let's go.'

'You've paid the driver?'

'Yeah. C'mon, it's cold out here.'

A man steps forward to hold the door while Jay pushes Willy through. Rachel is there waiting. One of the students, a young woman in a black cocktail dress, steps up to them. She has a badge, *Amber Tressage – Enabling Companion*.

She leans down to Willy. 'Hello. How are you today?' She doesn't wait for an answer. 'Are you Mr Keel?' She speaks with unnatural enunciation.

He's not deaf.

Willy nods.

'Okay.' Amber says, 'I'm your designated companion. I'll be looking after you today.' She turns to Jay. 'Thank you but I'll take over now.'

Jay shakes his head. 'Did you know about this, Willy?'

Willy shrugs. 'They called to ask me about my chair and whether I would have a companion. I said no.' He spreads his hands palms upward. 'What'm I gonna do? You go. Let this young lady look after me.' He's smiling broadly as Amber wheels him away.

Jay takes Rachel by the arm. 'Come on. Let's take our seats.'

Only minutes after they settle, the orchestra strikes up and Jay feels his spine tingle. He's nervous for Ben but prepares by reminding himself that it's only a High School show. Ever since he knew the school had chosen to perform *Cabaret*, he's been concerned about how they would deal with the explicit

278

nature of the sex. He hadn't dared say anything, in case Rachel thought it was inappropriate even to consider it, but as the MC appears for the opening number with the 'girls' behind him Jay is reassured.

You may be reassured. I am not so sure. This boy playing my part is not subtle at all. All this camping it up. Ambiguity. We're looking for ambiguity.

Yes, the boy playing the MC is overdoing his mannerisms but it's not enough to shock a New York audience. The senior girls who play the chorus line *are* dressed in what could be defined as lingerie, but their camisole tops and silk shorts, while exposing the straps and gussets of robust underwear, give more coverage than what they'd wear for a pool party. He need not have worried.

Meanwhile, I am being most troubled. The boy is murdering my song – and with such a bad accent.

Sally Bowles makes her first appearance for *Don't Tell Mama.* The girl playing her has the voice to rival Liza Minnelli's but she's at least three dress sizes bigger. Her version of the famous 'bowler' outfit is more like a skirted swimming costume. But none of this detracts from the enthusiasm of the young performers and Jay is soon lost in the love stories of Bradshaw and Bowles and Schultz and Schneider.

We're nearly there, Jay. Sit up.

His blood slows when the boy playing the MC brings a gramophone onto the stage. The air is bloated with anticipation. Jay clenches one fist inside the other. He resists the urge to lower his head between his knees.

It's as clear as a crystal bell when Ben's voice, without accompaniment, comes in from the wings: 'The sun on the meadow is summery warm …' A pause, and the quiet is so intense it hurts Jay's ears. The voice comes in again, melancholy, keening: 'The stag in the forest runs free …' And so it goes for the first two verses. It's masterly direction to have the disembodied voice sing at the pace of a funeral march. The audience is willing him to speed it along but he stubbornly refuses.

At the end, when the boy playing the MC leers the words 'To me ... ', the house is plunged into darkness and the audience explodes into a cacophony of whoops and screams. Jay thinks that a British audience would have maintained a silence suited to the mood.

No. This is better. We need the high emotion. Imagine what they'll be like when Ben sings the song to close the first half.

Further scenes play through until two students, stooped and with their smooth skin lined haphazardly in black pencil, act out the awkwardness of Herr Schultz's proposal and Fraulein Schneider's acceptance. Then on to the engagement party where the American writer Bradshaw discovers he's been an unwitting courier for the Fascists. Herr Ludwig, a Nazi who is at the party, learns that Schultz is a Jew. He tells Fraulein Schneider not to marry Schultz – 'he is *not* a German,' Herr Ludwig declaims.

Even I lose myself in this moment. But soon it will be Ben on stage.

Seeing that Frau Schneider is not going to be warned off, Herr Ludwig grabs his coat and is about to leave. Jay tenses. The song is close. It's usually sung by the Fraulein Kost character as an act of revenge against her landlady and to ingratiate herself with Her Ludwig. But in Mark Costidy's version, Ben, as Fraulein Kost's younger brother, arrives at the party and stands in Herr Ludwig's way as he tries to leave.

Fraulein Kost takes Ben's hand: 'Herr Ludwig, wait! You're not leaving the party so early.'

H. Ludwig: 'I do not find the party *amusing*.'

F. Kost: 'But it's only just beginning.' She pulls Ben centre stage. 'Come, my brother is here, we will make it amusing, ja? The three of us, Herr Ludwig, ja?' Her eyes wander contemptuously over the assembled cast. She nods to Ben and he unbuttons his coat. She turns to the Nazi. 'Herr Ludwig? This is for you.'

This is it.

Jay feels the tension build around him. As his tongue passes across his lip, he tastes electricity in the air. He reaches out and grips Rachel's hand.

The first descending chords of the song mimic the movement of Ben's coat as it slips from his shoulders. The boy is in the uniform of the Hitlerjugend. The notes drift downward as if responding to gravity. Ben stands straight-backed and stiffens. The lights on the rest of the stage dim, leaving only the spotlight illuminating Jay's son.

His voice is strong and sharp. It cuts through the silence. Behind it, the notes of the accompaniment are like the burbling of a brook underscoring the evening trill of a blackbird. Jay feels the hairs on the back of his neck prick into life. It sends chills down to his backside. His legs tremble. There is an almost overwhelming urge to stand. Jay controls it, knowing that the buzzing in his head, the rush of electricity along his limbs is the effect of a massive adrenalin dose.

Tears well up in his eyes. His throat is constricted. He never knew his son's voice could carry such emotion.

Fraulein Kost and Herr Ludwig join in for the second verse and when, in the third, the words, 'The Blossom embraces the bee ...' sound out, the cast and orchestra join in. The sound of it nearly lifts the scalp from Jay's head.

On stage, only the Jew, his new fiancée, the American and the Brit are silent. They stand, confused and aghast at this display of fanatical, patriotic aggression.

In the final verse, 'Now Fatherland, Fatherland, show us the sign ...' the crescendo and the descant combine to take the volume and intensity to even higher levels. And as the last 'Tomorrow belongs to me ...' fills the hall, the boy playing the

MC, now in full SS uniform, goose-steps to centre stage, stands alongside Ben, Fraulein Kost and Herr Ludwig. They start with their right arms straight by their sides but then raise them slowly, palms facing down, in what is clearly going to be a Nazi salute. When their arms are at waist-height the lights go off and the black void of the stage is lost behind the fast-dropping curtain. The house lights come on.

Yes! This is everything I expected and more.

The silence lasts for less than a second before the audience is standing and roaring its approval. The applause is loud and the whooping and hollering continues even as those keen for refreshment or a cigarette start to leave their places. It's as if the show is over.

Chapter 34

Hello, Jay. It's me, Willy. I'm typing this on the same Remington that Cameron used to record the story of our lives together. I've posted it to you so you'll read it after your son's show. It will explain.

Cameron writes at the end of his story about the guilt - the guilt because he left me to my fate in Berlin. But what could he have done? If he had come back from London one day earlier - who knows? He would have died less tormented, yes. But when would he have died?

Is it not more likely that his crazy scheme to smuggle me out as his brother would have failed? That we would have both been caught? We might have died together in a concentration camp. What a waste it would have been.

After the war started it was enough to survive. I've thought about this so much since you started coming to see me. It's all been about survival. Frau Guttchen survived Berlin's destruction and so did the Green House. Miraculously, the English passport was still there when I returned.

A British passport with my picture, my name as Cameron's brother - it had expired. If it had been valid and I had money, who knows, I could have got out in the chaos of 1946. But I had to wait until another survivor, Bernie Gunther, found me. It was Gunther arranged for a wartime renewal stamp on my charmed passport and he introduced me to his old flame - the rich widow Gerda Hardt - my Geraldine. Her survival - another miracle.

So many individual stories of survival against the odds. Without them there would have been no flight through Europe - no marriage - no stepson to bear his mother's maiden name.

And this is the thing, Jay. Out of such darkness that enveloped Europe, out of the shadows of so many broken lives, someone darker emerges. This man who talks of his destiny. Fifty years ago Cameron gave him a home and, like a father, I gave him unconditional love. Yet, after his mother died, he spat insults in our faces and made false accusations that, if the authorities had listened, would have seen me imprisoned again.

He claims he is religious but his message is one of hatred. He preaches the subjugation of a race. He lectures the town about the dangers of symbolism but he won't sleep until the Star of David flies on every rooftop from the Mediterranean to the Jordan River. He has to be stopped or where will it lead?

If Hitler had been killed during the Bierkellerputsch in 1923 there would have been no war, no Holocaust. Sometimes a man has to die in order to deflect history from its path.

I hope, Jay, this helps you understand.

Willy Keel
(Wolfgang Koehler)
December 2001

Chapter 35

They're in the lobby outside the auditorium where 'Friends of Jefferson High' sell refreshments on trestle tables. The Gagliano family, which owns the White Plains restaurant, has donated the pastries. Rachel and Jay stand accepting the congratulations. 'You must be *so* proud of your son.'

It's a triumph, Jay.

'It's something of a triumph, Rache. Isn't it?' he whispers.

There's a crashing sound and Jay turns to see that a man stands inside the double-doors.

Here he is – Rabbi Stern. Willkommen, bienvenue, welcome!

He's alongside one of the parents who's prostrate on the floor. The rabbi stoops and helps him up. 'I'm sorry,' he says, as he flicks at the man's jacket to remove some dust. 'But you shouldn't have tried to stop me.'

All faces have turned to watch him. He removes a thick coat and stands in a black jacket extending to his knees. There's a collarless, white dress shirt beneath it. His head is covered by a wide-brimmed fedora.

If he had ringlets it would be a caricature. Fremde, étranger, stranger. Glüklich zu sehen, je suis enchanté, happy to see you, bleibe, reste, stay.

To the left there's another commotion. A wheelchair emerges from the crowd around one of the tables. 'Push me to him, Amber. Now – before it's too late,' Willy says. Amber steers him in the direction of the rabbi. Jay recognises Willy and steps forward.

Rabbi Stern addresses the people gathered around. 'I know what's just happened in there. I could hear you from the car park. I know how the first half ends. You've been screaming and shouting your support for Nazism. You've been applauding a Jewish boy wearing the Hakenkreuz. You should be ashamed.'

Now my cast is assembled ...

Willy Keel is in front of the rabbi and saying, 'Brake, Amber! Put on the brake.' And as she fiddles with the handle he's already struggling to stand. 'David!' he says. 'You're the one should be ashamed.'

It unfolds exactly as to my direction.

The rabbi looks at Willy and his eyes widen as if he's in the presence of an apparition, 'Wolf!' His voice is dull, registering resignation rather than surprise.

Willy is now standing upright. His right hand is hidden inside his jacket, Napoleon-style.

... holding the gun.

'*You're* the one in the wrong here! You're the bigot – the fascist!'

'You silly, old fool. You dare to call this to *me*.'

'I saved you, David,' the old man hisses. His right arm moves. 'Did we survive – your mother and me – to put you here ... in this place?'

Yes. You served your purpose, Willy. And now, Jay, it's your time.

Jay takes another pace forward. He's responsible for bringing Willy; he's the one to take him away.

'Oh yes. You saved me,' Rabbi Stern says, 'but you abandoned me as soon as Mom died.'

'You said I was an abomination! You lied about me! You and Zion and your fucking destiny. I can stop you ...' He's pointing a Luger pistol at Rabbi Stern – at his stepson. 'You're as bad as them ...'

Jay's heart stutters. The heat in his chest is furnace-high. He's lost his hearing as if his ears have popped.

Now!

Jay moves alongside the wheelchair and turns to face Willy. He sees out of the corner of his eye that Mr Costidy has come through one of the auditorium doors and is approaching. The performers of the play cluster by the entrance. They want to see what the fracas is about. Ben is there still wearing the Hitler Youth uniform.

Now each person is positioned on the stage exactly as I wish. It is just for the rabbi to say his final words:

'You sick old fool. With that gun drooping in your scrawny hand. You threaten me while filth oozes from your pores. You dirty faggot.'

Willy tightens his grip.

This is your moment, Jay!

Jay steps forward at the instant Willy's finger closes. The old man senses that somebody has crossed the line of fire but the signals travel too slowly in his worn-out nerves and he's unable to stop the muscles in his hand. His arm stiffens to absorb the recoil.

Jay's mind is once again back twenty years standing in his Student Union bar watching a stray dart embed itself in the soft panel of a loudspeaker. The unseen bullet plunges into his body below his ribcage. It snicks his aorta and bursts from his back amid a spray of blood and flesh particles. He falls to the floor.

The gun's explosion freezes the crowd. Their faces are empty – uncomprehending. One person steps forward. It's Ben. 'Dad!'

Rachel screams, 'Jay!'

My man is resigned for this moment. He understands that he's been living on borrowed time. He knows that Willy didn't mean to shoot him. Jay knows all of this and he knows none of it. I'm thinking for him.

Ben drops to his knees and cradles his father's body. Jay's heart is pumping faster, faster. It's not able to comprehend that this only causes the blood to spew more rapidly through the breach in his artery. A carmine puddle spreads on the tiled floor. As his blood pressure drops, Jay's heart pumps faster still. It's a race it can never win.

Jay's eyes roll and the insignia on his son's arm burns into his retina.

The bullet that mortally wounded Jay was diverted from its original path barely at all. Its energy mostly spent, it hit Rabbi Stern in the chest with only enough force to lodge between two of his ribs. He fell because of the shock of the impact.

The MC stands by the rabbi and notices the reflection of Ben's uniform in Jay's glossy eyes. *Like so many of our tribe, Jay's last sight is the red, black and white of the swastika.* The MC makes this idea echo between Jay and the rabbi. It fades in one as a closing thought and assails the other as an opening salvo. *If the last thing you see as you die is the symbol that characterises evil – does this make you Jewish enough?*

But his hypothesis strikes a solid wall of resistance. There's no crack in the rabbi's certainty – no chink that the MC can exploit to worm his way in. He has to acknowledge that his role as destiny's agent is over. There's nothing left for him but to share Jay's fate. It's time to rest his weary spirit.

White greasepaint collects in the deepening crevices of his face; his lips turn from red to blue. A yellow star shines on his drab, striped garb. The stench, the dejected murmuring, the palpable fear of the shuffling queue overpowers them both.

Burford Buzz - 17th January 2002

Melissa Rosenberg was there when BL resident Jay Halprin was gunned down at Jefferson High

You all know what happened. A crazy old man shot Burford Lakes resident Jay Halprin during the interval of Jefferson High's final performance of *Cabaret*. At the time the *Buzz* went to press we understand that the alleged perpetrator will plead guilty to manslaughter.

Jay Halprin died in his son's arms. His wife was there. I saw her by the ambulance waiting to accompany her husband's body to the hospital. His blood blighted the finery she had worn in anticipation of her son's triumph. In her I saw the pale ghost of Jackie Kennedy – traumatised, shivering. The Halprins were visitors to our boro. It doesn't seem so fair, these days. You explain it. I can't.

When the police had finished interviewing witnesses I went back into the school's auditorium. The stage was empty, set up for the second half of a musical that would never happen. Neither will there be further scenes in the life of Jay Halprin.

We in Burford Lakes knew Jay as our 9/11 survivor. Yet he only lived another three months. We can't know why. We can only have faith that the God who blesses our sweet land and guides its destiny has His reasons.

Now the actors in our real-life drama have left the stage. Rachel Halprin came to our community as Jay's wife and left it as his heart-broken widow. She and Ben will attempt to re-start their lives in England. The alleged killer Willy Keel is an old man – he's going to die in jail. Rabbi Stern has already left us for his new life in Israel.

I sit here at my computer and, through my tears, I see across the street the home I still call the Halprin house. It's empty, awaiting new tenants. The Stars and Stripes is attached to the mailbox. I watched Jay fix it there after 9/11. It was good that our British neighbor stood shoulder-to-shoulder with us.

Jay was killed by a bullet alleged to have been intended for another man. September and January – editions of our community magazine that are the bookends to the life of a stranger in our country.

The first heavy snow of the winter is settling around the Halprin house at the close of a year that has brought us so much tragedy. The mood I'm in is captured by words that were never spoken the night Jay died because the school's production never ended. In *Cabaret* the disillusioned American writer speaks them as the orchestra strikes up the finale. I've altered only the place-names:

There was a cabaret, and there was a master of ceremonies ... and there was a city called New York, in a country called America ... and it was the end of the world.

Acknowledgements

This novel started with the idea that a boy in the Hitler Youth probably would have sung a song similar to *Tomorrow Belongs to Me* in a German beer garden in the 1930s and that he could have been alive as we welcomed the 21st century. For this inspiration I have to thank Bob Fosse, the director of the film *Cabaret* and the songwriters, John Kander and Fred Ebb. They created something that makes my spine tingle every time I watch it.

As I wrote the chapters, I shared many of them with my colleagues in the *Severn Valley Authors* writing group: Chris, Linda, Tony, Annie and Izzie and they gave me positive support and many valuable suggestions. (Sorry for leaving you out last time, guys!) My writing chums Fiona Joseph and Bruce Johns have been constant sources of encouragement.

When I was researching Berlin I came across Philip Kerr's 'Bernie Gunther' novels set in the period. They gave me huge enjoyment and provided valuable insights. I'm grateful to Mr Kerr for allowing me to give Bernie a cameo role here.

I asked members of my family to read the first manuscript – thanks to them all for their contributions. They will see that the book incorporates their corrections and many of their suggestions. Andy FitzGerald deserves a special thank-you for reading two versions.

I owe a big debt to Patricia Borlenghi, founder of Patrician Press, for her positive reception of the manuscript and her detailed critique. Her input has improved the book hugely. Thanks to Charles Johnson for the stunning cover artwork and to Chris Smith for proofreading the final manuscript and his other suggestions that positively affected the final product.

Finally, Val, David, Ruth, Charlotte. Yay! We've done it again. Thank you.